Titles by Rebecca M. Hale

Cats and Curios Mysteries

HOW TO WASH A CAT
NINE LIVES LAST FOREVER
HOW TO MOON A CAT
HOW TO TAIL A CAT
HOW TO PAINT A CAT

Mysteries in the Islands

ADRIFT ON ST. JOHN
AFOOT ON ST. CROIX
AGROUND ON ST. THOMAS

Praise for *New York* ~~Times~~ author Rebecca ~~M. Hale's~~
Mystery in the Islands Mysteries

Afoot on St. Croix

"Hale's novels are elaborate puzzle pieces where plots at
first seem scattered and unrelated, but ultimately weave
together into one surprisingly unified storyline. Complex,
funny, and with darker tones that share more elements with
the black-comedy mysteries written by Tim Dorsey than
any cozy, *Afoot on St. Croix* entertains with its many self-
centered characters that are flawed, but all too human."
—*Kings River Life Magazine*

"Readers will be enchanted by the setting, intrigued by the
characters, and amazed by the writing in this island cozy . . . [A]
wonderful blend of the Caribbean in every chapter."
—*Debbie's Book Bag*

Adrift on St. John

"Intriguing . . . fans who want something different will enjoy
being *Adrift on St. John*." —*Genre Go Round Reviews*

"A perfect story to escape into . . . Just when you think you
have everything figured out, you don't! Enjoy!!"
—*Escape with Dollycas into a Good Book*

"This was an easy-flowing, narrative tale that took a different path in its storytelling . . . An intriguing and adventur-
ous jaunt on a tropical island." —*The Cozy Chicks*

continued . . .

Aground on St. Thomas

Rebecca M. Hale

BERKLEY PRIME CRIME, NEW YORK

THE BERKLEY PUBLISHING GROUP
Published by the Penguin Group
Penguin Group (USA) LLC
375 Hudson Street, New York, New York 10014

USA • Canada • UK • Ireland • Australia • New Zealand • India • South Africa • China

penguin.com

A Penguin Random House Company

AGROUND ON ST. THOMAS

A Berkley Prime Crime Book / published by arrangement with the author

Berkley Prime Crime Books are published by The Berkley Publishing Group.
BERKLEY® PRIME CRIME and the PRIME CRIME logo are trademarks
of Penguin Group (USA) LLC.

For information, address: The Berkley Publishing Group,
a division of Penguin Group (USA) LLC,
375 Hudson Street, New York, New York 10014.

ISBN: 978-0-425-25251-2

PUBLISHING HISTORY
Berkley Prime Crime mass-market edition / December 2014

PRINTED IN THE UNITED STATES OF AMERICA

10 9 8 7 6 5 4 3 2 1

Cover art: Shutterstock.
Cover design by George Long.

*To the Mojito Man from the Miami Airport,
my seatmate on the flight to St. Thomas.*

We knew the job was dangerous when we took it.

—Motto of the blog page "Crucians in Focus"

Government House
Charlotte Amalie
St. Thomas, US Virgin Islands

~ 1 ~

The Invasion

THE GOVERNOR STOOD on the balcony outside his office, surveying the city spread across the hillside below. A breeze brushed against his cheeks, the up-flow of the trade winds kissing off the sea.

This was his frequent perch. The three-story neoclassical building that housed the territory's executive branch provided an expansive view of Charlotte Amalie and the island's busy south shore.

For centuries, the rulers of St. Thomas had monitored their realm from this elevated location. The Government House balconies offered vantage points of ships sailing in and out of the harbor—and of citizens scheming on land.

The Governor rubbed his round chin, pondering the view.

At first glance, the town presented a typical Caribbean setting, a colorful mix of wood, brick, and mortar, overlaid with the humid layer of grit that accumulated between rainstorms. Tropical greenery laced its leafy fingers around doorways and windows, an insidious landscaping that without constant pruning rapidly engulfed entire buildings.

Down along the waterfront, street vendors plied the sidewalks, hawking T-shirts and kitschy trinkets to a few meandering tourists. Inside the air-conditioned alley shops, jewelers and watchmakers waited for the surge of day-trippers from the cruise ship docked at the nearby deepwater port. Drawn like sharks to fresh chum, gangs of pickpockets circled both areas with ease.

On the east end of the shopping district, old men set up backgammon boards on shaded picnic tables inside Emancipation Park. Dice began to warm in shaking cups as checkers were lined up across their proper points. With the first sips of coffee, grayed heads bent to discuss the latest news.

Beyond the regular bustle of gossip, commerce, and graft, however, historic events were about to unfold.

The scene that morning was anything but ordinary.

The Governor shifted his gaze to a flagpole whose mast trimmings waved a few feet above his balcony.

Over the ages, the posted symbols had reflected various shifts in control over this region of the West Indies, the change of colors an age-old measure of which country's influence was in ascendancy and which was on the wane.

With a grimace at the Stars and Stripes fluttering near his head, the Governor let out a rueful grunt.

Considering the size of the US Navy vessel that had pulled into the cruise ship terminal, the odds were stacked against his regime's future longevity.

THE GOVERNOR PLACED a hand over his brow, shielding his eyes from the glare of the sun as he once more focused his attention on the city streets below.

A number of black-clad federal agents skulked along the harbor's curving edge, rapidly closing in on the Legislature Building. Armed with arrest warrants for all fifteen of the US Virgin Islands' sitting senators, the team aimed to sweep through the meeting chambers and apprehend as many of the indicted suspects as possible. It was a deft plan of attack, one designed to shut down the government in a single blow, without casualty or bloodshed.

Despite their attempted stealth, the invaders were easy to pick out. Their dark uniforms made a stark contrast against the harbor's sunny water and the sidewalk's flowering bougainvillea.

No amount of subterfuge could mask the swiftness of their movements. Not even the arrival of a mega cruise ship loaded with cash-bloated tourists inspired such energetic activity among the island's long-term residents.

The Governor squinted at a second group of agents advancing toward Emancipation Park, about five hundred yards south of his balcony.

These were the men who had been charged with infiltrating Government House—the men who were coming to arrest him and several members of his cabinet.

He had sent the other targets home to their families. The dispersal of the administration officials would delay their incarceration by a few hours and, he hoped, spare them the humiliation of a public capture.

He had afforded himself no such luxury.

Sucking in his breath, the Governor straightened his posture, bracing for the coming raid.

Inside Government House's white-painted brick-and-wood structure, the remaining staff had been briefed on what to expect next. The First Lady, ensconced in the Governor's Mansion on an adjacent hill, was prepared for the worst.

Any minute now, all transport on or off the island would temporarily halt. Air traffic control would be ordered to close the runways. Navy personnel would board the ferryboats that connected St. Thomas to its neighboring islands and prohibit the vessels from completing their routes.

Cell phone communications would be interrupted, landlines would fall silent, and traffic would grind to a halt.

The cruise ship passengers would be blocked from disembarking their ship, much to the dismay of the diamond dealers, the watch salesmen, and the sharp-eyed pickpockets.

If needed, the initial swarm of federal agents would be followed by a squadron of National Guard troops. Before long, the main government structures in downtown Charlotte Amalie would be seized by the US authorities.

The Governor had anticipated the operation's basic structure. The only question had been when the invasion would occur—and now the timing had been revealed.

He had done everything in his power to prevent today's action. He'd spent hours with the head of the local US attorney general's office. He'd granted interviews with the federal investigators assigned to the case. He'd flown to Washington to speak in person with the justice department officials overseeing the matter. He'd tried desperately to convince them to drop their meritless claims, to no avail.

The heady wheels of opportunism and advancement had gained too much momentum. An unseen force had pushed the judicial process past the point of no return. No one within the president's administration had the will or the political clout to stop it.

In recent days, a grand jury sitting in the district court for the US Virgin Islands had received the results of the attorney general's bribery investigation. The jury's decision to indict had triggered a court order granting the US federal government direct control over the Caribbean territory until the charges could be adjudicated, the alleged corruption flushed out of the islands' local institutions, and new elections held.

The Governor released the pent-up air from his lungs. His shoulders curved forward, bowed by the magnitude of the occasion.

It was a takeover of epic proportions, and he was helpless to stop it.

⌒⌒

WHILE THE GOVERNOR remained on the balcony, solemnly tracking the developments in the harbor, his closest aide paced back and forth inside the office.

The typically unflappable young man had worked himself into an agitated state. Muttering under his breath, he scanned the top sheet of a clipboard, as if searching for some tidbit of new information or a pending task with which to busy himself, but he had already read every piece of writing at least a dozen times. He had only one duty to complete that morning—the interminable wait.

He glanced down at his watch, cursing the second hand's slow movement.

A ringer sang out, and the aide pounced on the desk phone. A colored button on the handset indicated the call emanated from a secure line in Washington, DC.

Fresh beads of sweat broke out across his forehead as he spoke into the receiver.

"This is Cedric."

He listened to the voice on the opposite end. Then he pressed the mute button and turned toward the balcony.

"Sir," he called out tensely. "It's the attorney general for you."

Silently, the Governor shook his head, declining the call. The communication was a false courtesy, a last-minute request that he voluntarily relinquish his leadership position before it was forcefully taken away.

He would not give Washington that satisfaction.

The Governor's sturdy hand gripped the balcony railing. Despite the dire situation, he remained calm. He was ready.

With a gulp, Cedric set the receiver on the cradle, terminating the connection.

Almost immediately, there was a sharp knock at the door. The sound ricocheted through the office, causing the aide to jump like a nervous rabbit.

The Governor looked over his shoulder and nodded.

"Let them in."

Ashen-faced, Cedric straightened his tie. He tugged on his suit jacket lapels, smoothing the tailored seams. Then he grabbed the handle, turned it, and swung open the door.

The lone individual standing in the hallway bore no resemblance to the federal agents storming the city from the harbor.

He was a thin man in a golf shirt and khakis. His clothing hung loosely from his frame, as if the garments were two or three sizes too big for his body. His narrow face was flushed pink from exertion, and circular wet marks soaked the armpits of his shirt.

A visitor's pass hanging from his neck identified him by a single name: FOWLER.

It took Cedric a moment to recognize the unexpected visitor. The last time they'd met, the man had been about two hundred pounds heavier—and his name certainly hadn't been Fowler.

Throughout the Caribbean, when powerful figures ran into trouble, be it financial, criminal, governmental, or otherwise, they called on a nebulous figure known only by the service he provided: the Fixer.

Today's mission had required a less obvious pseudonym.

Cedric frowned, puzzling over the man's presence. He had been with the Governor practically every waking minute for the past two weeks as they strategized, fruitlessly, on how to avoid the looming crisis. There was no way his boss could have contacted the Fixer—or Fowler, as the case may be—without Cedric's knowledge.

The Fixer was a recourse of last resort, one that the aide had argued strenuously against on the grounds that his involvement would negate the Governor's asserted claims of innocence.

Not waiting to be invited in, Fowler pushed his way through the entrance and crossed to the balcony.

"Let's go, Governor. There's not much time."

~ 2 ~

The Escape

THE GOVERNOR TURNED away from the balcony railing, relief on his face.

He didn't seem the least bit surprised by the Fixer's arrival, Cedric noted, his own concern deepening by the second.

The aide watched, perplexed, as his boss bounded into the office.

Given the sedentary nature of his leadership position and the frequency of job-related eating engagements, the Governor wasn't in great physical condition. The combination of inactivity and constant eating had widened his already bulky form. He suffered from innumerable aches in his joints and muscles and saw a chiropractor, acupuncturist, and a masseuse with regularity.

None of these oft-cited infirmities appeared to hamper his mobility on this occasion. Cedric had never seen the big man cross a room with such vigor.

"Thank you for coming." The Governor glanced at the name tag and added with a smile, "Fowler." He clasped the newcomer's shoulders and gave him a firm hug. "I'd almost given up hope."

"Don't thank me yet," Fowler replied with a glance toward the harbor. "You're not out of the woods. Not by a long shot."

"Let's get going, then." The Governor reached for a hanger attached to a hook on the back of the door.

Fowler stopped him before he could slip on his suit coat.

"You won't be needing that, Guv." He lifted a tote bag from his shoulder, reached inside, and pulled out a T-shirt, shorts, and a pair of worn tennis shoes. "Better change into these. You need to be less conspicuous, and, uh . . ." He looked skeptically at the Governor's wide girth. "We might have some hiking to do."

As the Governor loosened his collar and unfastened his cuff links, Cedric resumed his worried pace around the office. The aide was unnerved by the sudden change in circumstances. The situation was spinning out of control—and he wasn't referring to the incoming feds.

Fowler folded up the Governor's shirt and slacks and tucked the clothing, along with his loafers, into the tote. As the Governor stood from tying his shoelaces, Fowler handed over a white visor printed with the logo from a New York–based tennis tournament.

It wasn't much of a disguise, Cedric thought, surveying the improvised outfit. The Governor's chubby figure was well known throughout the territory, particularly in Charlotte Amalie. He wouldn't get more than a block or two from the building without being identified and called out.

Fowler was far more confident in the costume's chances of facilitating evasion. With an approving nod, he cracked open the door and peeked down the hallway. The Governor leaned forward, anxiously peering over the other man's shoulder.

Cedric stopped his pacing and stared at the pair crowded by the doorway. He shook his head, stunned by the rapid turn of events.

For the past six years, he had run the Governor's schedule, overseen his legislative obligations, and managed almost every aspect of his daily life. He'd been invited to family events and had dined regularly at the Governor's Mansion. He had been the only aide trusted to babysit the First Lady's beloved Chihuahuas. He'd been an essential part of the politician's very existence.

But if he didn't act fast, his services were about to come to an abrupt end.

With difficulty, Cedric swallowed his pride. He would have to set aside his qualms about the Governor's accomplice—no matter how much he disliked the thought of involving the Fixer.

"How can I help?" he asked meekly.

The Governor turned his head back toward the office and shifted the visor so he could see out. The tone of his voice matched the incredulous expression on his face.

"Aren't you coming with us?"

THE TRIO CREPT down the hallway, with Fowler taking the lead, the Governor following cautiously in the thin man's footsteps, and a bewildered Cedric bringing up the rear.

The group hugged the corridor's right-hand side so they wouldn't be visible through the opposite wall, which opened to the floor below.

A quiet hush rose through the building's empty center space, the collected bated breath of the Government House employees waiting for the raid to commence. Cedric veered left to peek down through the slats in the hallway's side railing.

Like most offices, theirs was a fractious workplace, particularly behind closed doors and turned backs. Feuds were often fueled by jealous speculations about who was in favor and who had fallen out.

As the Governor's trusted aide, Cedric discreetly monitored the building's verbal traffic. He could usually squelch the most damaging rumors before they reached the newspapers.

Over the years, he had overheard countless disgruntled discussions from hidden positions on back stairwells, inside bathroom stalls, and behind copy room doors. The complaints ranged the gamut, from perceived inequities in pay and workload to suspicions about the administration's ethical policies and practices.

But at this moment, none of that rancor was in evidence.

As Cedric looked down at the employees gathered in the lobby below, the faces reflected back a wall of undivided loyalty. Their innate aversion to the imposition of foreign troops combined with the Governor's attempt to elude the invaders had forged a temporary unity.

That allegiance wouldn't last more than thirty seconds after the big man left the building.

At least, that's what Cedric was counting on.

In recent months, the trusted aide had turned on his employer.

He was now the star witness in the federal government's case against the Governor.

FOWLER THREW BACK his hand, halting the train of followers behind him. From the top of the building's central curving staircase, he angled his head to see through to the front lobby.

A woman had been posted to serve as lookout for the approaching federal agents. She stood next to the security scanners in an area dedicated to a display of the territory's past leaders. The lobby's homage included portraits of both elected and appointed governors, going all the way back to the Danish Colonial era. On the near wall hung a pair of Pissarro paintings, a tribute to the famed Impressionist artist who was born on the island in 1830.

From her position in the lobby entrance, the woman had a clear view of the narrow one-way street running in front of Government House as well as the public gardens that dropped down the slope from the opposite curb.

Fowler puckered his lips and sent out a low whistle.

At the sound, the woman leaned forward for a last check through the glass doors. Then she glanced up toward the unseen trio and subtly nodded.

With that signal, Fowler ushered the Governor forward, and the group began a mad dash down the red-carpeted staircase, a wild scramble of thumping, slipping feet.

Cedric considered faking a fall that might slow their departure. But before he could gauge a safe tripping distance, a heavyset man with a build similar to the Governor's chugged up the steps to meet them.

Fowler hit the brakes, nearly causing a collision. As Cedric struggled to regain his balance, Fowler reached into the tote bag and tossed the man the Governor's formal clothes and shoes.

"Hold them off for as long as you can," the Governor said gratefully, patting the doppelgänger on the back.

Cedric turned to watch the man continue up the stairs and along the hallway to the Governor's office. Once more, he found himself wondering how all of this subterfuge had been arranged without his knowledge.

Clearly, the Fixer's sudden appearance wasn't the only unforeseen wrinkle in the day's schedule.

The aide hesitated on the stairs as the other two resumed the charge to the bottom. It was an unsettling sensation, being so uninformed and out of the loop. He had no idea what to expect next.

Even after the Governor's earlier urging, he wasn't sure how far he was invited to join in this improvised escape.

Swallowing his anxiety, Cedric trotted down the remaining steps. No matter what bizarre tricks the Fixer had up his sleeve, he couldn't afford to lose track of the Governor's position.

Not now. Not when he was so close to achieving his goal.

He caught up with the pair on the first floor, falling in line as they passed the receptionist, who buzzed them through a security gate leading to the rear of the building.

They were moments away from fleeing into the surrounding residential neighborhood.

Cedric straightened his tie, trying to convey a look of confidence, even as his mind reeled with anguish.

Months of careful planning had just been thrown out the window.

~ *3* ~

A Warm Island Welcome

CEDRIC TRACKED HIS boss through Government House, following the man's bobbing visor down a series of narrow corridors. Up ahead, Fowler took off into a maze of tiny rooms, an indirect but, Cedric presumed, less conspicuous course to the rear exit.

The building's floor plan had been modified numerous times since its original Danish construction, the 1860s format being incompatible with the functions of a modern-day office space. The resulting layout contained several odd-shaped hallways and closet-sized cubbyholes, the squeezed-off remnants from efforts to create a center open area.

Fowler's winding path took the three men through a servant's quarters that had been converted into a copy center and across a galley-style kitchen that now served as a break room.

It was a frantic pace, and Cedric found himself struggling to keep up. The Governor's bulky frame flashed in and out of view, moving with surprising swiftness and agility.

"Where did the Guv get all this energy?" the aide panted, but there was no time to ponder the question. In all the twisting and turning, Cedric temporarily lost sight of the hefty politician.

He stopped in a hallway intersection, puzzling at the circuitous route.

The Fixer must be lost, Cedric reasoned. He allowed himself a modicum of hope. Maybe they wouldn't make it out of the building after all.

But when he reached the exit a few minutes later, he found the two men kneeling on the floor, peeking out the door's upper screen.

"Where to next?" Cedric whispered, crouching beside the Governor's visored head.

Fowler replied with a raised finger to his lips.

The federal agents had reached the lobby and were conversing with the woman who had been stationed by the security scanners. One of the men demanded impatiently to be let through.

After a tense back-and-forth, the lookout stepped aside. She spoke loud enough to be heard across the first floor.

"The Governor is upstairs in his office."

Scraping chair legs and shuffling feet communicated the agents' progress through the building. Once the uniformed men started up the central staircase, Fowler pushed open the screen door and crept outside.

The trio tiptoed through a courtyard and across a path leading to a gate in the high-security fencing that encircled the back side of the property.

Surely, the feds would have covered the building's rear access, Cedric thought, internally exasperated.

But the area appeared to be clear. Fowler unlocked the gate and eased himself through to the other side. After checking around the far corner of the building, he waved for the others to follow.

Not wasting any time, the Governor jumped through the opening, joining Fowler on a sidewalk attached to a flight of stone steps that led up Government Hill. The public stairs cut between Government House and an adjacent structure, another Colonial-era building that served as the parsonage for a local church.

Cedric proceeded more cautiously through the gate, expecting that at any second he would hear the sharp whistle of an arresting federal agent.

To his dismay, he too crossed to the outer sidewalk unimpeded.

He poked his head around the edge of the building and looked down toward the waterfront, still in disbelief at the ease of their escape. Craning his neck to see over the intervening neighborhood, he scanned the shoreline.

By now, he reasoned, the watchful residents of Charlotte Amalie would have noticed that something was amiss. The cruise ship traffic in and out of the harbor was closely scrutinized by the island's taxi drivers, tour guides, jewelry shop sales force, restaurateurs, and everyone else tourism-employed in the up-slanted town. Many were no doubt wondering why the day-trippers had yet to disembark—and why a navy vessel was moored in the deepwater port beside the fancy cruise ship.

Cedric grimaced at the scene below.

Frustrated citizens stood on the sidewalks, waving their disabled cell phones in the air, grumbling about the sudden loss of signal.

Confusion reigned among the street vendors. Many of them had given up for the day and had begun packing their mass-produced goods into the plastic bags provided by the money-men who financed their shilling operations.

A truck drove through the downtown streets, cruising at a snail's pace with its windows rolled down. The vehicle's radio had been set to an earsplitting volume. The speakers pumped out the broadcast of a local station whose transmitter had so far avoided being shut off.

Cedric couldn't make out the broadcast words, but the message was heard loud and clear across Charlotte Amalie's lower downtown area.

The backgammon players pocketed their dice, gathered their checkers, and folded their game boards. The remaining street vendors rolled up their wares. In the high-end alley shops, staff and storeowners scurried to secure the iron gratings used to protect their merchandise at night. The pickpockets had long since disappeared into the back streets, keen to avoid the surge of federal agents.

In the distance, ammunition began to pop through the air, reminiscent of the island's annual New Year's Eve ritual when celebratory gunfire peppered the sky. The regular January barrage was scary enough, leaving citizens hunkered on the floors of their houses, fearful of stray bullets flying in their windows.

Cedric listened to the reverberations, counting the rounds. A scattering of police cars ventured into the streets, but the local officers wouldn't make much of a dent in the gunfire. As with the incidents that took place at New Year's, there simply weren't enough resources to track down every report of randomly fired shots.

Cedric had warned there would be unrest during the execution of the arrest warrants, but the woman at the local attorney general's office had dismissed his concerns. Her superiors in Washington were reluctant to bring in extra manpower.

The aide gripped the corner of the white-painted wall, staring at the movements along the waterfront.

He hoped the feds were prepared.

They were about to receive a warm island welcome.

"PURE CHAOS," CEDRIC said, pulling his head behind the building. "And getting more so by the minute."

His words hit the concrete sidewalk without reaching human ears. Fowler and the Governor were no longer standing behind him.

Startled, his eyes swept up the hillside steps.

He nearly laughed aloud at the sight of the Governor scrambling over a window ledge into an unoccupied residential building that was under renovation. The roof had been torn off, and the frame had been stripped down to a concrete shell. The Fixer crouched on the ground beneath the Governor, laboring to heft the larger man through the square portal.

What was he so worried about? Cedric thought with a grin. The plan had been thoroughly vetted. There was no chance the Governor would escape capture. He just had to keep track of him until the feds caught up.

What could possibly go wrong?

He sprinted up the steps.

"Hey! Wait for me!"

Golden Grove Adult Correctional
Facility and Detention Center
St. Croix, US Virgin Islands

~ 4 ~

The Lucky One

A HAZY INLAND swelter sank into a low valley on St. Croix's southern flank, the location for the largest incarceration facility in the US Virgin Islands.

The Golden Grove detention center occupied a flat field that had been scraped down to bare dirt and the occasional patch of short weedy grass. Concrete walls stood behind ten-foot fencing topped with looped barbed wire, an intimidating but ineffectual barrier that enclosed an underfunded, overcrowded prison dormitory.

The center's squalid living conditions had been the subject of multiple investigations, lawsuits, and court orders, but as yet none of the issued legal remedies appeared to have improved the physical infrastructure, stemmed the violence among the inmates, or slowed the notorious influx of drugs.

An electronic buzzer pulsed, followed by a blinking red light, signifying that a prisoner was about to be released. The screech of sliding metal sounded across the front courtyard.

The guards manning the entrance stepped back from their posts. Their heads dropped in a show of respect for the man in the orange jumpsuit who strode casually through the gate.

The facility's administrator slid a paper bag across the checkout counter to the departing inmate. The bag's top third had been folded over and stapled shut, but the paper was crumpled along the edges and had obviously been opened and restapled. A few items had been added to the prisoner's possessions in the thirty minutes since the center received the call ordering his release.

"Here you go, Nova. Everything should be in there." Tentatively, the administrator held out a pen and a sheet of paper. "If you could just sign the form."

The exiting inmate scooped up the sack and tucked it under his arm. With his free hand, he grabbed the pen and scrawled a barely legible signature—not his birth name, but the moniker by which he was known throughout the island.

Casanova.

He took far more care in his parting smirk, a superior gleam that confirmed his dominance over the administrator and everyone else who worked at the correctional facility.

His brief stint at Golden Grove hadn't diminished his confident swagger. His stance was that of a triumphant prizefighter.

No one could touch him. He was invincible.

In his thirty-three years of life, Nova had seen plenty of death. He had smelled its rank finality, tasted its thick splatter on his tongue—and wielded its force with his bare hands.

But he had never once feared it.

This wasn't his first stay at Golden Grove. It wouldn't be his last.

"See ya next time, Larry."

Nodding casually at the guards, Nova turned for the walkway leading out through the barbed wire fencing.

The morning sun streamed across his smooth brown face, illuminating the amber flecks in his eyes. High cheekbones, perfectly parted lips, and a nose with a delicate bridge that, despite numerous fistfights, had never once been broken, completed the picture. His muscles were sculpted into the type of toned physique artistically emulated by the ancient Greeks.

The effect was one of unnerving physical beauty.

True to his nickname, Casanova had no problem attracting female attention. Countless Crucian women had fallen for his handsome looks. They found him irresistible—despite his bad-boy reputation, his violent temper, and the menace behind the mask.

SWINGING THE STAPLED paper bag, Nova sauntered onto the main road outside the detention center and headed toward a beat-up taxi van parked on the gravel shoulder.

He pulled on the handle of the van's side passenger door and deftly slid it open.

"Nevis, you're right on time."

The driver looked anxiously over his shoulder as the man in prison garb climbed into the van. Reaching into his shirt pocket, the driver pulled out a cell phone and silently passed it back.

"You seen those Coconut Boys around lately?"

Still mute, Nevis shook his head.

The two homeless men had been missing for weeks. No one had seen the hapless fugitives since Nevis dropped them off on St. Croix's rugged northwest coast. In so doing, the taxi driver had inadvertently aided in the pair's escape from Nova's clutches.

During Nova's incarceration, his extensive Crucian network had learned of the taxi driver's role in the getaway. As punishment for this offense, Nova had sent word to Nevis that his taxi would serve as his personal transportation until the two runaways showed up and Nova exacted his revenge.

Leaving the driver to fret behind the wheel, Nova squeezed around the first two bench seats and flopped onto the third cushioned row. Ripping open the sack, he changed out of the jumpsuit and into the clean clothes that had been added by the prison administrator. He had just zipped up a pair of brand-new designer jeans when the cell phone dinged with an incoming text message.

"Nevis, it looks like I've got a call coming in. You don't mind if I take it back here, do you?" With a snide chuckle, he answered his own question. "No, of course you don't."

The phone rang seconds later. "Hey there, lovely lady. How are things in Charlotte Amalie . . ."

The driver kept his attention fixed on a metal charm hanging from his rearview mirror. The chicken-shaped trinket pivoted on its string, glinting as the tooled surface reflected the bright sunlight. He had no wish to overhear any aspect of the one-sided conversation taking place in back of the van.

Despite the driver's efforts to tune it out, Nova's voice carried to the front seat.

"I figured you had me bailed out for a reason. What'cha got in mind?"

The inaudible reply generated a rumble of laughter, a maniacal sound that made the driver cringe.

"I'm on my way."

Nova pushed a button, severing the connection.

"Get this bus moving, Nevis. We've got some errands to run."

Drumming his fingers across the second-row seat back, Nova began mentally assembling the crew he would take with him north to St. Thomas.

Still organizing his thoughts, he reached into the paper bag for one last item. The shiny black semiautomatic pistol had been well maintained by its previous owner, who likely hadn't yet noticed its theft.

A broad smile spread across Nova's face as he checked the ammunition chamber. Reinserting the loaded magazine, he caressed the handle.

"Hello, Governor." He pointed the pistol down the middle of the van, aiming it at the back of Nevis's head.

"Nice to meet you."

Miami Airport

Departure Lounge for the Last Preraid
Flight to St. Thomas, US Virgin Islands

〜

~ 5 ~

The Mojito Man

"MOJITO! MOJITO, PLEASE! Does anyone know where can I get a mojito?"

A feeble but persistent voice hollered into the otherwise quiet boarding area for the day's first flight from Miami to St. Thomas.

The surrounding passengers pretended not to hear the thirsty man in the wheelchair. As the appeal continued, a college student turned up the earphones for his mobile music device. Farther down the row, a businessman hunched over his laptop computer, staring at a spreadsheet while purposefully ignoring the clamor. The rest of the crowd migrated to the opposite end of the seating area.

After several more minutes of the haranguing mojito plea, the flight attendant working the check-in counter hurried over and crouched beside the wheelchair.

"Sir, it's eight o'clock in the morning."

The Mojito Man beamed up at her with a crooked grin that revealed swollen gums and whittled-down teeth.

"Is it, now?" he replied. His gaze dropped pointedly to the attendant's chest and the unhooked buttons at the top of her blouse. Despite the woman's admonishing tone, he was clearly enjoying her attention.

Lifting an anemic arm, he waved his hand at the wheelchair,

gesturing to his thin frame and spindly legs. His muscles had atrophied from lack of use, and the skin sagged from his bones. His narrow ankles looked as if even his diminished weight might cause them to snap should he try to stand.

The back of the man's head had been rubbed bald from weeks spent lying in a hospital bed. He wasn't old, at most middle-aged, but his body had worn out. The warranty had expired, and the pieces were falling apart.

"The doc says I have less than a month to live. I can't be worried about social protocols."

Self-consciously tugging at her shirt collar, the attendant issued a placating smile. "Just try not to disturb the other passengers," she said before scurrying back to the counter.

For a brief spell, the frail figure remained quiet. He watched the people milling about the gate. Then he rotated his chair so that he could observe the pedestrian traffic in the main corridor. His eyes began to glaze over, as if he might fall asleep.

But it was only a temporary reprieve.

An unwary author entered the waiting area and, oblivious to the previous outbursts, took one of the many open seats near the wheelchair. She removed a travel magazine from her backpack, flipped through to an article she had started earlier, and resumed her read.

Instantly wide-awake, the man leaned toward the hapless woman and whispered loudly, "Excuse me, miss. Do you know where I can get a mojito?"

~ *6* ~

The Call of the Mojito

THE DEPARTURE LOUNGE outside the St. Thomas gate filled to capacity as the time drew near for the plane to begin boarding. Several passengers milled about the entry lanes, maneuvering for position, eager to get space for their carry-on luggage. Others slumped in the rows of floor-anchored seating, yawning as they waited for the next intercom announcement.

There wasn't an open spot to be found—except in the space immediately surrounding the ailing man's wheelchair.

"Mooooo-jito?" he called out pathetically, his parched voice rasping.

For those trapped in the departure area that morning, the popular Cuban cocktail would never be the same. The classic image of a narrow glass filled with muddled mint leaves, light-colored rum, sugarcane juice, and a splash of lime was now inextricably linked with that of the alcohol-obsessed cancer patient, for whom any public sympathy had long since dissipated. For years to come, mere mention of the sweet drink would bring to mind the sight of the pestering man, disconcerting in both his overt ogling of every passing female and his corpse-like appearance.

As for the unwitting author who had drawn his attention, her mojito misery was just beginning.

WITH A VULNERABLE target identified and pinned within reach, the Mojito Man refined his approach. His plea was no longer directed to the departure lounge as a whole. Instead, he focused his efforts exclusively on the woman seated next to his wheelchair.

The author had missed her chance to find another place to sit. If she moved now, her only choices were to stand on the crowded floor space or to lean against a wall. Given the limited options, she'd decided to remain next to the wheelchair.

She had tried without success to shrug off her neighbor's pleas. She avoided eye contact with him, even shielding the side of her face with her hand. At one point, she lifted the magazine she'd given up trying to read, propping it like a fence between them.

This too proved an ineffective barrier.

The raised magazine resulted in a verbal pause from the wheelchair, accompanied by a strained shuffling sound. Seconds later, a twenty-dollar bill folded in the shape of a paper airplane flew over the magazine's top edge.

"*Mo*-jito! I beseech thee, beautiful lady. Please, bring me a mojito!"

The author checked her watch, estimating the minutes remaining until boarding would commence. She had just enough time to circle through the nearest food court. Capitulating, she slid the magazine into her backpack.

She suspected she was being sent on a futile mission.

While mojitos were commonly served throughout south Florida, she couldn't imagine where the man had come up with the idea that the drink would be readily available inside the airport. It wasn't the type of item served by the many fast-food burger joints and coffee kiosks that operated within the terminal.

She figured her best bet was to try one of the airport restaurants, but it seemed unlikely she'd find a bartender serving cocktails during the breakfast hour—or that she would be allowed to purchase an alcoholic beverage in a to-go cup.

She shrugged her shoulders. Given the harassment she'd endured during the past forty-five minutes, she didn't much care one way or the other.

She was, however, feeling a tad hungry. Maybe I'll get some-thing to eat for myself, she mused.

I'll take a bacon, egg, and cheese biscuit plus a mojito—to go, she thought wryly.

"Keep an eye on my seat," she said out loud, in what she knew to be an unnecessary request. Wearily, she hefted her backpack onto her shoulders and grabbed the handle for her roll-around suitcase. "I'll see what I can round up."

The man gave her a crafty grin.

"You're so kind. Thank you, love."

The Bishop of St. Thomas

AS THE MINUTES ticked by, the agents behind the check-in counter doubled and then tripled in number. While they waited for confirmation from the flight crew that the plane was ready to board, a great amount of effort went into fussing about the computers, scanning passenger printout lists, and speaking into an antiquated plastic phone—anything, it seemed, to avoid making eye contact with the crush of antsy passengers who had transformed the departure lounge into a three-ring travel circus.

It was a typical preflight scene, a mix of travelers in mental states from crazed to dazed and everything in between—with one isolated spot of serenity. For the first time in almost an hour, the Mojito Man sat peacefully in his wheelchair, quietly sipping his favorite drink.

With the help of a generous tip, the author had cajoled a waitress at an Irish pub into mixing up the cocktail and pouring it into a foam cup.

The only downside to the resulting silence, she reflected, was that the area around her seat had grown far more crowded than before. Fellow travelers stood within arm's length in every direction.

Most members of the encroaching mass were new arrivals, blissfully unaware of the earlier mojito siege. The author gazed up at them as she munched on her breakfast sandwich, envious of their ignorance but happy to have a chair.

The group included a number of curious characters, the most notable being a Miami socialite with a carry-on-sized lapdog. The woman and the tiny canine wore matching outfits: the owner a sparkling tank top, necklace, and sandals, the pet a shiny collar and vest.

With a smile, the author wrapped the remains of her breakfast, wiped her hands on a napkin, and reached for a small notepad she carried in her backpack. This was the type of detail that might come in handy for a future work of fiction. She scribbled a brief description, looked up to confirm her observations, and did a blinking double take. She had missed an item on the list of human/canine similarities.

The woman and the dog also sported matching pedicures.

After adding a bemused notation to the notebook, the author shifted her attention to a priest who had walked into her periphery.

His was a less obvious oddity, but it was still one that drew her interest.

The man was dressed from head to toe in a brown cassock—a monk's garb, if she had to guess.

That conclusion, however, didn't jibe with the rest of his outfit. Beneath the pious outer layer, he wore hand-stitched leather shoes. An expensive watch glinted on his wrist, a ruby ring garnished his index finger, and a gold chain hung from his neck. Even the simple brown cassock, she now realized, had been tailored with an elegant drape.

The author tapped her pen against the paper, trying to sort out the man's religious denomination. She hadn't met many monks in her life, so she had few comparisons in her memory banks, but she couldn't reconcile him into that category. His wealth, while discreet, was far from subtle.

No, she thought, intrigued as the jeweled hand reached into one of the cassock's hidden pockets and pulled out a high-end cell phone. This guy's in an entirely different income bracket.

She leaned forward in her seat, continuing to study the religious figure.

His hair had been shaved close to his head, accenting the round curves of his skull, and a pair of fashionable rimless eyeglasses rested on his nose. A goatee sprouted from his chin, the gray hair a contrast against his satin brown skin.

There was something grand and powerful about his appearance, an intangible quality that commanded respect.

Seeing the author's fascination, the Mojito Man gummed his straw, bent toward her, and whispered loudly in her ear.

"Bishop of St. Thomas," he said informatively.

"I doubt it." Her brow furrowed. "Wrong costume."

She glanced over at the check-in counter. The plastic phone was at last being put to good use. The settings had been adjusted to broadcast across the departure lounge. Anyone who needed assistance or extra time to traverse the gangway was now invited to board.

The author looked at her wheelchair-bound companion, expectantly raising her eyebrows. At first, he seemed not to have heard the announcement—or to comprehend that the pre-board invitation applied to him.

"Oh, right," he finally said after the agent repeated the message.

The author waved a relieved good-bye as he rolled his chair toward the counter.

Slipping her pen and notepad into the backpack, she muttered wearily, "I hope he's seated on the opposite end of the plane."

~ 8 ~

The Middle Seat

A HALF HOUR later, the author found herself in the plane's packed coach section, staring up at the ceiling. The Mojito Man sat beside her, hogging the armrest.

She groaned, anticipating the flight ahead. She was certain the assigned seating was not as he had insisted.

Midway through the boarding process, right after the author had taken her seat, her friend from the departure lounge had appeared in the adjacent aisle. He'd apparently stopped in one of the plane's tiny restrooms, negating his preboard advantage. He stood wavering in the narrow walkway, loudly proclaiming that he held a ticket for the middle spot in her row.

Out of necessity, she had offered him her aisle position, which was easier for him to access. His wheelchair had been left at the end of the gangway, and the walk through the plane had worn him out. His spindly legs shook as if they were about to collapse beneath him.

It took several seconds for the author to shift to the next spot over. The man moaned loudly throughout the wait, finishing with a painful grunt as he dropped onto the seat's flat cushion.

In the shuffling process, she'd glimpsed the number printed on his boarding pass. It was for the other side of the plane, one row back. She glanced across the aisle at the passenger who had silently slid into the open seat. He shrugged apologetically, but did not offer to switch.

Her unwelcome companion beamed with delight. "What luck," he said cheerfully. Instantly cured of his aches, he curved in his seat to face the author. "We get to spend more time together." He bent the straw from his cup, which he had miraculously managed to carry with him, and slurped the last sip of the drink.

"Stewardess," he hollered, pressing the call light over his head.

"Mojito, please!"

FOR THE DESPONDENT author, claustrophobia had already set in by the time the passenger doors closed and the plane pulled away from the gate.

Bumping and creaking along the tarmac, the aircraft began a slow roll toward the runway. The writer tilted her head, craning to look out the nearest window. Planes were lined up, for as far as she could see, waiting to take off. An on-time departure appeared unlikely.

It was going to be a long flight.

"My mother, rest her soul. She died a painful death."

The author did her best to manage a sympathetic smile.

"Cancer. That's what did her in. It was a horrible thing to watch. No one should have to go through that."

Her seatmate motioned toward his wasting limbs. "That's why, when my time comes, I'm going to finish things off real quick." Swinging his arm upward, he pointed two bony fingers at his temple. "Maybe I'll do it Hemingway-style with a gunshot to the head. I'm telling you, Hem knew what he was doing. Not like my poor mother, rest her soul."

The author shuffled her feet, trying to figure out what she'd done to provoke this unsolicited barrage of information—and whether there was any way of stopping it.

The answer to the second question appeared to be no.

"I can see it coming—death—like the headlights of a car that's about to run me over. It's driving straight for me. I need to get in front of this thing. Take control, so that I go out on my own terms."

He tapped the armrest.

"What do you think? How should I do it? What's your pre-ferred method of suicide?"

AFTER A TWENTY-MINUTE crawl across the tarmac, the plane approached the front of the takeoff line. The pilot announced that he had reached the number-two slot in the order and that the craft would be in the air momentarily.

The passengers in the coach compartment let out a sigh of relief, particularly those seated within the vicinity of 26D. The Mojito Man had been chattering nonstop throughout the excruciating taxi from the gate.

The pilot completed his final preflight check and revved the engines. At last, the plane began picking up speed on the open runway.

Then, suddenly, the aircraft slowed. The engines dropped down to an idle, and the plane turned off the marked route. After a crackle of static, the captain's voice came over the intercom.

"I'm sorry, folks," he said in a strange voice. "There've been some issues on the ground in St. Thomas. Our departure's been delayed . . . I'm not sure for how long. They've asked us to pull off to the side here for a moment. I expect we'll be headed back to the gate. I'll give you an update as soon as I have more information."

There was a confused pause in the cabin as the passengers exchanged puzzled stares.

Then a call light flicked on over row 26, and a plaintive voice summoned the stewardess.

"Ma'am? A mojito, please!"

The woman seated beside him looked up in despair.

"Make that two."

THE PLANE COASTED to a stop on an empty stretch of tarmac, a no-man's-land amid acres of painted concrete. Murmurs of concern floated down the center aisle as the passengers speculated about what sort of "issues" could have led to the aborted takeoff and the captain's cryptic message.

The author winced at a sharp elbow poke aimed at the side

of her stomach. Having garnered her attention, the Mojito Man pointed at a passenger seated a few rows ahead. The religious figure they'd seen in the waiting area removed a cell phone from his cassock and made a short whispered call.

"The Bishop will get us in the air."

"I'm quite certain that's not a bishop," the woman replied wearily. "And even if he is, I doubt he has that kind of pull."

But a minute later, the pilot returned to the intercom. "Good news, folks. It seems we've been given the green light again. Flight attendants, please prepare for takeoff."

"Told you." Her seatmate nodded, as if the sequence of events proved his earlier assertion.

"He's the Bishop of St. Thomas."

KRAT Roving Radio Station
Charlotte Amalie
St. Thomas, US Virgin Islands

~ 9 ~

I Smell a Rat

"HEY-HO, FELLOW ISLANDERS. This is Dread Fred and the Whaler. If you've picked us up, you're listening to KRAT, the *only* radio station currently broadcasting here on the Rock— that's St. Thomas, for all the G-men listening in."

A fake police siren flooded the transmission before the DJ resumed speaking.

"But, hey. This is no joke. We have some serious *cock-a-doodle-do-dah* going on down here this mornin'." He paused, his chair squeaking as he turned to address his fellow broadcaster.

"Whale-man, can we say that on the radio?"

"You can today, my friend."

Dread Fred grunted his agreement. "It looks like we've been paid a visit by the pasty boys from up north."

Whaler cut in. "Our brothers from another mother."

"Yeah, and a different father too," Dread added dryly.

"They came in their finest black-tie attire," Whaler sang out.

"*Ya-hmph.*" Dread smacked the table. "But they forgot to wear their ties."

KRAT'S DREAD FRED and Whaler were St. Thomas's most beloved radio celebrities. Caricatured images of the DJs could be seen throughout the island, on billboards, public benches, and bumper stickers. T-shirts bearing their slogans were top sellers in the local shops.

The pair's broadcasts were widely followed. As a result, DF&W endorsements were highly sought after, and sponsors vigorously competed for the show's advertising spots.

But while the men's voices were well known on the Rock—and often imitated, even parodied by their fans—the duo had taken great care to maintain the anonymity of their physical appearances. Their real-life identities were closely guarded secrets.

It was a necessary precaution.

Although much of the daily broadcast was devoted to jocular back-and-forth between Dread Fred and Whaler, the dialogue frequently touched on sensitive political topics. In the year since the show's debut, they had poked fun at several high-level government officials, the board of elections, the chief of police, and all fifteen senators in the USVI Legislature.

This explained the DJs' popularity and their security concerns. The same playful taunts that thrilled their fans peeved the island's power brokers.

AS A MEANS of self-preservation, the KRAT radio stars performed their shows in secret. Subterfuge was part of their regular routine.

While the station had a small brick-and-mortar studio in Charlotte Amalie's waterfront Frenchtown district, DF&W typically broadcast from less formal—less identifiable— locations throughout the city.

In addition, the men took care to devise on-air personalities who conveyed distinctly different traits from those they actually possessed.

Dread Fred, aka Dreadlocks, was, in fact, bald as a billiard ball. A light-skinned Puerto Rican, he came from a prominent St. Thomas family whose landholdings dated back to before the Danish transfer. While on the radio Dread frequently complained about the high prices of food, gas, and electricity, his alter ego was independently wealthy, having inherited a small fortune from his grandfather.

Cohost Whaler was the one with the voluminous hair,

although he kept his Afro mane flowing freely, untamed by combs, braids, or dreadlocks. It was a beautiful shaggy mop, about which the DJ had become quite vain. Whaler's frequent on-air admiration of Dread's fictitious locks was a thinly veiled commentary on his own wild coif.

"Say there, Dread. That's a mighty fine 'do you're sporting today. Man, I wish I could sprout a hat like that."

Dread Fred ran a hand over his bald crown. "Why, thank you, Whaler." After a short pause, he added with a grimace, "There's nothing wrong with your short crop, you know." He cleared his throat. "A lot less maintenance."

Whaler nodded his head, throwing his thick mane back and forth. "Yeah, I s'pose." He gave his cohost a smug grin. "But it seems like I'm always worryin' about the sun crisping my head."

MUCH AS WHALER loved his bountiful hairstyle, even he had to admit it had a downside. All that extra insulation caused him to quickly overheat.

Mobile KRAT had set up that morning inside an unused cistern (in the fervent hopes that it didn't rain). Whaler had already worked up a thick layer of sweat in the windowless concrete room.

He picked up a towel and wiped it across his damp forehead. The cistern's poor ventilation was a necessary drawback to the benefits of its hidden location. Given the subject of the day's broadcast, they were likely to ruffle more than the usual amount of feathers.

The current discussion topic was the US government's invasion of Charlotte Amalie.

After less than five minutes on the air, Dread had already nicknamed the black-clad federal agents the "pasty boys."

DREAD TOOK A sip from a can of generic diet soda before resuming his commentary. Even with his bald head, he was feeling flushed in the stuffy cistern. The tank's dank mildew smell wasn't helping matters.

"Friends and neighbors. If you've got any information about the pasty boys—what they've been up to, where they've been doing it, and to whom—send us a report. The cell towers on the island have been jammed, so you're going to have to go old-school. Bust out those carrier pigeons . . ."

Whaler cut in from across the room. He stood on a metal ladder attached to an open hatch in the cistern's roof where he had threaded the KRAT transmission lines. Holding his cell phone up to the hole, he confirmed his findings. "Switch your settings over to the BVI tower. Their signal's still working."

"A thanks to our brothers on Tortola," Dread intoned deeply. "They're the ones relaying our transmission."

Whaler returned to the fold-out table where the portable broadcasting gear had been set up. "Now, those brothers are from the *same* mother."

"Truth," Dread replied and then whispered a loud aside into the microphone. "We're keeping it mobile today in case the pasty boys get too close. Whaler's got his trainers on, ready to do a runner. If we go dark, stay tuned to this channel. We'll be back on as soon as we can."

He pushed a button, triggering a recording of their signature tune, a reggae cover of the classic blues hit "I Smell a Rat."

Dread bent over his laptop, checking their Internet feed for any updates, while Whaler returned to the ladder. Climbing up, he poked his head through the hatch to look around. "Coast is clear," he reported uneasily. "So far, anyway."

Whaler's cell phone buzzed in his hand, signaling an incoming message. He squinted at the display and read the text aloud. "Legislature shut down. Senators arrested."

Dread took another drink, this time gulping down the soda. "This is big, Whaler. Bigger than anything we've ever covered."

The two exchanged glances.

They were operating in direct violation of the court order that had been circulated to all of the territory's radio stations that morning. Their list of potential enemies was about to expand well beyond local politicians—and this time, they were breaking federal law.

The stakes of getting caught had increased dramatically.

THE "I SMELL a Rat" jingle was but a short intermission. As the tune wrapped up, Dread brought the microphone to his mouth.

"This just in from one of our listeners: the pasty boys have taken the Legislature . . ."

Whaler hopped down from the ladder. He scooted across the cistern and waved a hand in front of Dread's face, indicating he had a caller on the line. He had pinned a separate antenna for the cell phone to the edge of the hatch. A jerry-rigged cable connected the phone to the broadcasting equipment on the table.

Flicking a switch for an audio setting, Dread merged the cell phone audio into the live transmission.

A static-scratched voice came through the line.

"Hey, Dread, I'm watching the feds move into Government House right now. I've got my camera ready. I'll send you a pic of the Guv in handcuffs when they lead him out."

A second caller was soon brought into the conversation.

"We've been waiting a long time for this, Dread. Dem crooks are goin' to get what's comin' to them."

Dread smiled ruefully. A small but vocal segment of the listening base had been convinced of the Governor's guilt from the moment he was first elected into office. The accusation was one of global culpability—as to the specific nature of the alleged crime, the accusers typically failed to elaborate.

"Let's keep it going, folks. Give us a ring and tell us what you think. Better yet, tell us what you're seeing out there on the street."

Before he could switch to the next caller, a sizeable *thump* sounded against the roof of the cistern.

The DJs froze, staring at each other.

Whaler stood from his chair by the folding table and crept toward the hatch.

Dread pushed the button to start what he feared might be their last music break.

"I smell a rat, baby."

~ *10* ~

The Rolling Stones

ONCE MORE, WHALER approached the cistern ladder, this time, peering far more cautiously at the hole in the ceiling.

Dread rose from his seat at the table, disentangling himself from the many wires and cords cluttering its surface. He whispered across the room.

"What do you see?"

Whaler climbed onto the ladder's lower rungs, trying to look out the hatch without poking his head over the rim. His wild frizz of hair bounced back and forth as he twisted his neck sideways, first one direction and then the other. Finally, he glanced back at Dread and issued his report.

"Sky."

The Puerto Rican threw his hands up, urging his colleague to move higher for a better look.

Tentatively, Whaler lifted his left foot to the next rung. He was about to shift his weight onto the upper step when a small stone rolled across the roof, skipped over the edge, and *plinked* onto the concrete floor.

Startled, Whaler jumped to the ground, his flip-flops nearly catching on the ladder rungs as he dodged the falling object.

"What in the heck is this?" he said, bending to pick up the stone. He held it up so that Dread could see. The two men stared at what appeared to be an ordinary piece of gravel; then their gazes shifted back to the ceiling.

Had their broadcasting location been discovered? Were the pasty boys waiting for them in the courtyard above? Was this a ploy to flush them out?

Before either DJ could muster an answer to these questions, a second stone of similar size rolled through the hole and dropped to the floor.

Whaler stared at it for a long moment before offering his assessment. "*Hmnh.* Okay, I'm going up."

Dread inched toward the ladder as Whaler brushed the sweaty hair from his brow, resolutely firmed his lips, and grabbed the metal handlebars.

"Violation of a court order. What's the worst they can do to us?" Whaler asked as he hefted his slim frame toward the hatch.

Dread's reply caused him to shudder.

"Send us down to Golden Grove for a couple of weeks."

Whaler reached the ladder's upper rungs and began to raise his head through the hole. Three inches of frizzy hair had emerged from the hatch when Dread called out a caution that made Whaler duck like a turtle pulling into its shell.

"Make sure they know you're unarmed."

"Dread, man. This is not worth getting shot."

As Whaler hesitated, looking down into the cistern, a handful of rocks sprinkled through the opening, most of them landing on his head.

"Arrrrrgh!" The howl echoed through the concrete room. Whaler dislodged several pebbles from his scalp. "Okay, that's it," he growled, charging up toward the hatch. "I don't care if it is the pasty boys. No one messes with the 'fro."

Dread hurried the remaining distance to the ladder as Whaler surged out the opening, stopping with his midsection bent over the ledge. He looked across the cistern roof at the lawn outside the Lutheran church in downtown Charlotte Amalie, where they were located.

"Dread! It's a couple of punk kids!" His voice cracked with indignation. "I'm going after 'em."

"No!" Dread hollered up the ladder. "Forget the kids. You'll blow our cover."

There was no containing Whaler's outrage. The stress of the day's events had converted into aggression.

"Hey! Hey, you over there. You think you're funny with the rocks? I'll give you something to laugh about!"

Before Whaler could scramble from the hatch, Dread lunged for his legs. Sliding on the pebbles that had scattered across the floor, he managed to grab Whaler's bony leg.

Whug. Whaler's flip-flops slipped from the ladder rungs. He caught the rim of the hatch with his arms, but he was quickly losing his grip.

"Let go, Dread!" He reached down with one hand and smashed his palm against the top of the Puerto Rican's bald head.

The two swung, awkwardly, for two long seconds, before crashing to the bottom of the cistern.

The commotion caused the relay on the radio equipment to repeat the broadcast jingle as another pebble rolled across the roof and dropped onto the floor.

"I smell a rat . . ."

Legislature Building

Charlotte Amalie

～

~ *11* ~

A Belligerent Lot

FBI ASSISTANT SPECIAL Agent in Charge Gabe Stein entered the meeting chambers for the US Virgin Islands Legislative Assembly and shook his head in dismay.

It was only a quarter past nine, but it had already been a long day for the man everyone called Friday—the nickname was a better fit for his scratchy voice, deadpan demeanor, and just-the-facts-ma'am approach to law enforcement. His horsey face and buggy eyeballs had helped to make the moniker stick.

The Legislature's rectangular building jutted out into the harbor at the east end of the shopping district, not far from Government Hill. Previously painted a distinctive mint green, the structure had recently been redone in a more demure cream.

The color overhaul hadn't toned down the attitudes or emotions of the elected officials who met inside, Friday reflected. He surveyed the senators quarantined in the middle of the meeting chamber—and winced at the harassment they were inflicting on the federal agents guarding the perimeter.

He had a feeling that his day would get a lot worse before it got better.

WIPING A SLEEVE across his brow, Friday shifted his focus from the senators to his team. Like him, the agents were conspicuously dressed from head to toe in black: black combat boots, black pants, black T-shirts, and black caps. It was an uncomfortable uniform selection for an operation staged in the hot and humid Caribbean.

While the flushed faces all belonged to familiar agents, people that Friday trusted from years of service together, he would have preferred to have brought on board a little local expertise.

The agency had a division office in nearby San Juan and a Resident Agency office on St. Thomas, but Agent Hightower, the special agent in charge, had stubbornly refused to involve them. Citing the potential for leaks, Hightower had insisted the team be staffed only with personnel from the Northern Virginia office.

Just another reason Friday hadn't liked the look of this operation from the get-go, he thought with a sigh.

There were too many variables, too many unknowns, too many ways the whole thing could go haywire—and with several federal agencies weighing in on the process, too many career-minded individuals ready to point fingers when the inevitable glitches occurred.

The undertaking was a political hot potato.

"Operation Coconut," he muttered to himself. Even the code name sounded hinky.

FRIDAY REACHED FOR a bottle of water and guzzled down several gulps, as much to relieve the stress as to douse his thirst. Regardless of office affiliation, a much bigger team would have been needed to run this mission properly, but his requests for additional manpower had been summarily denied.

If necessary, a small unit of National Guard troops waited on the navy vessel docked on the east side of town. However, numerous restrictions had been placed on that resource. He had been instructed in the sternest possible manner that the Guard was only to be used as a last resort.

This was to be a peaceful, purely judicial action. The FBI was to do nothing that might escalate matters into a civil conflict.

Friday screwed the lid back on his bottle. Despite his

misgivings, so far the operation was proceeding according to plan. He hadn't yet heard from Hightower, who was leading the Government House group, but his crew had entered the Legislature with minimal resistance.

The primary obstacle had been a female security guard manning the front entrance. She had blocked the doorway, demanding to see the arrest warrant. Even after a close inspection of the paperwork, she had questioned their authority.

Friday had been on the verge of forcibly moving her to the side when she grudgingly allowed the agents through.

He rolled his eyes, remembering the woman's miffed expression when he'd declined her request that they run their weapons through her security scanner.

AFTER CLEARING THE entrance hurdle, Friday and his fellow agents had moved quickly through the building.

Each of the senators had their own office space, so it would take time to complete a thorough search, but they had already captured most of the elected officials on the list.

Therein lay the next challenge.

The senators were to be held in the Legislature's meeting chambers until arrangements could be made to safely transport them, along with the Governor, to the navy vessel. A local federal district judge would be arriving shortly to preside over the formal reading of the charges. A third circuit appellate judge had flown down from Philadelphia to handle any pressing disputes that might arise. For the moment, the senators would have to sit tight.

Easier said than done, Friday thought. With an internal groan, he returned his gaze to the center of the room.

It was a belligerent, complaining bunch, but then, he supposed he would say that about most politicians. The senators were not shy in expressing their opinions.

Every possible insult and allegation had been hurled at Friday during their brief confinement—along with several pieces of trash and any other easily throwable items within reach.

He rubbed a bump on the side of his forehead. One of the feisty senators had nicked him with a wooden gavel.

Friday rubbed the scruff beneath his chin. Some of the protestations of innocence were probably true.

The six-month investigation into the USVI corruption charges had been rushed to its conclusion. Nebulous sources from high up the chain of command had exerted enormous pressure to move the case forward.

Even though investigators were still working to untangle the various interweaving lines of bribes, payoffs, and influence peddling, a decision had been made to throw a wide net around the territory's entire elected government.

Friday pulled off his black cap and fiddled with the size adjuster strap, seeking to lessen the pressure against his pounding temple.

It wasn't within his purview to question the justice department's legal analysis, but the collected evidence looked flimsy to him.

Given all of the procedural oddities surrounding the case, he wondered if someone behind the scenes had orchestrated the situation as a de facto coup.

With a frown, he slid his cap back on his head.

They wouldn't have been able to get the indictments at all without the cooperation and sworn testimony of a highly placed source within the Governor's cabinet.

"That's a whole lot of credence to place on just one witness."

FRIDAY TURNED AS an agent approached with the current inventory of the arrested senators.

"We're missing two, sir." The man looked down at a clipboard.

"Senator Bobo from St. Croix. Apparently he's a reverend, although I'm a little unclear on the religious denomination." Shrugging, he moved on to the other name. "And Senator Sanchez from St. Thomas."

Here it is, Friday thought as he switched on an earpiece radio device and prepared to brief Agent Hightower.

The first crack in the Coconut.

Fort Christian

Charlotte Amalie

～

~ *12* ~

The Missing Senators

FORT CHRISTIAN SPRAWLED across a short rise just above the shoreline, a strategic position it had occupied for over three hundred years. Reputed to be the oldest standing structure in the Virgin Islands, the fort had anchored the first Danish settlements on St. Thomas.

Fort Christian stood with its back turned to the Legislature Building, as if shunning the upstart democratic institution. From the fort's inland-facing entrance, it was a straight path down the waterfront to Market Square, a forum that bore the shameful distinction of having hosted some of the largest slave auctions in the West Indies.

Looking up the gentle slope from the fort's crumbling front steps, additional historic landmarks could be spotted. The stately Frederick Lutheran Church was only a few blocks away. Farther up the hillside, Government House was easy to pick out. A slight squint at the overlooking peak brought into focus Blackbeard's Tower.

The oldest of the city's Colonial monuments, Fort Christian was in the greatest state of disrepair. Its storybook façade was best viewed from a distance, where the cracking red plaster took on the romantic blur of a relic from an earlier era.

Up close, it wasn't so pretty.

The fort had been closed for several years, pending a

much-needed renovation, but that work had stopped not long after it began. Disputes between the VI government and the job's contractor had left the project in limbo. After lengthy exposure to the elements, the unfinished repair work would likely have to be redone. Despite constant promises to the contrary, it would be some time before the building would be ready to reopen to the public.

As a temporary measure, a small volunteer-staffed museum had been set up inside the fort, but given the curators' competing obligations, the hours of operation were sporadic.

In its prime, Fort Christian had cut an impressive figure. Named for one of Denmark's many kings, the massive walls soared up to Gothic arches and a top edging of crenellated battlements. A clock tower rose from the front wall, pointing timepieces at both the town and the harbor.

But nowadays, padlocks secured the building's rotting wooden doors. The windows were barred or boarded over. In the park that flanked the front entrance, a mishmash of telephone wires and power lines dangled from the limbs of battered trees.

Over the centuries, the fort had served as the seat of local government, a church, and a local jail.

Currently, it wasn't used for much of anything—except as a hiding place for two renegade USVI senators.

～～

IT WAS HOT inside Fort Christian's center courtyard. The sun beat down on the concrete-covered ground, its heat radiating up into the feet of Senators Bobo and Sanchez.

After evading capture inside the Legislature Building, the panting pair had sprinted across the street to the rear of the fort.

The fort's back parking area was blocked off with chain-link fencing and marked with warning placards. Perhaps due to the lengthy absence of the construction crews, parts of the fencing had sagged. A two-piece gate that stretched across the vehicle access had twisted at its midpoint to create a hole big enough for a full-sized adult to squeeze through.

Senator Bobo had hopped between the loosened gates like a seasoned rabbit, as if accustomed to the maneuver.

Senator Sanchez had followed him inside—with great hesitation.

JULIA SANCHEZ TURNED a slow pivot in the fort's courtyard, staring at the construction debris and abandoned scaffolding.

She had grown up in a residential area a few miles out of town. Like most children on the island, she'd visited the fort on school field trips and summer camp outings, but it had been more than a decade since she'd been inside the structure. The place looked far more run-down than she remembered, but, she supposed, childhood memories were often like that. Certainly, the dilapidated fort was a stark contrast to the recently painted Legislature Building across the street.

She shifted her attention to her fellow senator. "Lucky for us, you had a key to that back door."

"I've been volunteering in the museum," he replied, patting the pocket where he'd stashed the key ring. Solemnly, he tapped the four corners of a cross on his chest. "The good Lord looks out for Bobo."

Sanchez gave the man a dubious look.

"And the gate?" she prompted skeptically.

Reverend Bobo gave her a sly wink. "Providence provides to him who is prepared."

SENATOR BOBO LIVED in Frederiksted, a small community on the west end of St. Croix. He had taken the commuter seaplane up to St. Thomas earlier that morning in order to participate in the day's legislative activities.

He was a devoutly religious man—at least by all outward appearances. He ran a tiny but well-attended church in his neighborhood. It adhered to a strict conservative doctrine, but it was unaffiliated with any organized sect or denomination. As such, Bobo had never been officially ordained, but he had formally changed his first name to "Reverend," allowing him to use the title freely.

This deficiency (or perhaps, delusion) appeared not to matter to his loyal followers. The close-knit group had been instrumental to his repeated election to the Legislature, the clan tirelessly campaigning and fundraising for him. The other senators generally considered him a kook, but they rarely expressed this opinion out loud.

Bobo's political clout had been proven time and time again.

Sanchez glanced at the rainbow-colored scarf looped around Bobo's neck, an accessory he wore almost everywhere he went. The rest of his regular outfit comprised a white linen tunic draped over matching harem pants and, on his feet, huarache sandals. A musky coconut oil kept his frizzled gray hair swept back and the thinning strands plastered against his skull.

It was a distinctive look, one designed to stand out from the crowd.

The hair oil scent made the female senator want to gag.

"Bobo," Sanchez muttered to herself. "How did I get stuck with Bobo?"

JULIA SANCHEZ SHUFFLED sideways, increasing her distance from the fragrant hair oil. She was no stranger to the spotlight, but she preferred a more refined approach to publicity.

About five years earlier, she'd snagged a job as a junior weather girl for the island's main television station. The position had given her plenty of media experience and public exposure. She was accustomed to performing for cameras. At a moment's notice, she could switch from a pretty smile and a cute giggle to a solemn a-Cat-5-hurricane-is-coming-our-way expression.

After working her way up to senior weatherperson, she had channeled her growing popularity into politics, narrowly winning her first senate seat in the last election cycle.

It had been a nasty race, with a number of aspersions cast against her ethnicity. While her mother was a native Virgin Islander, her father was a Puerto Rican immigrant, leading some groups to insist on categorizing her as "other."

She had weathered the storm, so to speak, with class, dignity and the backing of her mother's family, who had deep roots in the West Indian community.

Despite the heavy makeup and flirty demeanor that had

been required for success in the television industry, she was a tomboy at heart. She wasn't easily pushed around by chauvinistic newsmen, fractious politicians, or the daily rough-and-tumble of the USVI Legislature.

Or, for that matter, Senator Bobo.

~ *13* ~

Hog-Tied

SENATOR SANCHEZ STRUMMED her fingers against the shoulder strap to her satchel-style briefcase, reflecting on how she'd wound up trapped in Fort Christian with Reverend Bobo.

JUST THIRTY MINUTES earlier, she'd been hurrying down a hallway inside the Legislature Building, the leather pouch of her briefcase bouncing against her hip. She was late for a subcommittee meeting and in a rush to get to the designated location.

A few feet from the committee room, she stopped to straighten her skirt, whose snug fit had twisted around her hips during the dash in from her car. Reaching up, she unhooked the clip that held back her wavy hair. With a quick head shake, the shoulder-length locks fell free. She tucked a few strands behind her left ear, smoothed her silk blouse, and prepared to march, unflustered, into what would likely be a quarrelsome meeting.

A half step past a cleaning closet by the room's entrance, a stiff hand grabbed her arm and pulled her inside.

She recognized her fellow senator almost instantly. A surge of indignation stifled her impulse to scream. She was about to knock Bobo over the head with her briefcase when he held a finger to his mouth and pointed to the two-inch crack he'd left open in the closet door.

Pushing aside a mop bucket, Bobo crouched to the ground and peered through the opening. Sanchez hesitated but eventually knelt beside him. She watched, stunned, as two black-clad federal agents moved stealthily through the corridor.

She gasped at the sight, causing Bobo to jab her with a shushing elbow.

"What's going on?" she whispered at the first break in the hallway's foot traffic.

Bobo mouthed the letters *F-B-I*.

"Why are they here?" she asked, troubled. "And why are we hiding?"

He leaned toward her so that his lips were practically touching her ear.

"They're after *us*. All of us." He raised a hand in front of her face and rubbed his fingertips together. "They think we're on the take."

Sanchez nearly choked on the smell of Bobo's hair oil. "But I'm not, I mean, I haven't . . ." she protested and then cut short her remark.

Another set of footsteps sounded outside the closet door, this time moving directly toward the senators' hidden position. The rubber soles on the agent's black combat boots squeaked, ever so slightly, against the tile floor.

Bobo gripped Sanchez's arm, squeezing it tightly.

Scrunched down in the closet, her leg muscles cramping and her head swimming from the proximity of Bobo's hair oil, Sanchez decided she'd had enough closet foolishness. It was time to put a stop to this nonsense.

She hadn't received any bribes during her short term in office. She would simply step forward and proclaim her innocence. Wincing, she released herself from Bobo grasp and prepared to stand.

Before she could move, a voice called out, "Hey, you!"

It belonged to Gilda, the guard from the Legislature's front entrance. The woman had worked in the building for decades and was a stickler for protocol. No matter a person's rank or seniority within the senate, Gilda insisted that everyone abide by the full set of security procedures, each and every time they entered the building.

In the few months since Sanchez had taken her senate seat, she had been subjected to Gilda's stern lectures more times than she cared to remember. Any deviation from the established protocol was met by rigid rebuke. She could only imagine Gilda's rage at the sight of federal agents running roughshod over her domain.

Gilda moved in front of the closet and gestured down the hallway.

"I saw them run around the corner," the security guard said in a convincing tattletale tone. "The two you're looking for— they went that way."

The rubber-soled boots jogged off toward a separate wing of the building.

"Stupid pasty boy," Gilda grumbled under her breath. Then she rapped on the closet door. "Hurry up. You can't stay in there forever."

Bobo pushed open the door and leapt into the hallway, nearly knocking over Sanchez in the process. "Can you get us to the side exit?"

The guard nodded grimly. "Come with me."

Sanchez stumbled out of the closet. "But I haven't done anything wrong."

The guard put her hands on her hips. "You think that matters? You want to end up like the rest of your lot? They've got 'em hog-tied in the main meeting chambers. Every last one 'cept for you two. I heard 'em hollering for their lawyers, but the pasty boys aren't letting anyone in."

"Hog-tied?" Sanchez repeated, in obvious disbelief. Surely, Gilda was exaggerating.

But suddenly, she didn't feel quite so willing to announce her presence to the arresting agents. Maybe it would be best to slip out of the Legislature Building and regroup. She could make herself available for questioning at the courthouse— accompanied by her lawyer.

"All right," Sanchez sighed, relenting. "Let's get out of here."

Sanchez slipped off her heels and crept barefoot down the hallway, her painted toenails treading behind Bobo's worn huaraches. Following the guard's hand-waving instructions, they made their way toward the building's north flank.

Gilda strode about ten feet in front of the senators, casually glancing from side to side, jauntily swinging her baton. It was a good act, Sanchez thought wryly, but the guard was perhaps enjoying her role in the subterfuge a little too much.

At several points along the way, they picked up snippets of the ongoing protests in the meeting chambers. While it didn't sound as if anyone had been tied up, the captured senators obviously weren't happy about their confinement.

For Sanchez, the raucous audio confirmed her decision to flee. The Legislature was a contentious decision-making body; discussions over the most mundane policy matters could evolve into shouting matches. She cringed at the thought of being cooped up with the other thirteen accused. She'd made the right decision to sneak out.

Now all she had to do was lose Bobo.

Sanchez spied the rectangular exit sign above Gilda's head. One last stretch of hallway to traverse and they'd be out the door.

She reached into her briefcase, feeling around for her cell phone. She'd call her lawyer, have him meet her, and then . . .

Bobo suddenly slid sideways into a recess created by a square column that jutted out from the nearest wall. Before Sanchez could object, she found herself yanked into the cramped space beside him. The Reverend's repulsive hair oil once more clogged her sinuses as the linen sleeve of his tunic wrapped around her neck.

"You have *got* to stop doing that," she hissed, trying to pull free of his grip.

"Shh," he replied, spitting into her ear.

The familiar squeak of rubber soles on tile emerged from an intersecting hallway—accompanied by a man's gritty voice. He appeared to be speaking into a wireless device.

"This is what we get for calling it Operation Coconut . . ."

"Agent Friday," Gilda greeted him with regimented formality. She tapped the exit door with her baton as if checking to see that it was secure.

The man's distracted reply was followed by the gradually disappearing squeak of his rubber-soled boots.

Sanchez squirmed free of Bobo's arm as Gilda jogged back to their hidden position.

"You two are going to get me fired," she sniped, signaling for the senators to come to the exit door.

Sanchez noted the harried expression on the guard's face. The game had lost its appeal. Another close call and she'd blow the whistle on them.

"You're on your own now," the guard said as she dismantled the security alarm and ushered the pair through the opening.

"Bless you, Gilda," the Reverend intoned in his placating preaching voice. He leaned in, as if to kiss her on the cheek, but the guard adeptly evaded his overture.

"Don't touch me, Bobo," the woman spat, wrinkling her nose from the acrid hair oil.

As the guard pivoted back toward the building's interior, she issued a last piece of advice.

"Get off the streets, fast as you can."

~ 14 ~

Blessed by God

THE WORLD OUTSIDE the Legislature Building was not the one Julia Sanchez thought she'd left a half hour earlier.

How had she missed the navy vessel docked at the cruise ship terminal on her drive in to work? Had she been so focused on her upcoming committee meeting—and so worried by the fact that she was running late—that she'd missed the anomaly in the harbor?

If so, she was one of the few. By now, the presence of both the navy ship and the FBI had been noted by almost everyone in Charlotte Amalie—along with the abrupt termination of the island's cell phone service.

Sanchez now joined in this last discovery. Still barefoot, she stood on the sidewalk outside the Legislature Building, punching buttons on her phone, trying to get a signal.

Bobo shook his head. He pointed down the block to a couple of taxi drivers cursing at their phones. "Forget it. It won't work. Best to turn it off. They'll only use it to track us."

As Sanchez powered down her phone, she saw a pair of FBI agents, crossing at a streetlight not more than a hundred feet away. She sucked in her breath and instinctively stepped backward.

Another duo in black clothing soon appeared at the next corner.

Escaping the Legislature, she realized, was only the beginning of their ordeal.

"This way," Bobo said, jogging across the street to the rear of Fort Christian.

Sanchez dropped the phone into her briefcase, tugged on her shoes, and scampered after the Reverend—immediately regretting her decision to follow when he hopped through the gap in the fort's rear fencing.

"IT'S A MIRACLE we made it here without getting caught," Sanchez summed up from her position inside the fort's courtyard.

"Blessed by God," Bobo replied, once more touching four points across his chest.

"Right," she replied, trying to keep the sarcasm from her voice. "What do we do next?"

The senators listened to the noise outside the fort. The air carried a volume of angry voices overlaid with the repeating *pop* of ammunition.

Bobo nodded toward the base of the fort's front tower. "There's a ladder inside to access the clocks. Let's climb up and see what's going on."

WEAVING AROUND PILES of discarded construction material, Bobo and Sanchez picked their way across the courtyard.

As they passed the little room that had been set aside for the museum, Sanchez caught a glimpse of a well-tended display area with exhibits dedicated to various aspects of the island's heritage. There were black-and-white photos, framed documents, maps, and, hanging on the far wall, one of the ubiquitous cutlasses that had been used to cut sugarcane.

Someone had taken a lot of care with the layout, she thought as she followed Bobo through to the fort's front foyer. It was a shame the rest of the structure was in such disrepair.

The Reverend reached the open shaft that contained the clock tower's rusty ladder. He slung his rainbow scarf over one shoulder and began pulling himself up the steps.

Sanchez looked at the shaky rungs and decided to once more

abandon her heels. She waited until Bobo made it to the top and stepped onto an adjacent platform before she began her climb. Leaving the heels on the floor beside her briefcase, she hiked up her skirt and scaled the ladder.

A narrow ledge ran around the tower's outer circumference, just a few feet below the clock face. Sanchez crossed the platform, ducked through an opening in the wall, and joined Bobo on the outside ledge.

They had views to every direction, including the harbor, the downtown waterfront, and Government Hill.

"Good grief, they're everywhere," Sanchez said as she watched another group of FBI agents gather outside the Legislature. If she and Bobo had been a minute later leaving the building—or crossing the street to the fort—they would have been captured.

Turning, she rotated her gaze to look toward the central downtown shopping district.

Just past a line of fire trucks and emergency vehicles parked against the fort's west wall, she found the now-empty vendors' plaza. Across the next intersection, a pricey jewelry store that occupied a prime corner lot had been locked up and secured with its nighttime barriers.

"What is going on?" Sanchez asked, stunned by the scene.

Bobo intoned as if speaking from the pulpit. "Hellfire and damnation are raining down on this island, that's what."

Sanchez scowled in frustration. It was unheard of to see Charlotte Amalie's downtown shuttered on a day when a large cruise ship was in port. But the only pedestrians on the street were disgruntled locals. It appeared the passengers—and their dollars—had been kept on board the vessel.

The thought of all that lost revenue made her blood boil.

She thrust her arms in the air, gesturing at the agents outside the Legislature Building. "Do they know how much damage they've caused? What kind of bribery investigation results in a complete government takeover?"

Bobo offered a noncommittal shrug. "I'm still trying to figure out how all those people were on the take." His voice sounded almost offended. "If someone was handing out money to senators, they sure didn't give any to me."

Sanchez dropped her hands to her sides, slapping her palms against her hips.

"Look, Bobo, we need a plan."

A pickup drove past the empty vendors' plaza, blaring its radio at full capacity. Enormous speakers had been hinged to the back bed so that they could be rotated outward. The rear tires bulged from the extra weight; the bumper nearly dragged on the ground.

Despite the static feedback, Sanchez recognized the KRAT broadcast.

"The pasty boys are still looking for the Governor," Dread Fred reported. Whaler let out one of his distinctive high-pitched whistles and added, "We've got a signed T-shirt for the first person who sends us a picture of the big man in handcuffs!"

Dread squeezed in a last comment before the broadcast jingle started to play.

"Run, Guvvy, run."

Legislature Building

Charlotte Amalie

~ *15* ~

The Man in Charge

AGENT FRIDAY STATIONED himself in a hallway outside the meeting chambers, safely shielded from the senators detained inside. He'd had enough heckling for one day—and his head still hurt where the gavel had nicked him.

His team had combed the Legislature Building from top to bottom. Senators Bobo and Sanchez were nowhere to be found. The entry logs indicated that both senators had passed through the security scanners that morning, but the pair must have sneaked out during his team's initial sweep.

Operation Coconut had officially dropped the ball.

Bobo, he thought wryly as he lifted his cap to massage his left temple. What kind of a name is Bobo?

The woman from the St. Thomas branch of the attorney general's office stepped into the hallway and handed him a walkie-talkie.

"Hey, Friday," she said with a toss of her head. "You'd better take this."

Despite the AGENT STEIN tag pinned to his shirt, it had taken the locals less than thirty minutes to pick up on his agency nickname. Even the testy security guard from the front entrance was now calling him by the moniker.

With a sigh, he took the receiver.

"This is Friday."

The call was from the advance team tasked with arresting the Governor and his cabinet. One of the agents under Hightower's command had dropped back to send a discreet warning.

As Friday listened to the report, the lines on his face deepened into ruts.

"What do you mean you just got to Government House? I can see it on the hill above us. How did it take you thirty minutes to hike a couple hundred yards?"

The response caused his expression to sour further.

"The mission is to secure the Governor. He can't arrest everyone he comes across who's carrying a weapon."

Friday's eyes rolled toward the ceiling.

"Yes, of course I hear the gunshots. They're not shooting at you, though, are they?"

He crammed his cap back down onto his head. Operation Coconut was falling apart, and he would no doubt be held responsible for the mess.

"Tell Hightower I'm on my way."

Government House

Charlotte Amalie

~ 16 ~

The Gorilla

SPECIAL AGENT IN Charge Reginald Hightower, aka "the Gorilla," charged toward the Government House front steps, accompanied by the rest of his advance team. The agent who had dropped back to radio Friday sprinted to catch up to the rest of the group.

"We're here for the Governor," Hightower announced boldly as he powered into the lobby.

He was a beefy, overmuscled man who spent an inordinate amount of time lifting weights in the gym. His bulky shoulders hunched forward, as if pulled down by the weight of his biceps. With his closely shorn head and top-heavy physique, it wasn't hard to see the animal resemblance. But his code name was inspired by more than his similarities to the simian shape; many thought of it as a reference to his quick, often irrational temper.

In addition to sporadic fits of rage, Hightower was also prone to distraction—as demonstrated by the numerous diversions that had taken place during the short trek up from the shoreline. The team had stopped several times to investigate potential "subversives." Half their number was still stuck in Emancipation Park, interviewing the increasingly hostile citizens Hightower had ordered to be detained for questioning.

Hightower's unlikely advancement through the FBI to

special agent in charge was a mystery to the rank and file. Within the last six months, he had been plucked out of relative obscurity and elevated to a senior leadership position. A less qualified candidate had never been so rapidly promoted. Rumors of backroom payoffs and high-placed political pressure circulated with every accolade and award.

The choice of Hightower to head Operation Coconut was a puzzle—and a concern—to the agents under his command that day in Charlotte Amalie.

"Sir," one had suggested on their final approach to Government House through the public gardens that covered the hillside below. "Perhaps some of us should go around back to cover the rear of the building."

Hightower had replied with a withering glare. He pointed up at the suited man who had just appeared on the second-floor balcony outside the Governor's office.

"Don't bother," he said dismissively. "We've got eyes on the asset. Look at him. This guy's not running anywhere—except maybe to the ice cream store."

He laughed at his own joke.

The rest of the team exchanged worried glances as they followed their leader into the lobby.

AFTER A HEATED exchange with the woman standing by the security scanners, Hightower wasted no time thumping up the carpeted stairs to the second floor.

This is going to be a piece of cake, he thought as he reached the top step and turned down the hallway toward the Governor's office.

The other agents closed in around him, positioning themselves against the outer wall and the inner side railing, moving in tandem to clear the area of potential threats.

Hightower waved them off.

The place was silent and still. No loyal bodyguards lurked in the corridor to protect the head of state. No vigilantes had camped out to challenge the agents' authority.

"I got this," he growled softly.

Motioning for the other agents to trail him at a distance, Hightower strutted toward the executive suite's marked entrance.

The door had been left slightly ajar. Hightower stopped outside the threshold, listened briefly, and then eased his shoulders through the opening, gun at the ready.

It was a long room, ornately decorated. Paintings in gilded frames hung from the textured walls. Plush red throw rugs stretched across a dark wooden floor. The Governor's wide mahogany desk occupied one corner, while a liquor cabinet and a display table for a marble backgammon set filled in another. A wall of windows framed the far end next to an open door that led out onto the balcony.

Hightower's gaze skimmed over the décor, checking for any third parties that might give him trouble. Seeing none, he shifted his focus to the man he'd seen from the public gardens below Government House. The target still stood on the balcony, looking out over Charlotte Amalie.

Unless the Governor was blind, he would have seen the feds swarming the Legislature Building on the shoreline as well as the activity of the black-clad agents in Emancipation Park. Hightower's arrival wouldn't be a surprise. The Governor had apparently decided to capitulate without a fight.

The Gorilla's chiseled face eased into a sly grin. This would be the biggest arrest of his career, résumé-building material that could catapult him into the agency's upper echelons.

He glanced over his shoulder at the agents hovering in the hallway and mouthed a stern *Stay back*. He wasn't going to share this glory with anyone else.

Hightower pressed forward into the office, his footsteps muffled on the evenly spaced floor rugs as he crossed to the balcony. The audio of the anticipated accolades played in his head.

We are here today to award the department's highest commendation to SAIC Reginald Hightower, for deftly taking down the corrupt leader of a rogue state . . .

Oh, heck, he thought, don't let facts get in the way. Let's just call him an oppressive dictator.

Ready to get down to business, Hightower hit the pause button on his internal commentary and crept to the edge of the balcony.

The Governor's build was slightly less bulky than Hightower had expected, based on the photos in the briefing file he had flipped through on the trip down to the island. His shoulders didn't quite fill out the tailored lines of his suit. Perhaps the strain of the past few weeks had taken a toll on the big man's appetite—or his wife had cut off his ice cream supply.

Hightower could barely suppress mental chuckle.

Regardless, nothing was going to prevent the successful completion of this mission.

As he stepped onto the balcony, the clatter of plastic on wood sounded from inside the office.

Hightower flinched, resisting the urge to look back to see which agent had knocked the picture frame over on the Governor's desk.

The suited man slowly turned from the balcony railing.

"Good morning, gentlemen."

Hightower leapt forward with his handcuffs.

"Governor, you have the right to remain silent."

The suit looked even more ill-fitting when viewed from the front, but the man inside the clothes was perfectly at ease. He held out his hands to the agent.

"Yes, of course."

Hightower snapped the cuffs around the man's wrists. "Anything you say can and may be used against you . . ."

"Oh dear."

The mocking tone riled the Gorilla's temper, taunting his inner beast. Already irritated by the subordinate's picture frame fumble, his face turned red with rage.

Swallowing a curt retort, Hightower continued the mandatory listing of the arrestee's Constitutional rights. "You have the right to an attorney . . ."

"Sounds like we better call him."

A strained cough interrupted before Hightower could spit out a response.

"Sir."

An agent stood by the desk, holding a picture of the territory's head of state standing next to his wife, the First Lady.

The agent frowned at the image and then compared the photographed face to that of the man in the handcuffs.

"You got the wrong guy."

"What?"

Meekly, the agent cleared his throat. "That's not the Governor."

Hightower spun around, stomped to the desk, and snatched the photo from the agent's hands.

His expression cycled through disbelief, realization, and then back to rage.

Cursing, he threw the frame onto the floor, cracking the glass fronting.

~ *17* ~

The Betrayal

GRUMBLING INTO THE two-way radio, Agent Friday huffed up the road to Government House. He was accompanied by a handful of agents that he had snagged on his way out of the Legislature Building.

The group had nearly completed the short hike to Government Hill, skirting Fort Christian, Emancipation Park, and a large post office en route.

While climbing a flight of public steps north of the post office, they received word that the Governor had given the slip to the team responsible for his arrest.

Alarmed, Friday had increased his pace to a brisk trot.

He rushed through the Government House front entrance just as a fuming Hightower shoved the handcuffed doppelgänger out of the Governor's office and down the hallway toward the stairs.

Friday joined the sea of upturned faces watching from the first floor. He clenched his teeth, hoping the Gorilla wasn't about to throw the man over the hallway railing.

He tried to catch Hightower's attention, but his hand-waving was ineffective. His polite verbal attempts were drowned out by the senior agent's belligerent rant.

"No one plays me for the fool and gets away with it. I'll book you on impersonating."

The doppelgänger merely smirked. He knew Hightower was bluffing.

"I believe I asked for my attorney."

"Oh, I'll get you your attorney. He'll have to use dental records to identify you . . ."

"Agent Hightower, *sir*," Friday called out, straining his voice to be heard. "I thought we might be of assistance."

Hightower jerked the doppelgänger to the side so that he could see down to the lower level.

"Friday," he replied without the least bit of embarrassment. "Good of you to join us."

FRIDAY SENT A subteam to scour the rest of the building for the real governor while one of the other agents took custody of the doppelgänger and carefully marched him down the stairs.

Hightower directed his ire to the employees who had been gathered in the lobby. With Friday's assistance, he corralled the onlookers into a center seating area for questioning.

It was a crowded assembly. Workers from a variety of positions were represented, from senior policy advisors to administrative clerks and cleaning staff.

Hightower was confident he would be able to elicit the Governor's location from one of the employees.

Agent Friday wasn't so sure. Despite the wide range of socioeconomic backgrounds, there was a stony similarity in the expressions on these West Indian faces. Whatever fractures of loyalty that might have existed within the group had been sealed over by Hightower's rough display on the second-floor hallway.

Friday stepped back and observed, but remained ready to jump in if needed. He'd been saddled with the awkward job of preventing his boss from making any further errors in judgment.

Operation Coconut, he thought bitterly. This is the last time I take an assignment named after a hairy piece of fruit.

The Gorilla moved clunkily from one suspect to the next, passing over the suited bureaucrats for the administrative staff and cleaning crew. The latter employees he deemed more likely to rat out their boss.

After unsuccessful interrogations of a janitor, a copy boy, and a secretary, Hightower focused on a cleaning maid seated in the middle of the group. The large unhappy-looking woman wore a cotton dress with a high frilly collar. A hairnet covered her tangled hair.

She sighed uncomfortably as Hightower bent over her chair, flexing his beefcake muscles for intimidating effect.

The maid fiddled with her cheap drugstore eyeglasses, nervously pushing the plastic frames into the soft cartilage of her nose.

"I think *you* know where the Governor ran off to. Don't you?"

Like the rest of the employees, she at first refused to speak or even look at him. She crossed and recrossed her unshaved legs, shuffling the flimsy rubber sandals that were squeezed onto her chunky feet. But after a few minutes of Hightower's steely-eyed stare and badgering questions, she pursed her lips and silently rotated her head. Her eyes looked pointedly northwest, in the direction of the public stairs that led up Government Hill.

It was a wordless communication, but an effective betrayal, nonetheless.

"Friday!" Hightower hollered, thrusting his arm to point at the building's rear exit. "Get moving!"

An Abandoned Construction
Site on Government Hill
Charlotte Amalie

⌒

~ *18* ~

The Hideout

IN AN ABANDONED construction site up the hill from Government House, Cedric kept a watchful eye out the window through which Fowler had hefted the Governor less than an hour earlier.

The aide wiped his sweaty face with a damp handkerchief. He was standing next to the building's only open portal; the rest of the doors and windows had been sealed up, likely to prevent just this type of incursion.

Government Hill was a pricey neighborhood with several historic homes built into its steep slope. Key selling points were the area's proximity to downtown, the facilitating access of multiple public staircases, and the stunning harbor views. The most appreciated feature—by both the current inhabitants and the original settlers—was the breeze that filtered up the hillside, helping to break the humidity.

"No luck on that today," Cedric muttered as he glanced over his shoulder at the gutted interior. Despite the building's missing roof, the high walls blocked any cooling respite the wind might have provided.

THERE WASN'T MUCH left of the residential home that had been co-opted as the Governor's hideaway.

The structure was undergoing a major renovation and had been stripped down to its concrete shell. From the look of things, work had been stopped for several months. The interior had been left exposed to the elements, and weeds had sprouted up through cracks in the concrete. A permit issue had probably tied up the construction, Cedric mused.

It was a perfect spot for the Governor to lay low, he had to admit. With the exterior walls still intact, they were hidden from the public staircase that led down to Government House. That same walkway had ensured the Governor's minimal exposure en route. Once they ducked out the back gate, it had taken just a few minutes to get here.

His only complaint: with no roof, the concrete floor was baking hot.

LOOSENING THE TOP buttons of his collared shirt, Cedric glanced over his shoulder at the fugitive hiding farther inside the building.

The Governor had tucked his body into a shaded crevice in one of the kitchen walls, an opening designed for a sink or a stove. Capped wires and cut-off piping poked out from the framing. Seeking shelter from the sun, he had crawled as far back into the hole as possible. Not much of the man was visible, other than his sneakered feet, which had drooped sleepily sideways.

Whatever burst of energy had inspired the wild sprint through Government House and the hike up the hill had been depleted.

Cedric grinned as a snore droned out of the kitchen cubbyhole.

Now *that* was the Governor he knew.

Cedric shifted his gaze to Fowler, who hunched by the Governor's shoes like a pit bull guarding a bone.

Fowler stared across the construction site, an unreadable expression on his flat face. Sweat drenched his oversized golf shirt and dotted his loose-fitting khaki pants.

Cedric found himself wondering, yet again, how the Governor had managed to contact the Fixer without his knowledge.

In the weeks leading up to the indictments, he had carefully monitored the Governor's movements, always staying within earshot, if not closer. Whatever means they'd used to communicate had somehow slipped past his radar.

His eyes narrowed as he pondered Fowler's interference in the day's proceedings.

The day hadn't turned out quite the way he and his coconspirators had planned. Now that he'd had a moment to reflect on the situation, however, he could see that the damage wasn't nearly as bad as he had initially feared.

They had yet to achieve their primary goal—the Governor's arrest—but it was only midmorning. The Guv couldn't possibly elude his pursuers for long. Operation Coconut was off and rolling. The feds wouldn't stop until they had their man.

CEDRIC RETURNED HIS focus to the window and the view through to the public staircase on the opposite side. Although all sorts of commotion rumbled up from Emancipation Park and the city's waterfront, the walkway outside the construction site was quiet and—frustratingly—unoccupied.

There was no indication that the federal agents inside Government House had sounded the alarm and begun a wider search.

Cedric tried to ignore the tantalizing weight of his cell phone in his pocket.

If only he could send a text message with their location to the woman from the local attorney general's office, the information would be routed to the FBI, and agents would be swarming up the stairs in a matter of minutes.

But with the Fixer lurking less than ten feet away, it was too great a risk to try to access his phone. While the man's eyes appeared to be glazed over, Cedric had the distinct impression they were sharply trained on his position by the window. He couldn't chance it.

He shrugged off the thought.

All but essential phone lines in the territory had been shut down. Even if he could sneak his phone out of his pocket, he probably wouldn't be able to send the message.

More important, he had a cover to maintain. The general

public need never know that he was involved in the Governor's downfall.

He took in a deep breath and slowly let it out.

By now, the doppelgänger in the Governor's office should have been exposed. Surely, one of the many backstabbers at Government House would have snitched on which direction they'd fled, if not the exact location of the hideout.

It was only a matter of time before the feds began sweeping the hillside. Sooner or later, the agents would track them down.

With a tense sigh, Cedric stared out the window.

He wished they'd hurry up.

He'd been waiting months for the Governor's ouster. His patience had reached its limit.

~ 19 ~

Seeking a Schism

IT WAS NO small thing, plotting to unseat the elected governor of a US territory. Even as Cedric sweltered in the hot sun, restlessly anticipating the arrival of the federal agents, he knew that he had to remain calm and let the situation play out.

This was but the latest scheme hatched by the aide and his fellow conspirators—the goal of each initiative had been to trigger a groundswell of social upheaval that would cause a permanent schism between the territory and its US overseer.

Separatist movements had been present in the US Virgin Islands for decades, going back to the 1917 transfer of ownership from the Danes to the Americans. But in recent times, the independence ideal had lost all momentum. Despite a neverending stream of complaints, most islanders had concluded that the benefits of US citizenship outweighed the drawbacks of their limited federal representation. After years of thwarted ballot initiatives and waning political support, the separatist agenda had petered out—on the surface, that is.

A secretive offshoot from the lone surviving independence coalition, Cedric's cabal was alive and kicking.

CEDRIC AND HIS conspirators had abandoned all attempts to achieve a separatist mandate through the ballot box. In their view, subterfuge had a far better chance of manipulating public perception than stump speeches and door-to-door canvassing. They aimed to create a provocative event that would rile local sentiments and sway enough opinions, if only temporarily, to effect the desired change.

As in any modern municipality, there were plenty of fears and prejudices upon which to play. The easiest for the cabal to exploit revolved around Native Rights, a belief among a vocal minority that preferential treatment should be given to islanders who could trace their ancestry back to West Indians living in the territory at the time of its US transfer. The proposed list of rights included tax exemptions, homestead land grants, voting privileges, and qualification hurdles for those seeking elected office.

Frictions between those who could claim the Native Rights heritage and those who could not were regularly vented in election debates and on the floor of the Legislature. The contentious issue had even torn apart the most recent effort to draft a USVI constitution.

The populace was primed for an explosive outburst. It was just a matter of finding the right wedge, the right nerve to expose and trample.

IT TURNED OUT social engineering was a difficult science, a delicate process of trial and error. Despite their best efforts, the cabal's previous schemes had failed to achieve the desired results.

Indeed, the most recent project had nearly ended in disaster.

Intended to spark civil unrest on St. Croix, a plot to engineer the racially motivated murder of a Saudi grocery store owner had gone awry when the sacrificial perpetrators, two luckless coconut vendors, had disappeared from the crime scene at the last critical moment.

Cedric shook his head at the memory. They were lucky their man on St. Croix had taken the fall for that caper. Otherwise, the entire cabal could have been exposed. Casanova had been sent to Golden Grove to serve a minimal sentence. Given his connections, he would no doubt be released soon.

The cabal had continued its work, unabated.

Crouched next to the concrete wall inside the abandoned construction site, Cedric listened to the chaos bubbling up from Charlotte Amalie's lower downtown area. He could hardly suppress his inner glee.

The attempt to remove the Governor from office was their most promising effort yet. It was bolder and more direct than anything they had tried before.

And this time, it was working.

WIPING ANOTHER LAYER of sweat from his forehead, Cedric reflected on the inspiration for the day's ploy.

The idea had occurred to him a few months back, when he read a news story about a controversy brewing in the Caribbean islands of the Turks and Caicos. The territory's residents were railing against a VAT (value added tax) that their caretaker governor had threatened to impose on all goods and services.

It was the notion of the appointed governor, imposed by the overseeing British government, that had piqued Cedric's interest.

He vaguely remembered the corruption allegations against the elected premier that had triggered the British takeover, but T&C was too far north of the Virgins to draw more than a passing mention in the local press.

Intrigued, Cedric quickly plowed through every news article about the T&C crisis he could get his hands on.

After a police inquiry into enormous bribes being paid to develop public lands, the T&C's premier had suddenly resigned and fled to South America. The UK promptly suspended the islands' government and replaced it with one led by the British caretaker governor, who would serve until the corruption issues were resolved and new elections could be organized.

The initial British takeover met only muted resistance, but by the end of the interim governing period, the appointed leader had plummeted in popularity.

The threatened imposition of the VAT drew a firestorm of criticism. The caretaker governor eventually withdrew his tax proposal, deferring the issue to the incoming elected government, which had since taken control—and summarily dismissed the hated tax.

CEDRIC HAD OBSESSED over the story.

What would it take to wake Virgin Islanders from decades of subjugated complacency? Could a similar scenario be devised to provoke a US takeover—one that would prove so distasteful the residents would finally rise up and throw out their overlords?

The question was tantalizing. He'd spent several days plotting out a strategy.

Then he shared it with the separatists.

Like a boulder careening down one of Charlotte Amalie's steep hills, the project had been gaining momentum ever since.

~ 20 ~

The Rabbit Hole

IT WAS A long and winding path from devoted public servant to devious revolutionary, from starry-eyed intern to subversive malcontent.

Cedric had made the full conversion.

The man he once idolized, he had come to despise.

The system that had provided his life's most valuable opportunities, he now loathed and labored to dismantle.

A vigilante's blinkered zeal steered his vision.

He thought of the events still to come, the chips yet to fall, and relished his role in the Governor's demise.

He was a complicated man with complicated ambitions.

But it hadn't always been that way.

GROWING UP, CEDRIC was a studious sort, an awkward adolescent who tried hard to fit in but somehow always found himself outside the norm. His efforts to assimilate made him stick out all the more.

A fragile soul, he soldiered on, closely watching his peers for signs of acceptance that would never come, at least not in the demonstrative form that would satisfy his thirsty ego.

That perceived rejection wounded him to the core.

Emotionally closed off, he was a puzzle to his parents and

the few friends he had accumulated. He could be openly hostile, frigidly polite, or, in his more desperate moments, unnervingly obsequious.

The alienation fed an isolation-induced vanity. In that coping mechanism sprung the seeds of the duplicitous adult he would become.

In politics, he was a natural fit.

CEDRIC STARTED WORKING for the Governor on his first campaign, volunteering as an entry-level intern. Eager to please, he worked tirelessly, making himself available for extra duties after hours and on the weekends. He made himself useful and then, inevitably, indispensible, soon earning a paid position as a junior staffer.

Latching on to the Governor's broad coattails, Cedric gradually weaseled his way into the politician's inner circle. His duties expanded into his natural area of expertise: data consumption and on-demand delivery.

Long an observer of local politics, Cedric was an encyclopedic resource on the topic. His brain was wired with an infinite capacity for minutia. He knew the pros and cons of every policy issue, the professional and private details of every actor engaged in the legislative process. Most important, he could disgorge these facts at a moment's notice. This last ability, in particular, gained him the highest level of access to the Governor—and the informal title of "right-hand man."

Maintaining this database, however, required constant study, intake, and observation.

It was while diligently collecting information that he slipped down the rabbit hole.

CEDRIC WAS ON his way home from another busy day at Government House when the first wayward step occurred.

He had stopped at Emancipation Park, where the separatists were holding a sparsely attended meeting. It was an innocuous gathering, clearly the dying sputterings of a dysfunctional organization.

But as he prepared to leave, one of the members touched

him on the shoulder and whispered in his ear, extending an invitation to a far more select committee that would be convening later that evening.

Skeptical but intrigued, Cedric wrote down the location.

At the designated time, he wandered into the waterfront alleys and found the address of the jewelry shop he'd been told was hosting the event.

From the narrow walkway, he tried to peek through the grate-covered glass. Like the rest of the stores in the downtown area, it was locked up tight. There was no indication that anyone else was around.

Cedric rang the buzzer, not expecting a response. But after a few silent seconds, the furtive shopkeeper peered out through a hole in the protective grate and reluctantly let him in.

The aide was surprised at what he found inside—or more specifically, who. In a dimly lit room behind the display area, he encountered a cluster of the island's most influential citizens, native Virgin Islanders with tremendous economic and political clout.

Then he was introduced to the woman at the center of the group, a charismatic figure of immense prestige. Due to the sensitive nature of her public position, her role in the organization had to be kept confidential, and she could only attend private meetings with closed access.

He left that evening unsure of how to process what he'd observed or of why he had been entrusted with such an important secret.

Nevertheless, he omitted mention of the meeting from his briefing the following day.

The next time the Governor asked for his thoughts on the separatists, Cedric dismissed them as irrelevant.

From that moment on, the schism slowly grew between Cedric and his mentor—even as the Governor remained unaware of the rift.

CEDRIC PIVOTED AWAY from the window in the concrete shell of the construction site on Government Hill. He turned as if to check on the Governor and Fowler. In reality, the aide was looking up over the far wall to the mansion perched on the adjacent hill, about twenty degrees around the city's upper perimeter from the worksite where they were hiding.

Visible from almost every angle within Charlotte Amalie, the Governor's Mansion looked down on the whole of the city. Flagpoles in the south yard framed the stately white-painted structure. Surrounded by a mass of jungled greenery, the building stood alone atop the steep slope, its columned front emulating the president's living quarters in Washington, DC.

Cedric had visited the gated property numerous times during the Governor's tenure. His admiration for the fine furnishings, manicured lawns, and expansive view had followed his overall transition, morphing into envy-tainted desire.

His was a patriotic mission, a matter of pride and heritage. But if he played his cards right, he would soon be moving into that mansion—as the new head of state.

The woman leading the conspiracy had assured him as much.

The Attorney General's Office
Washington, DC

~ 21 ~

Buster

THE US ATTORNEY general sat in a top-floor office cluttered with stacks of legal files and document-laden banker's boxes, pensively staring at a collection of papers spread across his desk.

He was a wolfish man with a lawyer's worn-down look. Worry lines had aged his once-boyish face. A pair of smudged eyeglasses sat haphazardly on his nose, the lenses needed to correct the vision that Harvard Law School and fifteen years at an ultracompetitive Manhattan law firm had irreparably damaged. While the speckled gray of middle age made some men more attractive, his color change only lent an air of frazzled exhaustion.

It was late morning in the nation's capital, but the country's chief law enforcement officer had been up half the night. The lack of sleep—along with the accumulated wear from several decades' worth of nocturnal deprivation—had taken their toll.

He reached for a bottle of antacid tablets, tilted the container to knock the last pink squares out into his palm, and popped them into his mouth like candy. The tablets crunched between his teeth, disintegrating into a thick powder that he swallowed without water. The chalky taste was no longer bitter or off-putting. Just another part of his daily routine.

The potent combination of stress, caffeine, and aspirin had

worn his stomach lining to the point of constant irritation. The condition was exacerbated by his nightly relief, a cocktail—or more typically, cocktails—at the bar around the corner from his DC apartment.

The downtown digs had originally been meant as temporary housing, to use when work kept him too late to bother with driving home. The apartment had quickly become his permanent residence.

His wife and dog lived in the family's townhouse in Old Town Alexandria. The wife had long since given up on the marital relationship. She accompanied her husband to obligatory work functions and social events; otherwise, the two rarely saw or spoke to one another.

A picture of the happy golden retriever was propped on the corner of the AG's desk, facing his chair for easy viewing. There were no mementos of the wife.

The AG was the epitome of professional success. His career had been lauded by colleagues, fellow alumni, and myriad bar associations, but he rarely felt any satisfaction in his achievements or that his life's sacrifices had been worthwhile.

A few months down the road—perhaps sooner, given the mess that his department had just created down south— someone else would take over this office.

After that, he doubted anyone would remember that he was ever here.

THE ATTORNEY GENERAL swallowed the last chalky bits of antacid and chased the pink paste down with a gulp of stale coffee.

He flipped over one of the top sheets of paper on his desk, cursed under his breath, and shifted his gaze to the framed photo of the dog.

The room was nicely furnished, fitting for his rank, but the décor was hidden behind the boxes and piles of paper, giving it a closed-in feel.

The AG was one generation removed from the modern trend of paperless record-keeping. While he was comfortable with a computer and at ease with the various forms of tablet technology, he still preferred to read a document on printed paper. He wanted to write notes in the margins, highlight important words and passages in the text, or, if the need arose, crumple the sheet up and throw it across the room.

When he walked into the tidy offices of his junior attorneys, he couldn't help but feel suspicious. How could they work in places that were so clean? Where was the evidence of their diligence?

When these same attorneys handed him their legal briefs, he often asked to see their background notes. He still found it unconscionable when they handed him a tiny jump stick instead of a Redweld crammed with dog-eared court cases. The worst offense, of course, happened at the end of each day as they walked toward the elevator, carrying nothing but a thin brief-case and a laptop computer.

He still lugged a banker's box home each night.

Of course, in times like these, with his career on the line and an increasingly unstable situation unfolding in the Caribbean territory his department had decided to seize, he just slept in his office.

The AG shivered, pulling on a cardigan he kept draped over the back of his chair.

An electronic wall setting allowed him to control the room's temperature, but it seemed he could never get comfortable. It was always either too hot or too cold.

As the air-conditioning unit cycled on, blowing frigid air down onto his desk, he thought about the events unfolding a thousand miles to the south on humid St. Thomas.

"We've really stepped our foot in it, Buster," the attorney general muttered to the dog's flat photo image.

~ 22 ~

The Green Light

THE US ATTORNEY general rubbed his temples as he reflected on the circumstances that had brought about the day's arrests on St. Thomas.

Attempted arrests, he corrected. The Governor and two senators were still missing.

The case had come up through the department's Virgin Islands division, championed by the woman who led the branch office in Charlotte Amalie. Wendy the Wunderkind—that's what the AG called her. She was one of his best and brightest recruits, an attorney who brimmed with the ambition that had all but drained from his being.

Despite Wendy's stellar reputation and the merits of the case, the AG had shied away from the USVI corruption allegations for months—and for good reason, he could almost hear the dog's picture reminding him.

But Wendy had persisted.

He'd finally been convinced by the analogies to the situation in the Turks and Caicos. Wendy had assisted the British government in their case against the T&C's former premier, whom Interpol had tracked down to a beach in Rio. The fugitive politician had been extradited back to his homeland to stand trial on corruption charges. The suit involved bribes worth millions of dollars, some paid by US nationals, made in exchange for discounted purchase prices and facilitated development clearance for publicly owned land.

By all accounts, the premier had changed, seemingly overnight, from a man of relatively modest means to a lavish millionaire playboy. His rapid wealth accumulation had occurred in conjunction with his election to the territory's highest elected office. Not long after taking the position, he began traveling the world in private jets and holding extravagant parties for movie stars and other celebrities. To top it off, he built a jaw-dropping private estate on one of the island's most pristine and sought-after beachfront locations.

Despite the circumstantial evidence of the T&C premier's flamboyant lifestyle, it was the testimony of the man's ex-wife that dealt the fatal blow. As payback for her husband's many infidelities, the glamorous American model had provided crucial evidence to the British Parliament. The investigating committee subsequently issued a damning corruption report on the premier.

Rather than face a full inquiry, the premier fled the country. A British caretaker governor was put in place to clean up the territory's rampant corruption and supervise new elections.

All in all, the process of takeover and release went smoothly. The transition was completed in just under three years. The Turks and Caicos reformation was now touted as an example for other countries with pesky post-Colonial Caribbean holdings.

Of course, the premier's decision to flee his post had facilitated the procedure. There had been a few rough patches during the caretaker governor's rule, but the hastening of new elections had muted those criticisms.

With this precedent in place, the US attorney general had faced a difficult and pressing question.

If the technique had worked so well for the British territory, why not use it in the US Virgin Islands?

THE CASE AGAINST the USVI Governor and the Legislative Assembly came together quickly. The parallels with the situation in the Turks and Caicos were too numerous to be ignored. While the Governor was not as showy with his allegedly ill-gotten wealth, the bribery allegations were nearly identical in substance and scope.

The attorney general had worried endlessly over the matter. An indictment of the entire USVI government would look bad for his president, who had numerous ties to the islands, but—as Wendy had pointedly reminded him only the day before—the president was halfway through his second term in office. The AG had his own reputation to think about.

Over the past several months, the president's administration had been plagued by an endless stream of leaks. The released information had included sensitive details about several of the justice department's ongoing investigations.

If the AG declined to prosecute the USVI Governor and the Washington press corps found out, he would be in for a public grilling of epic proportions.

In the end, he felt he had no choice.

The portfolio of evidence was irrefutable. The primary witness was one of the Governor's closest aides. The whistleblower had provided voluminous testimony that was buttressed by a slew of incriminating documents. It was one of the most iron-clad indictments against a politician the department had ever handled.

And, of course, they couldn't give the British an excuse to call their American cousins complacent.

After a vigorous evaluation and several tense discussions with the president, the AG had reluctantly given the action a green light.

It was a decision he already regretted.

But once started, the process could not easily be undone.

FROM THE GET-GO, the prosecution was fraught with difficulties. There was no budget for a full-scale military action. The arrests would have to be handled by the FBI, using the utmost discretion and respect for the affected islanders. A small number of National Guard troops had been allocated to provide support, but they had been told they were unlikely to see any action and that they were essentially going on a tropical vacation.

Wendy had met up with the FBI team when the navy vessel

docked at the cruise ship pier earlier that morning. As the justice department liaison, she had been on-site ever since, monitoring events.

So far, her reports had not brought good news.

Snippets of their phone conversations, the last one ended moments before, replayed in the attorney general's head.

"It looks like two senators managed to escape from the Legislature Building, Bobo and Sanchez."

The AG had stroked his chin, pondering. "Well, that's not so bad. They were low on our list of priorities anyway."

The next call had caused him to fluster.

"A couple of local DJs are stirring things up with their on-air commentary. I'm afraid they're calling this a federal invasion."

"I thought we had clearance to shut down all local broadcasts while the feds were moving in. Why are they still on the air? KRAT? What kind of a radio station goes by the call letters of a rodent?"

The third report generated stomach-churning consternation.

"Hightower arrested the wrong governor!? How did that happen? Doesn't he know what the man looks like?"

The last call, he had received with exhausted resignation.

"A flight from Miami just landed? How did they get clearance to take off from Florida? Should you send them back? No, that'll get too complicated. Let the people off the plane, but tell them the city's been shut down. Make them register their whereabouts. We've got bigger problems to deal with."

The mental recap caused the AG to dig divots into the side of his head.

He directed his next comment to the framed photo of the retriever.

"The Brits would never have called it Operation Coconut."

Groaning, he pulled open a desk drawer and broke the seal on a fresh bottle of pink tablets.

Cyril E. King Airport

St. Thomas, US Virgin Islands

~ 23 ~

A Bumpy Landing

OF THE 146 passengers on board the Miami flight as it landed on the bumpy runway at the St. Thomas airport, no one was happier to see the approaching ground than the woman in seat 26E.

The author leaned forward at the welcome screech of brakes, relieved beyond words as she felt the forceful drag of the upturned wing flaps.

The two-and-a-half-hour flight from Miami had stretched on interminably. At one point, she had unbuckled, squeezed around the Mojito Man, staggered up the aisle, and shut herself inside the bathroom, just to have a few minutes respite from his ongoing chatter.

Earphones were no use. There was no setting loud enough to drown out his persistent commentary, which vacillated among three main topics: the graphic details of his painful illness, the gruesome means he might use to hasten his impending death, and—by far the most disturbing—his attempts to lure the writer into a romantic rendezvous.

"Why don't you join me for dinner tonight on St. Thomas? I'll take you somewhere nice."

The woman fixed a blank expression on her face, hoping he would think she hadn't heard the question—to no avail.

"I'll pay," he insisted, undeterred. "I've got plenty of money and just a few weeks left to live." He paused for a mojito-scented burp. "No point in holding back now. I can't take it with me."

He waited through only a short silence before trying another tack.

"I've booked a room at Blackbeard's Castle. It's a nice place up on a hill. Great views. You could stay with me for a while. Come on, what do you say?"

She pulled the earphones from her head.

"I'm headed to St. John," she replied tersely. It wasn't the first time she had tried to convey this information. The geographical distance and intervening span of water between the two islands appeared not to faze him.

"How about dinner, eh? I'll take you to the nicest restaurant on St. Thomas. I've got wads of cash to spend, and not much time to do it in."

He paused, a faraway look in his sunken gray eyes, but after constant repetition, the accompanying phrase had lost all dramatic effect.

"Within a few weeks, I'll be dead."

"UH, WELL, BYE-BYE, then," the author said to her seatmate as she hurried down the rollaway steps that had been pushed next to the plane's side door.

She sprinted across the tarmac to the terminal, her backpack swinging from her shoulders, her suitcase bumping wildly across the asphalt.

A frail voice called after her.

"Come see me at Blackbeard's!"

Her muttered reply was directed at the pavement.

"Not on your life, buddy."

A QUICK DEPARTURE for the St. John ferry, however, was not to be.

Uniformed policemen blocked the terminal entrance. One of them held up a stern hand, halting the author at the doorway.

"St. Thomas is on lockdown. You need to stop here and register."

"Excuse me. What?"

"The US government has temporarily taken control of the island."

"What?" she asked again, this time in stunned disbelief.

"Which hotel are you staying at?" he asked, clearly wishing to avoid another "what." "We can only allow you to go directly to your hotel, nothing more."

"But I'm staying on St. John," she said, a lump growing in her stomach.

"No ferries are leaving today, miss. Talk to the woman organizing the taxis. She can get you a room in Charlotte Amalie."

Woefully, the author walked outside to the taxi stand.

"Where are you headed?" the matron asked, tapping a pencil against her clipboard.

"Anywhere but Blackbeard's Castle," she replied with a groan.

TWENTY MINUTES LATER, the author watched in despair as the Mojito Man joined her in the line of people waiting for a local taxi. The drivers wouldn't leave the airport until they had accumulated five or six passengers who were heading into the city.

The midmorning sun beat down like a hammer, as relentless as her sickly suitor.

The Bishop breezed past the taxi line, following a private driver to a waiting car. The author stared numbly at the swishing brown cassock, trying to ignore her traveling companion's jubilant greeting.

"Hey there, partner. You look like you could use a drink!"

The Governor's Mansion

Overlooking Charlotte Amalie

~ *24* ~

The First Lady

THE FIRST LADY of the US Virgin Islands sat on a bench in the gardens outside the Governor's Mansion, sipping a glass of iced tea as she watched the last commercial flight from Miami land at the St. Thomas airport. The short runway on the south shore was just visible from the mansion's elevated perch above Charlotte Amalie.

Formally known as Villa Catherineberg, the chalk-white mansion occupied the summit of one of the city's flanking hills. Anchored in place by red retainer walls, the property sat behind a tasteful line of security fencing. Stately columns and a wide portico that looked out over the harbor completed the typically tranquil scene.

A ring of tropical greenery isolated the mansion from the high-density housing that crowded the rest of Charlotte Amalie. Accessed by a curving asphalt road that swept around the hill, the estate presented the image of an elegant retreat.

Today, however, the property was under siege.

THE FIRST LADY set her glass down on a decorative iron table next to her chair and took inventory of the personnel now occupying the residence.

An armed guard stood watch less than ten feet away. He

was a member of the regular entourage that protected the first family, so at least his was a trusted face—as evidenced by the relaxed attitudes of her two Chihuahuas. The dogs, both wearing jeweled collars, played in the grass near her feet.

Additional guards from the territory's regiment manned the front gates and strolled the grounds, but there was little pretense that they were monitoring the hillside for potential intruders. Their attention was focused inward, on the black-clad invaders who had swarmed the premises.

The FBI agents had arrived about an hour earlier, rolling up to the front gates in a convoy of black SUVs. After a tense standoff with the gate attendants, they had grudgingly been admitted—to the fierce barks and threatening growls of the Chihuahuas.

The First Lady had been excluded from the long list of federal indictments, and she had offered no response when the agents informed her of her husband's arrest. Nor had she expressed surprise when the agents later announced he had eluded capture. As to the questions they put to her about where he might be hiding, she simply replied, "I don't know."

THE FIRST LADY had been placed under surveillance in case the Governor attempted to contact her. She was, in effect, a prisoner in her own home—a home she was likely to lose in the coming days, if not hours, whether or not the FBI managed to track down her husband.

The couple owned a private estate on the island's west end, a lavish but much more homey abode.

By contrast, the official mansion had the feel of a museum. Priceless artwork adorned the walls, and plush carpets covered the marble floors. Its primary function was to serve as a venue for hosting foreign dignitaries and for other government-related entertainment.

She and her husband had sprinkled only a few personal touches around the place: a couple of knickknacks, a handful of family photos, and a backgammon set her husband had recently purchased.

For the life of her, she couldn't understand his sudden fascination with the game. She'd always seen it as an excuse for old men to sit around and gossip. She'd said as much after he'd spent an afternoon staring at his new board and the various checker pieces.

"This is a game of strategy," he'd replied. "An exercise of the mind."

If it was exercise he was after, she thought wryly, he would have been far better served by a jog down the hill and back.

IT WAS HER strategizing husband who had suggested they reside full-time in the Governor's Mansion over the past several months. He reasoned the move might prevent a full-scale invasion of their private quarters. So far, his plan had worked. Only a few federal agents had been sent to secure their estate.

The morning's coup had been anticipated for weeks. It was an eventuality for which the First Lady was well prepared. She was an emotionally solid woman, beautiful but sturdy, and not easily unsettled.

Picking up her iced tea for another cooling sip, she turned her gaze south toward St. Croix, the long flat island of her birth located about forty miles away. Obscured by the sky's thickening haze, the landmass wasn't visible that day, even from her hilltop overlook. That made no difference; she was tethered to her homeland by a force stronger than sight.

The First Lady was fiercely proud of her Crucian heritage. True to her roots, she had an independent spirit, and her relationship with the Governor was rarely tranquil. Despite their fiery exchanges, she was deeply devoted to her husband.

Their enemies would have to do far worse than this to break them, she resolved as she stared across the cupped hillsides at another prominent landmark of only slightly lower elevation than the mansion.

Black-clad agents scurried across the one-way street in front of Government House. One of the foreigners strolled onto the balcony outside her husband's office.

Her fingers wrapped around the glass, the only sign of tension in her otherwise composed figure.

She was willing to do anything to protect the Governor's legacy.

If she had to marshal her home resources, so be it.

The Caribbean Sea

Midway Between St. Croix

and St. Thomas

A Bullet for Every Occasion

THE CARIBBEAN SEA stretched across the horizon, a sapphire fan dotted with brown hues of submerged coral and rafts of floating seaweed. A heavy blue sky pressed against the water, the upper atmosphere streaked with plodding elephant clouds.

A midsized powerboat cut across the open sea, churning a foamy wake as it sped north toward St. Thomas.

The boat was functional and fast, the typical white-painted vessel common throughout the region. No bright decals or signature stripe marks decorated its hull; the generic design was easy to maintain and intentionally indistinguishable—unlike the man who stood at its helm.

Nova gripped the boat's front railing, his arms flexed like oiled pistons. Barefoot and brazen, he let the salty spray mist his skin.

He was joined by his ever-present team of brutes, Crucian toughs who followed his lead without question or complaint. It had only taken a couple of hours to round them up. They had quickly signed on for the trip to the Rock—and for anything else he commanded them to do once they arrived at their sister island.

A fearsome aura surrounded Casanova. The tales of his strength and cunning far exceeded his actual capabilities, but this was of no concern to the man at the center of the myth. He believed his own propaganda, a trait that made him all the more dangerous even as he flirted ever closer with disaster.

The boat hit a wave, leapt out of the water, and bounced down with a splash. Nova licked his lips, tasting the salt.

He envisioned himself a modern-day pirate, a mercenary for hire with allegiance to no one but himself. His natural advantages of physique and appearance entitled him to inflict misery upon others.

A deviant smile spread across his face.

He had left the nervous taxi driver behind at the Christiansted pier. The man from Nevis had been released from his unpaid chauffer duties—if only temporarily.

"I'll send word when I'm headed back," Nova had admonished darkly. "You'll meet me here at the boardwalk." He paused for a wink, a gesture that caused Nevis to shrink behind the taxi van's steering wheel. "That is, unless I happen to run into the Coconut Boys while I'm taking care of my other business on the Rock."

Still smiling, Nova reached inside his pants pocket and pulled out a handful of bullets. He rolled the smooth metal in his fingers, savoring the feel of the familiar round rods.

His parting comment had been more than just a cruel tease. He'd heard a rumor that the Coconut Boys had fled to St. Thomas. They certainly weren't hiding out on Santa Cruz—if they were, someone would have given him their location by now.

He selected two bullets and slid the rest back into his pocket. Holding up the metal casings, he tilted the points so that they glinted in the morning sun.

The Governor was the main focus of this trip, but if he could kill two birds with one stone, all the better.

"I'm sure she wouldn't mind a little multitasking," he murmured, thinking of the woman who had hired his services.

"This one's for Mic," he said, tapping his thumb against the far right rod.

Squinting at the shadow of St. Thomas in the distance, he shifted his thumb to caress the other casing.

"And this one's for Currie."

Coki Beach
St. Thomas

~ 26 ~

The Coconut Boys

IT WAS A lazy morning at Coki Beach. News of the turmoil in Charlotte Amalie had yet to reach St. Thomas's sleepy north shore. As the sun inched toward its midday zenith, the angled rays cast frond-shaped shadows across the sand where two scruffy West Indians sat enjoying the breeze.

"Currie-mon, can you get us a drink?"

Grimacing at the "mon" affectation, a stubby man—the shorter of the pair—popped up from his seat and walked over to a grove of coconut trees.

Currie selected a tree, grabbed a rusty machete, and hoisted himself up the curved trunk, expertly gripping the grooved bark with his bare feet. The palm's spindly frame bent and swayed as he reached the top. Wrapping his legs around the trunk, he dropped the rest of his body so that he could access the coconuts bunched beneath the crown of fronds.

The machete's ragged blade swung through the air, knocking loose a pair of green nuts that fell, one after the other, with a loud *thunk* onto the sand.

Currie slid halfway down the tree and then dropped the rest of the way, landing safely on the ground. Picking up the closest piece of fruit, he lopped off the top and took a sip of the watery juice inside. He swirled the liquid in his mouth, as if evaluating the flavor. With a satisfied nod, he passed the coconut to his long-legged friend.

"Here you go, Mic."

"Thanks, Currie-mon."

Currie rolled his eyes.

"No problem," he replied and then added under his breath, "mon."

RUNAWAYS MIC AND Currie had settled into their new life at Coki Beach, a popular tourist spot on the island's northeast shore. The Crucian pair had been living on St. Thomas for the past couple of months—ever since their dramatic departure from St. Croix.

Coki was a pleasurable place to camp out, with several leafy trees to sleep under when it rained, and an abundance of coconuts, which provided basic sustenance. Deep sand led to crystal-clear water with excellent snorkeling. Directly offshore, the blocking length of Thatch Cay protected the cove from the Atlantic's bigger waves.

But by far the most important benefit to their beach retreat was the concealment it provided from the man who was out to kill them.

So far, there had been no sign of Casanova.

COKI BEACH WAS located next to an aquatic theme park, whose white observation dome could be seen hovering over the water about a hundred yards away. The combination of pristine beach and entertaining sea life resulted in a high volume of visitors. This, in turn, attracted a number of enterprising vendors, most of them Jamaican in origin, giving the area a colorful flair.

The Jamaicans had flourished, expanding their commercial endeavors to a wide range of services.

All manner of beach-related equipment could be rented, from snorkel and scuba gear to lounge chairs and umbrellas. In addition to the typical rum and beer shacks that lined the waterfront, an assortment of palm readers, massage therapists, and hair braiders plied their trades.

It was this last profession that Mic had enthusiastically embraced. He sat next to a plastic box containing an assortment of colorful rubber bands and other hair-tying accessories.

Currie preferred to stick to coconuts, a medium with which he was more familiar. In addition to being their basic source of nutrition, the scalped nuts could be sold to thirsty sunbathers.

Mic passed the coconut back to his pal, and Currie stared down at the globe-shaped fruit, ruefully reflecting.

They had been selling coconuts on the Christiansted boardwalk when Nova approached them with his fateful proposal. It was a case of being in the wrong place at the wrong time. Currie sighed, wistfully missing his home island.

And yet, he was grateful to be alive.

CONCERNED THAT THEY might be recognized by visiting Crucians, Mic and Currie had tried to pass themselves off (generally unsuccessfully) as Jamaicans. As Currie took a seat on the sand next to Mic's hair-braiding operation, he slipped on a tattered wig of dangling dreadlocks, his main effort at disguise.

Mic had managed to grow three inches of the real thing, but at this point in the process, his stubs of twisted hair made him look more like a porcupine than a Rastafarian.

Mic had taken their Jamaican integration a step further. He had begun speaking with a strange lilted accent, and he sprinkled "mon" into his sentences at every opportunity.

It was an unconvincing imitation, but Currie didn't have the heart to tell that to his friend. As for the Jamaicans, they were amused by the pair's attempts at assimilation and had adopted Mic and Currie into their ranks.

"Currie-mon, hand me that other coconut. I've devised a new marketing tool."

Skeptically, Currie tossed the second round ball through the air. Mic caught the coconut in the palm of his hand and planted it in the sand by a placard advertising his hair-braiding services. Gently, he lifted a helmet of weaved palm fronds, plaited into braids, each one tied off at the end with a colored rubber band. Turning the helmet to its proper orientation, he placed it on top of the nut.

"I call her Cinderella-mon."

Currie shook his head.

"You can take the man outta St. Croix, but you can't take the Santa Cruz outta duh man."

WHILE MIC REVELED in his hairdressing duties, Currie remained vigilant, surveilling the beach and surrounding vendor areas for Nova and his cronies.

As a result of Mic and Currie's escape from the grocery store caper gone awry, Nova had spent several weeks at the Golden Grove incarceration facility on St. Croix.

Currie hadn't received any updates on Nova's status, but the gangster never stayed locked up for long. It was only a matter of time before they crossed paths again. Nova might be temporarily distracted by other matters, but he would never stop looking for the two men who had betrayed him.

Currie's gut told him they had gained but a temporary reprieve.

WITH ANOTHER GLANCE up and down the beach, Currie laid back in the sand. It had been a quiet morning at Coki. After a late night socializing under the stars, the full-time residents had taken their time starting their day.

As a few tourists rolled in from the nearby resorts, the Jamaican crew, along with the Crucian impersonators, began to casually hustle the arrivals.

"Hey there, bee-you-tiful lady-mon," Mic crooned to a passing tourist, a rather large woman in a strapless halter top. "Let me run my magic fingers through your hair."

From a nearby rum shack, a battery-operated radio released a sharp feedback of static, followed by lead-in music that was instantly recognized by the locals on the beach.

"I smell a rat . . ."

Downtown Charlotte Amalie

~ 27 ~

Calling Senator Bobo

INSIDE THE UNUSED cistern that was serving as KRAT's temporary broadcast studios, yet another loud *thunk* sounded against the ceiling. A rock rolled across the roof, slid through the open portal, and plopped onto the concrete floor.

Whaler glared up at the ceiling, threatening the perpetrator with a clenched fist.

"If that kid throws another rock at us, I'm going to go out there and . . ."

Dread cut in, waving him off. "Any other day, and I'd help you squelch the little bugger. But we've got bigger fish to fry."

He pointed to the transmission line that Whaler had been trying to fix before the last rock was launched. "We're barely hanging in here, signal-wise. How's it coming with that line?"

Whaler looked dubiously at a piece of aluminum foil he'd been using to try to amplify the signal.

"That's the best I can do. We're too low to the ground. All this concrete is a bother. We should probably try another location." He scowled once more at the ceiling. "Plus, I don't like that punk knowing we're in here."

Dread shrugged his agreement.

"All right. I'll give another shout-out. Then we'll pack up and move."

He flicked on the mike and resumed the broadcast.

"If anyone out there has information on the Governor or the two missing senators, we'd love to hear from you." He glanced at the news feed he'd captured on his computer screen. "It's Bobo and Sanchez who have so far eluded the pasty boys."

"Bobo," Whaler sighed. "That's just what this day needs, a Bobo sermon." The hyperreligious senator was a frequent guest on the radio show. Unlike the other local politicians, he appeared not to mind the DJs' mocking commentary—or he had calculated that the exposure was well worth the jabs he received.

Crossing to the broadcast table, Whaler leaned over the mike.

"Hey, hey, Bobo. Give us a call." With a wink at Dread, he nodded toward the ceiling, a reference to the Lutheran church outside.

"We're in a perfect place for preachin'."

Between a Fort and
a Hard Place

SENATOR SANCHEZ WIPED her brow. The view from the walk-way along Fort Christian's upper wall was surreal but, with the sun beating down, the perch was unbearably hot. Reverend Bobo had spread his rainbow-colored scarf over his head, blocking the direct rays, but even his face was flushed from the heat.

While the fort's height allowed the two rogue senators to see across the whole of Charlotte Amalie, they were equally exposed, should any of the federal agents patrolling the streets look too closely at the boarded-up building's top echelons.

"We can't stay up here." Sanchez pointed to the navy vessel docked next to the cruise ship and the National Guard troops that had begun marching along the shoreline into the city. "They're going to be looking for us."

For a moment, Reverend Bobo appeared not to hear her. His gaze remained focused on a spot north of the fort.

Scanning the mayhem below, Sanchez tried to determine what had drawn his interest.

At first, she thought Bobo was staring at the action in Eman-cipation Park. The public square was located just inland from the vendors' plaza, across from the fort's front green space.

A cluster of concerned citizens had formed at the park's west end near an iron sculpture depicting a rebelling slave. The

Freedom Statue was one of a set that had been commissioned to commemorate Colonial-era uprisings. Similar statues could be found on both St. John and St. Croix. With one hand, the figure held a conch shell to his mouth. His swelling cheeks indicated he was blowing into the shell's mouthpiece, generating a bellowing blast that was often used to signal the start of a revolt. The slave lifted his opposite arm toward the sky, waving a machete.

Sanchez shuddered at the implied symbolism behind the gathering point. The slave rebellions had been violent affairs of bloodthirsty revenge. She hoped the FBI realized how easily their intervention might be misconstrued.

Additional crowds had gathered by the park's grandstand, a round stage with a pinwheel roof that was used for festival events, concerts, and the occasional speech. It was the last category that was being employed that morning. An improvised sound system had been set up, allowing individuals to step onstage and voice their opinions about the federal troops. Angry words, both pro and con, floated through the air toward the fort.

Sanchez pursed her lips, afraid the Reverend was about to suggest they head to the grandstand, a move that would certainly lead to their arrest. But after studying the angle of Bobo's scarf-covered head, she concluded his vision was directed a short distance up the hill from Emancipation Park.

Tracing his line of sight, she homed in on the iron gates of the Lutheran church. Beyond the fence, a concrete walkway led into the church grounds.

Two tiers of brick steps provided access to the sanctuary, a sturdy structure with a practical square-shaped steeple. The cream-colored bricks were paired with white trim, a red iron roof, and red-painted windows and doors. A concrete cistern took up much of the side yard.

Despite the locked outer gate, the sanctuary's front doors were swung open, an invitation to the breeze—and, apparently, the Reverend.

"Bobo?" Sanchez prompted. "What are we going to do?"

His face broke into a reassuring smile. Pointing to the church, he said, "I know a place that will take us in."

Sanchez was unconvinced. "Are you sure they won't call the feds?"

"We are like brothers," Bobo replied confidently. He pulled the scarf from his head and pointed at the striped colors.

Still she resisted. "Do you know the presiding priest?"

Bobo grinned, as if sharing the punch line to a joke. Sanchez shook her head, puzzled. If there was some underlying humor reference, it wasn't one she understood.

"Better," he replied with a chuckle. "I know the Bishop."

~ *29* ~

The Mysterious Monk

DREAD FRED AND Whaler prepared to make their departure from the church's empty cistern. They had narrowed their options for the next broadcast location to a short list and would select the best one based on the street conditions when they emerged from their bunker.

As Dread folded up the plastic table, he took a close look around the concrete room. He didn't want to leave anything behind. It might be a while before they were able to return.

Whaler released a lever on the canvas camp chair he'd been sitting in, triggering it to collapse into travel mode. Then he turned to work on Dread's. The chairs compressed into rod-shaped bundles that fit into a narrow sack that he strapped onto the side of his backpack.

No sooner had Whaler threaded the second chair into its bag than a scraping noise sounded on the roof.

"That's it!" Whaler yelled, lunging for the ladder. "I'm gonna get that kid."

"Relax, man," Dread said, hefting a pack filled with transmission equipment onto his shoulder. "I'm sure we'll find you someone to punch on our way through town."

A shadow darkened the hole in the ceiling, one created by a larger presence than the skinny kid who had been throwing rocks at them.

Both men froze. They were standing in an empty tank. There was only one way out and nowhere to hide. If the federal troops had tracked them down, they were about to be captured.

This might be the end of the Dread Fred and Whaler radio show—for good.

A foot stepped onto the ladder's top rung. The light shifted, revealing a polished oxford with hand-sewn leather uppers.

Not a combat boot.

The DJs released their pent-up breath, and then immediately drew it back in as the foot was followed by the swish of a brown cassock.

A man dressed in a strange costume, somewhat reminiscent of an affluent monk, descended the ladder. He had dark brown skin, but his nationality was distinctly foreign, not West Indian.

"Good morning, gentlemen."

His voice confirmed his outsider status. He had an odd accent that neither of the radio personalities recognized. Although he spoke in English, his words carried a slight inflection, as if the language wasn't his mother tongue.

Regardless, he appeared to be familiar with both of St. Thomas's local celebrities. Their anonymity was blown with him.

"Dread Fred, I believe," the man said, crossing the room to extend a hand. The jeweled ring on his finger sparkled even in the cistern's dim light.

"And you must be Whaler," he continued, turning toward the second DJ. "It's a pleasure. I'm a real fan of your work."

The pair shook the man's hand, but stood in stunned silence until Dread finally found his voice.

"And you are?"

The newcomer smiled.

"You can call me the Bishop."

~ *30* ~

Anti-Denominational

SENATORS BOBO AND Sanchez climbed down the clock tower and returned to the rear of Fort Christian. They exited the same door they'd entered, the only one for which Bobo had a key. Cautiously, they skirted around the building to a side yard and slipped through a gap in the fencing.

Hiding behind the scarred trunk of the nearest tree, the pair looked out across the fort's battered lawn. Past the east edge of Emancipation Park and up a narrow street, they could see the gates of the Lutheran church.

A couple hundred yards at most separated them from their next destination.

But there was quite a bit standing in the way.

Emancipation Park had filled to capacity. The grandstand had been commandeered by four different speechmakers, each one struggling to be heard—both over the competing microphones and the surrounding din.

Intermixed with the locals, a smattering of National Guard troops had arrived in the downtown area. The soldiers appeared somewhat lost, as if their marching orders had come unexpectedly and they were ill prepared for the abruptly initiated task. Certainly, they were unequipped with proper navigational guidance.

Sanchez spied a soldier holding a tourist brochure, staring

at the tiny map configured in its corner. He turned the colorful paper one way and then another, trying to orient himself within the stylized rendering.

A second uniformed man held a stack of office copy paper, which he began peeling off and distributing to the other soldiers. One of the sheets caught the breeze, flew up into the air, and floated toward the fort.

Sanchez waited until the soldiers had moved to the next street corner before scampering across the lawn to retrieve the discarded flyer.

She returned to the tree and smoothed the crumpled sheet against the trunk. Bobo looked over her shoulder as she held up a paper printed with the black-and-white images of their two senate profiles.

The photocopying had been hastily done on a low-resolution printer. Sanchez wore a simple blouse, and her hair was slicked back into a neat bun. Bobo was depicted in the same white linen outfit he wore to every senate meeting.

Sanchez felt a hand ruffling through her hair, messing it into tangles.

"Hey! Stop that!"

"There," Bobo said with a last toss of her hair. "They won't make you now."

"Okay, thanks, I guess," she murmured as Bobo began working on his own appearance.

He took off his rainbow scarf and tucked it into Sanchez's briefcase, but there was no obvious way to hide his distinctive tunic and trousers. After a moment's reflection, he began lifting up his tunic.

"What are you doing?" Sanchez demanded, instantly alarmed.

"Distancing myself from that photo," he replied, pulling the shirt over his head. He flexed the muscles on his scrawny chest, causing clumps of gray hair to pump up and down.

Rolling her eyes, Sanchez looked away. She quickly turned back as he began running his hands around the loose waistline of his pants.

"Bobo, don't you dare."

"No one will recognize me in my skivvies," he protested.

"I would," she replied with a visceral shudder. "And that's an image that would stay with me for the rest of my life."

WITH BOBO'S DIMINISHED wardrobe and Sanchez's mussed-up hair, the senators started off down the fort's front path—and then immediately stopped and looked at each other.

"We probably shouldn't stay this close together," Sanchez said nervously.

Bobo nodded in agreement. "I'll go first."

She watched him stroll down the walkway past a pair of Guard soldiers holding printed flyers. Seconds later, his bare torso disappeared into the throngs that had spilled over onto the street outside Emancipation Park.

Sanchez dug around inside her briefcase, sliding her hand beneath Bobo's scarf and tunic, and pulled out a pair of sunglasses. Wrinkling her nose at the musky scent released from the Reverend's clothing, she began to casually walk along the path toward the park.

She found herself tousling her hair, adding additional tangles to the ones Bobo had initiated, particularly when a couple of befuddled soldiers stopped to converse by the lawn's last tree. Trying not to look conspicuous, she stepped off the curb at the end of the walkway and weaved her way into the Emancipation Park crowds.

Immersed in the park's edgy atmosphere, her grip tightened on her briefcase shoulder strap.

The garbled speeches from the grandstand threw out harshly spoken words and phrases.

". . . cowards been stealing from us . . ."

". . . dare take over our government . . ."

". . . if I catch that Governor, I'll tell you what I'll do with him . . ."

"Hey, you, pasty boys . . ."

With relief, Sanchez reached the opposite side of the park's overflow crowd and hurried up the narrow street to the church.

Alone outside the locked iron gates, she looked back toward the park. There was no sign of Bobo. She wondered if he'd been picked up by the Guard.

"Gotcha!"

Sanchez jumped as Bobo grabbed her shoulders. She cringed at the touch of his naked skin.

"Bobo, get off me.

"I mean it. Now."

AFTER SEPARATING HERSELF from Bobo's bare-armed bear hug, Sanchez returned her attention to the church. The chapel's massive hurricane-strength doors were swung open, but there was no other indication that the place was currently staffed. The courtyard was empty, and the rosebushes looked as if they could use a drink of water. The cistern in the side yard must have run empty.

It had been a mistake to come here, Sanchez thought. But as she reached for her cell phone to attempt a call, Bobo poked her in the ribs.

She looked up to see a man in a brown cassock and gold chain crossing the inner courtyard. She wasn't sure where he had come from, but he was now walking briskly toward the locked gate.

"Who's that?" she whispered.

"Bishop of St. Thomas," Bobo replied with a knowing nod.

A lifelong Catholic, Sanchez attended mass almost every Sunday. She knew most of the local clergy, but this man was unfamiliar. It wasn't the Catholic bishop or the equivalent Episcopalian leader. There were dozens of independent religious organizations on the island. Perhaps he was a member of one of those—but surely she would have heard of a bishop.

"Bobo. I think you're confused. That's not any bishop of St. Thomas that I've ever met."

Her fellow senator pumped his eyebrows.

"Oh, I assure you. He's the Bishop all right."

Charlotte Amalie Harbor

~ 31 ~

Through the Looking Glass

CASANOVA MOTIONED FOR the motorboat to slow as it approached the outer fringes of the Charlotte Amalie harbor. Keeping a safe distance from the cruise ship port and the docked navy freighter, the Crucian craft veered toward the west side of the protected bay.

The commercial ferries had been halted, but as Nova's source had assured him, there was little policing of the hundred or so smaller craft in the area.

The boat slipped easily behind Hassel Island, a onetime peninsula that had been cut off from the mainland in the 1860s to create a shipping lane.

The ever-expanding size of Caribbean cruise ships placed constant pressure on harbor officials to maintain and widen the water routes to Charlotte Amalie's deepwater dock. While such alterations remained environmentally controversial, the island's lifeblood depended upon regular visits from the floating cities and their thousands of cash-dropping passengers.

Even with the harbor modifications, the massive ships moved through the designated passage points at a snail's pace, their captains fearful of straying from the narrow course and beaching on the adjacent shoals.

No such turtle traffic cluttered the area that day. The lone cruise ship stranded at the dock had sent a clear message to those scheduled for late morning arrival. The next several days' worth of vessels had already diverted to other destinations. There were plenty of islands within range happy to host an extra cruiser.

The Crucian powerboat edged around the far side of Hassel Island and slid through the cutout channel. The motor cut back to an idle as Nova whipped up a pair of binoculars and surveyed the shoreline.

His magnified lenses skimmed over the shuttered waterfront shops to the Legislature Building, whose front entrance was guarded by a pair of FBI agents. Across the street, the crumbling rear walls of Fort Christian retained their typical forlorn and abandoned stance.

Shifting his view up the slope, Nova scanned the crowds packed into Emancipation Park. National Guard troops from the navy ship had encircled the perimeter and were trying, without much success, to maintain order.

Moving another notch higher in elevation, Nova's glasses picked out the Lutheran church and, just above its metal roof, the easy marker of Government House. Skipping up the adjacent public staircase and past an abandoned construction site, a zoom of the binoculars captured the lookout tower for Blackbeard's Castle.

As Nova's scope swept across the hilltops toward the Governor's Mansion, he homed in on a taxi van speeding along a curved road at the city's upper outskirts.

He kept the lenses trained on the vehicle, following it back to the center of the upturned city, where it stopped in front of Hotel 1829, a historic accommodation at the bottom of Government Hill.

Hotel 1829

Charlotte Amalie

~ 32 ~

Room at the Inn

THE AIRPORT TAXI van screeched to a stop, blocking the one-way street outside Hotel 1829.

With a weary wave to the other riders, the author climbed out and met the driver at the rear cargo doors. She paid her portion of the fare, grabbed her roll-around suitcase, and watched the driver shuffle back to his slot behind the wheel.

She saw the wince on the driver's face as he pulled open the door. The interior's cool blast of air-conditioning couldn't mitigate the ongoing commentary of the Mojito Man in the front passenger seat.

Seconds later, the van squealed off. The driver was eager to make his next delivery as quickly as possible.

His next stop was around the corner and up the hill at Blackbeard's Castle.

THE AUTHOR EXTENDED her suitcase handle and rolled it toward the hotel's front steps.

The drive into Charlotte Amalie from the airport had been far from routine. Near the downtown area, the van had encountered a number of pedestrians on the streets. The driver had slowed the vehicle to a crawl, carefully pushing the bumper through the roaming crowds. He hadn't used his horn, perhaps fearing retribution. The day's events had understandably left the populace on edge.

A number of low-riding pickups, many with stereo speakers hanging out their rear windows, had further blocked the roads. After taking to a sidewalk to get around a snarl of parked trucks, the driver had finally detoured up into the surrounding residential hills in order to gain less impeded access to Government Hill.

Like the rest of the van's passengers, the author had been unable to get any updates on the lockdown situation. Her cell phone didn't appear to be working, and the taxi van's radio had been drowned out by the Mojito Man's constant yammering.

All she knew is what she'd been told at the airport. The territory's elected officials had been indicted on bribery charges. The FBI had moved in to arrest them, but the Governor and two senators had so far escaped capture.

Still standing by the hotel's front steps, the author turned to look down at the waterfront. She had a partial view overlooking several flights of stone and brick steps that tracked down the slope to a post office, which, like the adjacent jewelry shops, had been locked up and barricaded.

Most of the action was happening the next block over in Emancipation Park, where bullhorns and portable microphones amplified the noise from the crowd. It was difficult to discern the actual words, but the tone was clearly one of anger and concern.

Beyond the park, the occasional pop of gunfire echoed through the air.

It was a tense, uncertain scene.

She wondered if she'd made a mistake coming into town.

THE AUTHOR ALMOST didn't make it out of the airport.

The taxi concierge had managed to secure a viable phone line, but it had taken several attempts to get through to a hotel. Due to the telecommunications outage, none of the resorts were reachable. With the help of the officers stationed at the airport, the concierge had reached a police station located across the street from Hotel 1829. Using this relay, a room had been held for the author.

There were relatively few lodging options within the city limits, even without a government siege. For many tourists, Charlotte Amalie was a place for passing through. The town hosted about a hundred thousand cruise ship passengers per year, but those visitors came for the day, spent their money in the shops, and, at the signal from their ship—a hooting whistle that could be heard across the entire downtown—returned to their staterooms for the evening. The next day they'd disembark at St. Maarten, St. Barts, or some other cruise ship–friendly destination with a deepwater port and repeat the process all over again.

Another flow of tourist traffic used Charlotte Amalie as a connection hub to neighboring islands. The ferryboats that docked along the waterfront provided transport to St. John and the chain of British Virgin Islands to the north.

Even those tourists planning to spend their vacation on St. Thomas rarely overnighted in Charlotte Amalie. The expansive resorts that dotted the northeast shore provided everything a guest might need or want, from relaxation to water sports and casual to high end dining.

With resort lodging unavailable, the author had been lucky to secure a room in town.

Of course, the Mojito Man had offered to host her at Blackbeard's Castle, but she had immediately rejected that suggestion.

She recalled his offer with a shudder.

"I would have preferred a mat on the airport floor."

THE AUTHOR LOOKED up at her temporary home—for who knew how many nights.

As the name suggested, Hotel 1829 had been around for a while. The date was a reference to the year of the building's original construction.

Painted coral pink with white trim, the multistory structure was built into a steep slope at the bottom of Government Hill, just two doors down from Government House—which presumably explained the presence of the FBI agents on the street.

As a pair of boot-stomping agents jogged past the author and up the hill, the hotel's front gate opened. A cheery man with a sandy-gray mustache and a matching ponytail issued a hearty welcome.

"You must be the writer. Come on in!"

~ *33* ~

The Gym Membership

IT TURNED OUT the hotel's check-in clerk was also the bartender—or, more accurately, the bartender did double duty as the receptionist. The check-in counter was a wooden table inside the bar.

He was a cheerful bloke. The smile behind the mustache was one of genuine contentment, the kind often found among older expats living in the Caribbean. After years of a regular nine-to-five job up in the States, he had chosen to work where he vacationed, so that every evening was a tropical sundown and every day off offered a potential swim at the beach.

Once the author signed in, he handed her a key and motioned toward a doorway leading through to the building's inner courtyard.

A younger man with an athletic build brought in a bucket of ice and dumped it into a bin on the serving side of the bar's long counter.

"I'll take her up," he offered, setting aside the bucket.

"Number fifteen," the mustached man replied, tossing the key. "Your morning workout."

"I'm on it."

"It's not that heavy," the author said as the second bartender reached for her roll-around suitcase.

Bemused, she followed him into the courtyard—and then she understood the exercise reference.

The building's open interior scaled up the hillside, with the guest rooms accessed by a daunting array of crisscrossed staircases. A small pool had been built into a narrow landing around the slope's midpoint. The lower level where she now stood held just a small patio, with most of the space taken up by a splashing waterfall.

"Where's number fifteen?" the author asked, looking up, her eyes wide.

The young man grinned his response. He threw the suitcase over his shoulders and nimbly leapt up the first set of stairs. She panted to catch up as he summited the second flight. By the third, she'd given up trying to keep pace. When she finally arrived at the top of the fourth, he was waiting to show her into her room.

"No need for a gym membership," he said with a smile.

THE AUTHOR TOOK a few minutes to freshen up. Then she loaded her camera and computer into her backpack and returned to the bottom level.

The trip down was much easier than the one up, but the hotel's steep architecture was just as much a marvel on the descent.

She stepped inside the bar and slowly looked around, absorbing the details she'd missed on her first pass through.

While the room now served as a casual entertainment area, it had originally been the building's main kitchen. A brick fireplace big enough for several people to step inside took up one end of the space. Vintage cooking utensils were displayed above the hearth. Other mementos from that earlier time frame could be seen throughout the bar, with assorted brass pots hanging from the ceiling and plaques and black-and-white photos mounted onto the brick walls.

A heavy wooden table in the center of the room displayed an oversized backgammon set with a marble board and a matching dice-throwing cup. The author paused to study the game pieces. Given the position of the checkers, it looked as if play had been stopped midgame.

She turned to the bar itself, a solid structure of deep mahogany with brass detailing, set her backpack on the floor, and climbed onto the nearest stool.

The bartender leaned over his counter and pumped his mustache, inquisitively waiting for her order.

"Hi, I'll have a . . ." she started and then groaned at a dreaded itch on her arm. Swatting her elbow, she caught a bloodsucker still attached to her skin.

After only a few hours on the ground in the Caribbean, she'd already accumulated a small rash of mosquito bites.

The bartender eyed the welts. "Wow, they must love you." He pointed to a pair of bug-spray bottles on a shelf by the cash register. "Help yourself."

He reached beneath the counter and brought up a pair of citronella coils. He lit one on either side of her barstool and returned to his counter.

"Now, what can I make for you, hon?"

"Whatever you like," she replied and then added, "Just so long as it's not a mojito."

~ 34 ~

The Clamshell

THE AUTHOR SLUNG her backpack over her shoulder and walked onto the hotel's veranda. In her free hand, she carried a frozen mango daiquiri, a drink she hoped would help soothe the itch from her mosquito bites and erase the tiresome memory of the day's travels.

The bartender soon followed with the burning citronella coils. He positioned them strategically around her table and returned to his station.

About ten feet up from the street, the porch caught a nice sea breeze. There were plenty of seating options, with two rows of wicker tables and chairs, either pushed up against the building's coral pink wall or adjacent to the planters that lined the veranda's front railing.

The author selected a spot and powered up her laptop, but her gaze quickly drifted from the computer to the scenery. Sipping on the cool drink, she gazed out at the surrounding city.

LIKE COUNTLESS OTHER travelers, her previous visits to St. Thomas had been brief, a necessary stopover on her way to other locations. But even from those limited encounters, she knew Charlotte Amalie was different from the typical Caribbean port.

Many cruise ship destinations had become nothing more

than cardboard cutouts, façades created for the amusement of day-trippers, with little of substance existing underneath. Each morning, the tourist-catering businesses and related infrastructure were rolled out like a rug, the pieces neatly polished and positioned, an illusion of a colorful Caribbean scene.

The moment the cruise ship's afternoon whistle began to blow, the entire enterprise was closed down, packed up, and carted away. Umbrella operators cleared the beach, jewelry shops shuttered their glass windows, and tour operators folded up their sidewalk sandwich boards.

Charlotte Amalie had all that superficial dressing, most prominently on display at the vendors' plaza and in the alley shops, but beneath that commercial shell lay a foundation of culture and history.

Although the nonstop cruise ship schedule had driven out some of its long-term residents, Charlotte Amalie was still a real town where people actually lived. It was a thriving microcosm, with the diversity, economic strata, and inevitable frictions of a modern Caribbean society.

And because the territory's seat of government provided almost as much local employment and income as the passing cruise ships, the town was far more varied than most in terms of drama and intrigue.

Even with a population of almost twenty thousand, it was a place where everyone knew everyone else. Cupped in the palm of the hill, the actors could wave to one another across the vertical stage.

The city was a clamshell propped open for observation, each property visible to prying eyes—it was just a matter of finding the right angle.

Taking another sip from the ice-cold daiquiri, the author directed her gaze past a looping power line and through a screen of spreading tree branches to the distant shoreline where she could make out the stranded cruise ship and, beside it, the navy vessel.

She suspected the last item had drawn a great deal of scrutiny from the surrounding hillsides that day—along with the government offices located two doors down from her hotel—as the residents of Charlotte Amalie wondered what had happened to their missing Governor.

Government Hill

~ 35 ~

Caught

TIRED OF STARING through the window to the vacant public stairway, Cedric began to pace across the flat concrete floor inside the abandoned construction site. Despite the heat baking down on his head and shoulders, he couldn't help it. The repetitive movement was an instinctive habit, his conditioned response to stress.

And right now, he felt his stress level rising.

Despite his earlier reassurances, he was beginning to have doubts.

They had been holed up in the construction site for over an hour. Surely, by now someone had been sent to look for them. The doppelgänger inside the Governor's office shouldn't have fooled the federal agents for more than a minute, maybe two. They couldn't possibly have fallen for that ploy . . . or could they?

He reached up with a handkerchief to dab a drop of sweat from his chin. On the subsequent downward motion, his hand brushed against the cell phone wedged into his front shirt pocket. He had transferred the device to his shirt a half hour earlier when he slipped out of his suit jacket and folded it neatly on a concrete ledge.

For the duration of their concealment inside the construction site, the aide's thoughts had repeatedly returned to that phone.

He would be struck by a sudden inspiration on how he might contort his limbs and sneak a text message to Wendy, his contact at the local attorney general's office.

Every contemplated scheme, however, was quickly squashed, deemed too risky by Cedric's practical inner voice. He couldn't risk being seen by the Fixer.

(The Governor, of course, had long since drifted off to sleep. Judging by the volume of the snores emanating from his cubbyhole, he was enjoying quite a snooze.)

The message probably wouldn't go through anyway, Cedric concluded for the umpteenth time.

But as the minutes dragged by, desperation grew closer to parity with his sense of prudence.

Keeping an eye on Fowler—who, in turn, obliquely glowered back—Cedric gradually expanded the path of his pacing, with each cycle veering farther toward the open window overlooking the public steps.

On his third pass by the window he spied a flash of black clothing.

Finally, he thought with relief. This is it.

Seconds later, heavy boots could be heard tromping up the stairs.

"Get down," Fowler hissed.

Cedric dove to the ground, as slowly and as ungracefully as possible, sending loose pebbles scattering across the concrete.

Sprawled across the floor, his heart thumping a rapid drumbeat, he listened for the approaching agents. In his right hand, he clutched a pebble he'd grabbed during his overly dramatic fall. He tensed his arm, preparing to toss the stone toward the public stairs if needed to draw the agents to their position.

The skidding tumble had been sufficient.

The boot-generated footfalls deadened to silence, the sound replaced by the heavy pant of individuals who were unaccustomed to physical exertion in the tropical heat.

Through a narrow crack in the south wall, Cedric watched a man in a black T-shirt make hand signals to the rest of his team.

The horsey face looked almost comical behind the dark

sunglasses, but to Cedric, Agent Friday's homely mug was the most welcome sight he could have imagined.

FRIDAY MANEUVERED HIS team around the residential structure's outer concrete shell, sending pairs to either side to close off potential exits. Meanwhile, he and the remainder of the agents moved in on the open window where he'd glimpsed the Governor's aide diving for the floor.

The assistant special agent in charge showed none of the ego-driven zeal that his boss had displayed during the earlier storming of Government House. If anything, Friday's tone was hesitant, reflecting the serious nature of the arrest.

"Governor," he said, a slight falter to his voice. "Please come out, sir." He cleared his throat and added, "With your hands up."

~ 36 ~

The Magician

WITH A WHEEZE and a snort, the man who had been curled up in the kitchen's shaded cubbyhole rolled out into the full light of the open-roofed room.

Friday and his fellow agents swept into the construction site, swerving around Cedric's prone body. From all sides of the building, they closed in on their target as he slowly lumbered into a standing position, flapping his shorts and T-shirt, trying to unstick the clothing from his sweaty torso.

Two agents moved in with handcuffs while Friday began the regular litany.

"You have the right to remain silent . . ."

It was at this moment that Cedric realized the Governor's accomplice had disappeared. The aide pulled himself upright, whipping his head around, but there was no sign of Fowler's oversized golf shirt and chinos.

He must have slipped out of the construction site while Cedric was lying on the ground.

"How did he get by all the feds?" Cedric wondered, noting that some of the agents had charged in from the opposite end of the house. "The guy must be some sort of magician."

Despite the missing accomplice, Cedric felt his spirits lift. It was if a great weight had been removed from his chest.

The Governor was in custody. This arrest location was even

better than Government House. He would now be led, hand-cuffed, down the public staircase—in full view of the surrounding city.

Operation Coconut was a success.

Cedric and his fellow conspirators couldn't have asked for a more inflammatory photo opportunity. If the photogs hadn't been tipped off to the fed's activity at this location, he would take a pic with his cell phone.

That was justifiable, even while maintaining his cover as the Governor's loyal aide. After all, someone had to document the injustice being done to the territory's leader—or at least that's what he would say if anyone questioned him.

Cedric picked up his phone from the concrete, where it had landed during his fall. He checked the settings, relieved to find that the electronics still worked.

As he had suspected, the St. Thomas cell tower was blocked. He'd made the right decision to leave his phone in his pocket.

After dusting off his pants, he turned toward the construction site's exposed kitchen. With the Governor secured in hand-cuffs, the agents began to step away from the prisoner, giving Cedric a clear view of the big man in the visor, T-shirt, shorts, and sneakers.

He was unable to speak for several seconds. His shock was genuine—not part of any ruse.

Finally, he found his voice.

"That's not the Governor!"

"AINT NO CRIME here, pasty boys."

The impostor in the white visor who had been huddled in the kitchen cubbyhole for the past hour and a half dusted off his substantial backside. "I was just taking a nap."

The federal agents stood on the hot concrete, staring at each other in puzzlement. Friday turned to Cedric, as if seeking clarification.

The aide threw his hands up and shook his head. He still couldn't believe he'd been duped. He didn't have any idea when the switch had happened or, worse, where the real governor might be now.

The tension of the past several months now returned tenfold.

Exhaling in frustration, Cedric tilted his head skyward. In that moment, his sun-glared eyes picked out a man in a golf shirt and chinos standing in front of a bank of bougainvillea about fifty yards up the hillside.

Cedric's mouth fell open as he was struck with a second stunning blow.

Agent Friday's visual question had confirmed the aide's complicity in the operation.

The Fixer nodded his acknowledgment before slipping around the corner of the nearest dwelling.

Cedric croaked to the agents, trying to alert them to the location of the Governor's accomplice.

Even as he pointed, he knew the attempt was futile.

By the time they turned to look up at the bougainvillea, the Fixer had vanished.

~ *37* ~

The Seduction

AGENT HIGHTOWER PACED back and forth across the Government House lobby, waiting for news from Friday and the agents who had been sent up the hill to search for the Governor.

Hightower was not a patient man. He took a demanding approach to life, his sole purpose being the relentless pursuit of self-gratification. No payout, bonus, or reward could come fast enough.

The Gorilla wasn't the type to sit around.

He needed a backup plan in case Friday failed to find the Governor.

With a threatening glare at the husky maid in the frilly-necked dress who had given them the lead on the Governor's whereabouts, Hightower started up the stairs to the second floor.

Perhaps he might find some useful intel in the Governor's office.

HIGHTOWER SCALED THE steps two at a time. Reaching the top, he turned down the hallway and strode to the open door at the end.

He blustered into the office. His boots thumped across the red throw rugs as he prowled the room, searching for a clue that might shed light on where the Governor was hiding.

His beady eyes briefly roamed the rectangular space before coming to rest on the liquor cabinet pushed against the side wall beside the backgammon table.

Hightower had no interest in the checkers placed at seemingly random locations across the board's painted points. He'd never had time for board games.

It was the cabinet that soaked up his full attention—more specifically, the short glass sitting on its surface and the sizeable volume of dark rum that had been poured inside.

He blinked, trying to remember. He was sure the glass hadn't been there before . . . but then, he'd been focused on the impostor standing on the balcony. Perhaps he'd missed it.

His nose sucked in the liquor's rich scent—it was one of his favorite brands. He could gauge the make and year almost by sight.

It was a familiar sidekick, one that he had aggressively tried to lose.

But oh, how he'd missed it. He'd missed it every day of the past six months of sobriety.

He crossed to the credenza and stared down at his old demon friend.

It was almost as if someone had left it there especially for him.

Of course, that was silly, he told himself. He should just turn around and walk away.

The smell was stronger now, wafting up from the glass like a seductive siren. The temptation was too strong to resist—even for a man with the strength of a Gorilla.

Hightower's hand shook as he reached for the drink. His fingers wrapped around the glass, pressuring the surface with his grip.

His eyes closed as he brought the glass to his lips, tilted it back, and tossed the rum down his throat.

The effect was almost instantaneous. His head spun as the high-proof alcohol hit his bloodstream—and the office search soon became a ransacking.

~ 38 ~

So Close . . .

AGENT FRIDAY STOOD in the concrete shell of the house on Government Hill, pondering the Governor's latest ploy.

He rubbed his chin, scratching the uneven stubble.

The furrows in his face made it difficult to achieve a close shave. By noon each day, scruffy tufts could be seen growing out of the deeper grooves, giving him a rough, haggard look— one that, at this particular moment, matched his mood.

He unhooked his two-way radio from his belt, punched the talk button, and braced himself for a volcanic eruption.

"Hello, sir. We don't have the Governor in custody. Not yet. I thought we had him . . ."

Friday never made it to the "but" portion of his sentence. He shifted the radio away from his ear and waited for Hightower to stop shouting. The Gorilla was almost incomprehensible. When he eventually paused for breath, Friday broke in with his explanation.

"It turned out to be another charade."

This merely provoked a second tirade, which, at least, wasn't directed at Friday.

Hightower's parting remarks could be heard by every agent on the hill.

"Get back here. Now."

Amid belligerent protests, Friday and the rest of his team

led the second doppelgänger out of the construction site and down the public staircase. Still in handcuffs, the Governor's impersonator objected every step of the way.

Friday maintained a tight-lipped expression, but he knew the man's complaints were valid. The only charge they could hold him on was trespassing, and they could hardly pursue that minor offense while ignoring Cedric's identical infraction.

It was a short walk to Government House—far too short, from Friday's point of view.

"Operation Coconut," he muttered. "What a cursed piece of fruit."

AT THE BOTTOM of the public stairs, Friday led his team into Government House. He left the doppelgänger and the rest of the agents in the lobby, where the building's employees were still being held, and resignedly climbed to the Governor's office on the second floor.

The special agent in charge had made himself at home. He sat kicked back in the Governor's leather recliner, his combat boots propped up on the desk.

Friday glanced across the office. The place was in complete disarray. It looked as if it had been hit by a tornado. Pieces of furniture had been moved out of position, and several pictures now hung askew. The backgammon board had been upended; dice and checkers were scattered across the floor.

Some sort of search had taken place, but it was impossible to discern if anything had been found.

Friday spied an empty glass on the liquor cabinet and frowned.

With a loud *clomp*, Hightower dropped his feet to the floor.

"So did that maid downstairs send us on a wild-goose chase?" His words were slurred. The glass had apparently been filled—and emptied—since Friday left Government House to follow the fake lead up the hill.

"It's hard to say, sir. She could have been misled, the same as the Governor's aide."

The response sent Hightower into a rage. Stomping across the room, he grabbed an office chair and dragged it out onto the balcony. He hefted it over his head, held it there for a few wavering seconds, and then threw it over the railing. The chair fell through space, crashing with a *bang* onto the street below.

The Gorilla was in rare form, Friday mused.

The outburst did little to temper Hightower's anger. Friday cringed with the announcement that another interrogation was in order.

Hightower stormed out the office and down to the lobby, Friday in close pursuit.

Friday was almost relieved when a scan of the restless employees revealed that the manly maid was not among the detainees—until he saw Hightower's purple face.

Friday gazed up at the ceiling, tuning out the next tirade, wondering all the while: How had this lunatic been appointed head of the mission?

ONCE THE RANT ended, Hightower returned to the Governor's office, presumably for another shot of rum.

Friday appointed two agents to stay with the employees in the lobby—mostly to protect them from Hightower—and ushered the rest of his available manpower through the front entrance to the one-way street outside. With a wary glance up at the second floor, he repositioned the gathering point about twenty feet to the west—to ensure adequate clearance should anything else come flying over the balcony railing.

Commandeering the hood of a parked car, Friday spread a map of downtown Charlotte Amalie across the flat surface. He pulled a marker from his pants pocket and began dividing the downtown area into sectors.

"I'm going to break you into four teams. You'll each have a color. We're going to search on a grid, focusing first on the areas surrounding Government House; then we'll gradually work our way out."

He drew a rectangle that encompassed the waterfront immediately south of their position. "Team blue, you're responsible for this quadrant: Fort Christian, Emancipation Park, the Lutheran church, and anything this side of the Legislature Building. We've already got that secured."

He traced a second perimeter around the alley shops, reaching north up the hill to the one-way street where they stood.

"Green, you take this region here." Another jab delineated the next sector. "Red, start at the Legislature and move east." He folded the map and tucked it in his back pocket. "I'll take yellow and cover the hill."

As the groups set off on their assignments, Friday pulled a water bottle from his pack. They should have taken a tactical approach to this hunt from the get-go. Hightower was off his rocker—and getting drunker by the minute.

After a gulp, he wiped his mouth and tightened the plastic lid.

"Can't imagine this is going to do much good. The Governor's probably long gone by now."

AS AGENT FRIDAY marshaled his troops and sent the color-coded teams out into their designated search zones, he was unaware that an observer stood looking down at his map from the second floor of a nearby building—not Government House, but the structure immediately adjacent.

The Lutheran parsonage was a typical Caribbean-Colonial-style blockhouse with two tiers of breezeways assembled across its wide front. Built in 1725, it was one of the oldest continually inhabited residences on the island.

Its current occupant was the islands' most wanted man.

The Governor stretched his arms wide, enjoying the freedom of the loose-fitting brown cassock he'd found in a wardrobe positioned against the room's far wall. Sized extra-large, the garment swallowed his bulky frame. He had just changed out of the maid's costume, and it was a relief to be free of the dress's frilly neck collar.

Through the open doors that led onto the second floor's shaded balcony, the Governor watched the federal agents group around the map spread across the car hood below.

Everything was proceeding according to the plan. The game pieces were moving around the board in a predictable, orderly fashion.

He chuckled as the red, blue, and green teams dispersed.

But the sound died in his throat when he realized the yellow team was headed for the parsonage's front door.

~ 39 ~

The Parsonage

FRIDAY AND HIS team scrambled up the uneven steps leading to the parsonage's front gate. A cedar tree's spreading roots had disrupted the stairway's alignment, making the walkway difficult to navigate.

A pair of iron gates, one to the front terrace, the other to the side yard, were both locked. While decorative, the scrolling metal designs were effective impediments, blocking the agents' access.

Friday craned his neck to look up at the building. White with red trim, it looked as if it could use some maintenance, but it was obviously in use. One of the doors that led onto the balcony had been propped open, likely to facilitate airflow through the upper level. Someone must be inside or close by.

It was a long shot, but given the parsonage's proximity to Government House, it had to be checked out—even if they had to boost one of the agents over the security wall to get in.

Friday pushed a rusted buzzer mounted next to the front gate. A moment later, a church representative appeared on the road below. The elderly man climbed the lopsided steps with ease, despite the bulk of his flowing brown cassock.

"Hello, gentlemen. How may I assist you?"

"Agent Gabe Stein, sir." Friday's mouth twitched at the introduction. The use of his given name sounded odd, even to him. "We need to check your building for a fugitive."

The man surveyed the agents, solemnly noting the FBI insignia on their hats and shirts.

"You're looking for the Governor, I presume. I can assure you the premises have been locked all morning while I was at the church." He gestured toward the slope below the public gardens. The rear of the chapel was visible through the trees.

Friday straightened his shoulders. "We still need to look inside, sir."

"As you wish." Reaching into the cassock, the man pulled out a set of keys. He maneuvered around the agents to approach the lock, his movements fluid but not in any way hurried.

"Thank you. We'll be quick," Friday said when the gate finally swung open. He paused as the other agents moved through the passageway into the front terrace. "I'm sorry. I didn't catch your name."

The cassocked man responded without hesitation, meting out the job title as if it conveyed a clear identification.

"The Bishop of St. Thomas."

～

THE GOVERNOR SQUINTED through the parsonage's second-floor doorway, watching the interaction at the front gates with concern.

He was trapped.

It was too late to try to flee the building. And besides, even if he had been able to slip out before the agents entered, he had nowhere to go. The brown cloak would possibly explain his presence inside the parsonage. It wasn't nearly a good enough disguise to deter Agent Friday in a face-to-face meeting—or to conceal his identity from the prying eyes of his fellow islanders.

The Governor hadn't expected the agents to home in on the parsonage so quickly. Hightower's bumbling leadership—and predilection for fine rum—were meant to give him a little breathing room. He hadn't counted on the far more skilled lieutenant.

Panicked, the Governor glanced across the room. Then he dove toward the only available hiding place, the eight-foot-high standing wardrobe.

The closet was, unfortunately, already occupied with a

number of items. A full set of vestments hung from the upper rod, while several pairs of shoes and an assortment of pointed clerical hats cluttered the floor.

The hats took the brunt of the damage as the Governor clambered inside the wardrobe's base. Curling his body into a ball, he wrapped his fingers around the inside stub of the nail holding the outer knob in place and tried to pull the door closed. He tugged with all his might, but a two-inch gap remained between the facing and the outer frame.

The door bumped, a dull thudding sound as if something blocked its path.

He tried again.

Bump. Bump.

Voices echoed down the hallway outside the Governor's room. The agents had almost reached his location. He wedged the door into its flattest position and held his breath.

It was then that he realized that the hem of his cloak was stuck in the corner next to the hinge.

His eyes widened with alarm. How much of the cassock was poking out the bottom of the wardrobe?

The Governor froze in place. Any movement he made now would only draw attention to his hiding spot, but he felt certain he was about to suffer an embarrassing reveal.

Through the crack in the door, he saw the agents walk into the room. They were doing a quick sweep, but there was no chance they would skip a peek inside the wardrobe.

Two black-clad men strode out onto the balcony. A third circled the opposite side of the room.

Agent Friday approached the wardrobe.

His brow furrowed at the scrap of brown cloth snagged on the cupboard's bottom hinge. His hand reached for the knob.

He was about to open the wardrobe door when his radio squawked.

With an exasperated sigh, Friday pulled the receiver from his belt. His tone was far testier than his even-tempered disposition typically allowed.

"This is Friday."

Hightower's slurred voice came over the transmission.

"Agent Friday, where are you?"

Friday grimaced at the receiver before responding.

"In the Lutheran parsonage next door to Government House. I've got a small team with me . . ."

"Great." Hightower half suppressed a hiccup. "We've just received word. The Governor has been sighted up the hill from you at Blackbeard's Castle."

"We're on it." Friday sighed wearily. It sounded like another false lead, but there was no point in trying to convince the Gorilla of that.

"And Friday . . ."

"Yes, sir."

"This time, you'd better get him."

Friday clicked off the radio and hooked it back onto his belt.

The Bishop slid his hand into his robe, ensuring that his cell phone was securely tucked into its pocket, as the agents began filing past him into the hallway.

"Well, Bishop," Friday said, touching the brim of his cap. "Thank you for your assistance."

"Of course," he replied calmly. "Let me show you out."

THE GOVERNOR RELEASED his sweaty grip on the inner nail stub, and the wardrobe door eased open. One by one, he eased his cramped legs out onto the floor. He staggered unsteadily to the nearest chair and dropped into the seat with relief.

Wiping his forehead, he eyed the ceremonial hats that had been crumpled beneath his weight.

"Whew, that was close."

But who, he wondered, was the man in the cassock who had let the agents inside? The church's official pastor was out of town that week. This fellow wasn't a sanctioned replacement.

The Governor strummed his wide chin, pondering a bigger question.

Why had the cassocked man helped him avoid capture?

~ *40* ~

Blackbeard's Castle

AGENT FRIDAY WATCHED the Bishop shut the parsonage gate and lock it behind the last members of team yellow.

Friday was getting an odd vibe from the religious man. There was something strange about the Bishop's demeanor—something off about the whole parsonage experience—but he couldn't quite put his finger on it.

Shrugging, he pulled out his map and assessed the possible routes to Blackbeard's Castle, the location of the Governor's reported sighting. He slid his finger toward the upper north side of Charlotte Amalie. The resort was located almost directly above him at the top of the nearest hill.

There were two public staircases that would take him to the spot. He chose the one farthest from Government House—and Agent Hightower.

FRIDAY LED TEAM yellow down the one-way street to the stairway entrance for the 99 Steps.

The turnoff was marked by a colorful signpost highlighting the direction to various tourist destinations, with some labels pointing toward the lower downtown area and others indicating up the hill.

Friday picked out the upward arrow for Blackbeard's Castle,

uncomfortably aware that he was being watched from Hotel 1829, the property located on the opposite side of the staircase. A woman with a 35mm camera leaned over the hotel's veranda railing, snapping shots of the black-clad agents.

Remembering the attorney general's cautionary instructions, Friday cupped the brim of his hat, shielding his face from the lens.

Operation Coconut was meant to be a low-key operation, a government takeover with minimal visual impact. The sooner they captured the Governor and brought him into custody, the better.

The situation had the potential to turn into a media circus.

NOT WISHING TO provide any more photo opportunities, Friday steered his crew up the staircase.

Like many of Charlotte Amalie's slanted public walkways, the 99 Steps were formed out of bricks that had been transported from Europe as ship ballast, a balancing weight stored in the hull during transatlantic journeys. When used as staircase building materials, the bricks were positioned on edge and surrounded by a thick layer of mortar. Each step provided a minimal increase in elevation, a scheme designed to facilitate their use by the donkeys that once carried loads up the hill.

Three hundred years of heavy traffic had carved dipping ruts into the stairs; every square edge had been rounded from wear. Under dry conditions, the walkway was relatively easy to navigate; after a soaking downpour, the footing became treacherous.

Friday and team yellow hiked the stairs at a trot, passing a thick hedge of bougainvillea that formed an impenetrable barrier against the walkway's east side. On the opposite flank, the hotel rose with the steps, a terracing of coral pink structures behind a high concrete wall.

Each step in elevation provided a clearer view of the harbor, but Friday and his team didn't stop to look behind them. Their black clothing was quickly soaked with sweat.

Midway up the walk, palm trees took over the landscaping and the hotel gave way to other historic homes. They were soon even with the abandoned construction site where the second Governor impostor had been discovered.

Friday tried not to think about that fiasco as the team reached another multipronged signpost at the top of the stairs. He hoped they weren't being led on a similarly fruitless chase, but given the vagueness of the reported sighting, he remained skeptical.

A colored arrow pointed the way to their destination. The agents jogged up a curving road past a few more private residences. Then the hotel at the crest of the hill came into view.

Friday motioned for his team to drop into stealth mode as they approached the edge of the property.

He scanned the lower perimeter, pondering the best strategy to flush out the Governor.

BLACKBEARD'S CASTLE ENCOMPASSED several acres, much of it on a vertical slope.

A line of steps led up from the road, cutting into the hillside beside a rolling lawn. Midway up the grade, in the center of the grassy slope, stood a fountain featuring a ring of metal statues.

The fountain's spigots had been turned off, likely to conserve water, but the lack of spray did nothing to diminish the grace of the sculptures. Three young West Indian women stood in a triangle, each facing outward, poised as if searching through a wind-whipped night. One lifted a lamp, the next a torch, and the last a cutlass. The bronze figures were so lifelike, it was easy to imagine that they were on the verge of speaking, calling out the name of the person or object they so desperately sought.

Friday and his agents crept up the adjacent stairs, glancing only briefly at the fountain, their focus trained on the hotel above.

At the top of the lawn, a formidable concrete wall with spiked iron bars surrounded the main guest area. An arched entrance with a metal gate stood off to one side. Each half of the gate incorporated the image of a tower accompanied by the initials *BC*.

Closely followed by his team, Friday eased himself through the gate's open left-hand door. Yet another flight of steps rose from the entrance, this one wiggling toward the hilltop.

The switchbacks blocked the view of the upper horizon until the last rise revealed the hotel's signature landmark, the Skytsborg lookout tower, used during Colonial days to monitor the harbor and the surrounding sea for marauding pirates intent on invading Charlotte Amalie.

ST. THOMAS HAD a rather complicated relationship with pirates. Over the years, the swashbuckling sailors had been welcomed by some Danish governors, shunned by others, and, most recently, exploited as fodder for day-tripper tours.

Despite all this history—and the name attached to the hill-top property—it was unlikely that Blackbeard himself ever visited St. Thomas.

Regardless, it was easy to imagine the famous buccaneer hanging out at the entertainment area that surrounded the lookout tower.

A swimming pool abutted the tower's base and ran parallel to an open-air pavilion that housed an expansive bar. The elevated view provided a unique perspective of the city, the surrounding water, and the smaller islands that bumped up against the south shoreline. It was a great place to suck down rum, revel in the scenery, and watch the cruise ships navigate the harbor's narrow channels.

If that wasn't enough to inspire a person's pirate fantasies, statues of the Caribbean's most notorious sea criminals were scattered around the bar, the pool, a side yard, a gift shop, and the various guest room bungalows. The life-sized statues were as convincingly real as the trio of women in the fountain on the lawn below. Only close examination in the direct sunlight revealed the menacing scowls to be fixed in place and not alive.

In large part due to the pirate collection, Blackbeard's was a prime stop on the day-tripper circuit. On a regular port day, the tower and the surrounding hotel would be packed with visiting cruise ship passengers. The spiraling ladder-like staircase inside the tower was a bottleneck of aspiring lookers, with two-directional traffic vying for space within the single-width passage.

Costumed locals added flesh-and-blood characters to the statue display. Kitted out in hats, blousy shirts, pantaloons, and

boots, the hired actors posed for pictures, handed out bro-
chures, and provided the occasional pirate anecdote—
researched or made up: either way, it enthralled the guests.

But all that action had been shuttered for the day.

As agent Friday and team yellow reached the top of the last
staircase and advanced on the swimming pool, none of the
regular bustle was in evidence.

The pavilion was quiet, occupied only by a bartender cleaning glassware. The tower was locked, and the pirate imitators
had been sent home.

The lawn chairs spread across the flat side yard next to the
pool were empty—save one, occupied by a lone guest who had
booked all of the hotel's rooms for the next six weeks.

~ *41* ~

A Maligned Mojito

BLACKBEARD'S MOST RECENT arrival lay snoozing fitfully beneath a layer of wet towels that he had draped over his body to block whatever UV rays might penetrate through the sky's increasing cloud cover.

A glass with melting ice cubes rested on the grass at his feet. The consumed contents had represented the bartender's best effort at a mojito—minus the muddled mint leaves, which were currently unavailable.

The bartender glanced across the pavilion at the sleeping man and smiled at the empty glass. The improvised concoction had finally won the guest's approval—not bad for a drink that had received negative reviews before the ingredients were even mixed.

"NOPE. NO WAY, man. I'm telling you, that is not a mojito."

"Sorry, pal. Best we can do under the circumstances. Even if I could make it to the grocery store, it'd be closed by now. Locked up tight, and a guy inside with a gun ready to shoot first and ask questions later. Not worth the risk. How about we swing it to a rum punch?"

"I'm a dying man, and the best you can offer me is rum punch?"

With a sigh, the bartender had reached for a top shelf and

pulled down a bottle of aged overproof rum that was typically only used for special customers.

If ever there was an occasion to pour the gold standard, this was it.

"Trust me, mate," he'd said as he measured out a large dose and added it to the drink. "This one might just push you right on over to the other side."

WHETHER THE FORTIFIED rum drink had permanently relieved the Mojito Man of his earthly pain was still an open question.

The body beneath the pile of wet towels didn't move as Agent Friday and his team silently circled the pool to the grassy side yard, looking for their target.

The man on the lawn chair wasn't near large enough to be the Governor, but there was no one else in sight, the bartender having ducked beneath his counter when the agents cleared the top of the stairs.

Friday couldn't help but sigh at the relaxing scene. He would have liked nothing more than to jump into the pool and cool off—were it not for the matter of cleaning up the mess of Operation Coconut.

"If I ever get done with this case, I'm taking a vacation."

The faint mutter caused the hotel guest to wake with a start. Wet towels tumbled to the grass, revealing a pale human form in a pair of neon-colored swimming trunks. The advanced state of his illness was impossible to ignore.

Friday stepped back, instinctively repulsed. Trying to regain his composure, he directed his gaze to the ground beside the lawn chair, avoiding the skeletal face and wasted limbs.

"Sir, have you seen anyone else up here today?"

The man slowly sat up in the chair, gumming his dry mouth. With difficulty, he dropped his bedsore-ridden feet to the grass. He cupped a hand across his forehead, shielding his eyes. Blinking blearily, he stared up at the agents.

"Well, I've just seen you, haven't I? Hey, they called off the pirate party today. You boys can head to the beach. What do you say we all go? The pool is nice, but I'm hankering for some salt water."

He shifted his weight to try to stand, but Friday quashed his momentum with a slight tap on the shoulder.

"This is a serious matter, sir. We're searching for the Governor. He escaped arrest earlier this morning. We received word he's hiding up here at Blackbeard's."

The remaining towels went flying as the man tossed them into the air.

"Well, let's take a look, shall we? He must be around here somewhere. Now, where'd he go? Maybe we should look in the tower."

Friday frowned sternly. He didn't want to waste time dragging this poor soul down all the steps he and his team had just hiked up. But if the fellow had sent in a false report on the Governor's whereabouts, the agent would have no choice.

"Sir, do you have some clothes nearby? You're going to have to come with us."

"Whoa, whoa, whoa, there, G-man. You've got this all wrong. I don't know nothing about no governor. I've just been sitting up here relax-inating. I came here to die, man."

His face took on a pathetic, pitiful expression—which vanished when he noticed the empty glass at his feet.

He peered up at Friday and asked hopefully, "Do you think you can you get me a mojito?"

THE HOTEL MANAGER arrived on the lawn to provide an alibi for his guest. He'd been summoned by the bartender, who had slipped out of the pavilion while Friday suffered through a lengthy mojito monologue.

A survey of the property turned up no evidence the Governor had been there that morning. Friday was about to radio back to Government House to ask for more information about the source who had called in the reported sighting, when he noticed a color television mounted over the pavilion's bar.

The sound had been muted, but the picture on the satellite feed was tuned to one of the main news channels from the United States. Images of the Legislature Building and downtown Charlotte Amalie flashed across the screen, followed by footage of National Guard troops marching in formation down the walkway leading into town from the cruise ship dock.

In another clip, troops were shown jogging past a closed Prada store and a row of mega-million-dollar yachts. The occupants of the last category stood on their decks, gaping and snapping shots with their cell phones.

The bartender had returned to his station. Seeing Friday's interest, he turned up the set's volume, releasing a thunderous sound of combat boots thumping across the wooden boardwalk that wound through the shopping area.

Friday sputtered, incredulous. Spinning around, he turned to stare down at the harbor.

"Who let the Guard guys loose?"

Legislature Building

~ 42 ~

The Dignity of the Law

IT HAD SEEMED like such a plum assignment, the third circuit appellate judge thought as he stood on a dais overlooking the Legislature Building's meeting chambers.

He'd fly down to St. Thomas and perhaps officiate over a few minor procedural matters. Most likely, his services wouldn't be needed. Then he would spend a couple of days of much-needed rest and relaxation with his family at an all-inclusive beachside resort.

Operation Coconut. It sounded so quaint. What could be easier?

With a sigh, he crossed his arms over his chest. The black judicial robe he wore over his Hawaiian shirt and khaki shorts swung loosely around his short pencil-thin frame.

This is not what he had envisioned.

Chaos reigned in the makeshift courtroom that had been set up in the meeting chambers.

The indicted senators had refused to listen to the reading of the charges. They had rejected the public defense attorneys who had been offered, demanding instead that their own lawyers be brought in to provide counsel. With the arrival of the first private lawyers, the group had grown even more rowdy.

The local district judge had thrown her hands up and fled the building, leaving the appellate justice in charge. He'd had no better luck bringing the room to order. His tinny voice had been drowned out by the senators' continued jeers.

He wiped a hand across his cheek, rubbing at a sticky residue on his skin, the remnants of a rotting banana peel someone had thrown at his face.

The woman from the local attorney general's office gave him a sympathetic smile. Given the growing instability in the surrounding downtown area, she had arranged to have the National Guard troops activated to secure the streets outside the building, but there was little else Wendy the Wunderkind could do to help.

The FBI agents had retreated to a safe distance at the far perimeter of the room. The senators had cowed them with their persistent demands, threats, and verbal abuse.

There had been a few attempts to question the arrested politicians about their two missing members, but the effort had quickly been abandoned.

The impounded senators had nothing but venom for Bobo and Sanchez.

"Isn't it suspicious that they disappeared right before the troops arrived . . ."

"If they had a way out, they should have taken us with them!"

"Traitors! They must have known the feds were coming!"

If possible, the Governor was even more unpopular.

"He's a crook! I always knew it . . ."

"Thief! He's the one who's brought this on us."

It seemed unlikely this group had any information on the fugitives' whereabouts.

The justice thought of his wife and two children, who were resting comfortably at the resort. By now, they would be enjoying a nice tropical lunch. His wife, a woman nearly twice his size, was likely on her second or third mai tai.

He desperately wished he were with them.

WENDY MANNED HER post at the side of the room, occasionally sending a chagrined look to the appellate judge and the unfortunate agents tasked with monitoring the senators.

Every so often, the slight edge of a smile crept into the

corners of her mouth, but she quickly smoothed it out, careful not to let on that the day was unfolding just as she and her coconspirators had intended.

WENDY TURNED AWAY from the melee in the chambers and strolled into the adjacent hallway.

The head of the local attorney general's office, she had an impressive résumé and, to most observers, appeared to be headed toward a bright legal future.

Certainly, she had put in the time and effort required for such success.

Born and raised on St. Croix, Wendy had diligently worked her way through the island's public education system, earning a coveted seat at Georgetown Law School. After graduation, she had moved into public practice, clerking with several high-profile judges before obtaining a position with the justice department.

Despite the years of toil and sacrifice it had taken to reach her current status, she was prepared to risk it all for the cause.

Growing up, she had attended a small church on the island's west end. The preacher's favorite sermon topic was independence, specifically, the need for St. Croix to free itself from the clutches of its American overlords.

The message had stuck with her.

Now it was time to cut those binding cords for good.

AN AGENT TAPPED Wendy on the shoulder and motioned for her to join him by the window.

"Ma'am, you need to hear this."

Following him to the opening, she listened as a passing truck blasted the KRAT station from its speakers.

The broadcast had resumed—and this time, the DJs were joined by a pair of special guests.

The Lutheran Church

~ *43* ~

A Crowded Cistern

"HELLO, ST. THOMAS! The KRAT crew is coming back *at-cha* with some in-studio guests."

Dread Fred pushed the button for the "I Smell a Rat" jingle, giving his listeners a moment to return to their radios. He wiped the sweat from his brow and adjusted the headset clamped over his bald scalp.

The cistern had grown more crowded since the last broadcast's abrupt termination. Double the number of bodies now occupied the concrete tank, increasing the humid heat in the confined space. Little breeze filtered through the roof's open hatch.

It had taken the concerted efforts of both DJs plus Senator Sanchez to convince Bobo to put on his shirt.

Four was an uncomfortable squeeze in the cistern's close quarters, but it could have been worse. The fifth member of their group had excused himself not long after he introduced the two senators.

Dread Fred glanced up at the ceiling and the hole where the swishing cassock had disappeared moments earlier.

He wasn't an expert on Christian orthodoxy, but he had the distinct impression that the Bishop wasn't your typical religious leader.

THE RAT INTRO ended, and Dread Fred returned the audio feed to his headgear mike.

"Welcome back, islanders. Never fear, we're still here. For this next segment, we're bringing you a couple of special guests who have joined us in our studio. Voices from the front lines, so to speak. We think you'll be interested in what they have to say."

"And no, they're not the pasty boys," Whaler cut in with a second microphone, a wireless handheld device set up to pass among the guests.

Dread chuckled. "Or the Governor—but, hey, Guv, man, if you're out there, we'd love to have you on."

Whaler paced around the table, his fluffy mane of hair bouncing with each step. "Unless the pasty boys have nabbed you. In which case, keep your distance. We don't need to meet your new friends."

He paused and leaned over the table.

"No offense, big man, but we don't want to end up in the hoosegow."

JULIA SANCHEZ PERCHED on a fold-out chair next to Dread Fred, listening to the familiar banter. She still couldn't get over the DJs' physical appearances. The two men didn't look anything at all like what she had imagined.

Like everyone else on St. Thomas, she was an avid follower of the KRAT broadcasts. The cheeky duo had even interviewed her before the last election—but the entire transaction had been conducted by phone. She wondered if they'd been holed up in a cistern like this during that previous conversation.

Dread's deep voice cut into her thoughts.

"Now, Senator Sanchez," he said with an impish grin, "perhaps you could give us some insight into the day's . . . weather."

She issued a stern smile as Whaler handed over the mike. "Dread, I think we have far more important matters to discuss."

"Actually, I'm quite concerned about the possibility of rain," Whaler muttered, nervously eyeing a series of troughs feeding into the cistern's ceiling.

"All right, Senator," Dread allowed, "we'll put off the fore-cast for a moment. Let's move on to your current occupation. Why don't you tell us what happened over in the Legislature Building this morning."

Before Sanchez could speak, Bobo wrapped his hand around the microphone and tilted it his direction.

"If I may, Fred, it was a *dread*ful situation." He grinned. "Pardon the pun."

"Senator Bobo, I was about to get to you, but please feel free to jump in . . ."

Sanchez felt her chair slide sideways as Bobo maneuvered between her and Dread Fred.

"Today, the United States government descended upon us like a plague. A locust swarm of federal agents invaded the Legislature, fouling our hallowed hallways with their heavy-handed assault. These same fetid roaches now gnaw at the very foundations of Government House, even as they pursue our lawfully elected Governor. It is a dark day for the Virgin Islands, I tell you. A dark day indeed."

Dread opened his mouth, searching for something—anything—to say, but he waited too long to interject. Bobo wasn't finished.

"Today's unlawful action was a direct affront to our civil liberties, to common decency, and to the integrity of these islands. If this injustice is not remedied, if our government is not returned to the people, then a tempest will descend upon this land, blotting out the sun. The sea will turn to blood, and hordes of ravaging amphibians will fill the streets."

Throughout this soliloquy, Whaler stood behind Bobo's back, mocking each Biblical reference with facial contortions and exaggerated hand motions.

Dread struggled to maintain a solemn expression. "What do you propose we do to, uh, address this injustice and, perhaps most important, turn back the frogs?"

Bobo stroked the side of his head, reflecting. The action only served to further distribute the scent of his musky hair oil, which had begun to concentrate in the humid room.

"Well, Fred, I'm glad you asked. As you can imagine, I've thought about this a great deal. I believe we need someone to serve as interim governor until we can get this mess sorted out."

"Who do you suggest?" Dread asked, but everyone in the cistern had already anticipated the answer. Whaler shook his head as Bobo tossed the tail of his rainbow-colored scarf over his left shoulder.

"I humbly submit my application."

~ 44 ~

Governor Bobo

DREAD FRED STRUGGLED to maintain his composure, but Whaler made no such effort. His hoots echoed off the cistern walls.

Finally Dread managed his first follow up question.

"So, Senator Bobo, what makes you think you have the right qualifications to step in as governor?"

Sanchez watched the interview from across the room, where she had retreated after Bobo commandeered the microphone. The stench from his hair oil was overwhelming, even at a distance.

She stood with her arms crossed over her chest, suspiciously observing the proceedings. As Bobo disavowed any role in the alleged government corruption, she couldn't help but think that the Reverend was delivering a carefully rehearsed speech. This was a well-practiced presentation, not something that he had pulled together in the last few minutes.

"Look at me, Fred. Take a good close look. I live a pious life. If people were throwing money around, it wasn't at me! Check my accounts. You'll find nothing there, I promise you!"

The radio host appeared unconvinced. "We haven't seen the Governor's accounts yet either . . ."

"Fred, Fred, Fred. I take no position on the Governor's guilt or innocence, and I object to the manner in which he has been treated. Today's seizure was nothing short of a military coup."

"Then shouldn't we give the Governor a chance to defend himself?"

"In an ideal world, Fred, yes. Yes, we would. But I fear there's no time for that. The territory is under attack. We have to put our government back together immediately, so we can fend off these invaders. Let's select a new executive, one not tainted by the current allegations. Let's assemble a new Legislature, without the indicted senators." He paused, cleared his throat, and added, "Except, of course, for Julie here . . ."

Senator Sanchez knew the last allowance had only been made because she was standing across the room glaring at Bobo. He seemed to have conveniently forgotten that he too was among the list of indicted senators.

"And let's go forward with a new government . . ." Bobo licked his dry lips, moistening them for the finale.

". . . without the United States."

DREAD COVERED HIS face with his hands. He'd done a number of crazy interviews with Senator Bobo, but this one topped them all.

Whaler snatched the end of Bobo's rainbow-colored scarf and twirled it around the cistern like the tail of a kite.

Sanchez stared at the broadcasting table, stunned by the implications of Bobo's comments.

The Reverend wore a smarmy, contented smile that made her skin scrawl. He couldn't hide his satisfaction.

While the DJs appeared to have lumped the senator's last proclamation in with the rest of his wild notions, Sanchez had sensed a larger purpose to his final words—and she was beginning to suspect that Bobo was somehow secretly involved in the whole invasion scheme.

"This just in, folks." Dread looked up from his laptop and paused to clear his throat. "We're about to have a real circus on our hands."

Whaler released the scarf, letting it flutter down over Bobo's head. He peeked over Dread's shoulder to read the message on the laptop's screen and let out a whooping holler.

Dread shook his head.

"Pull out your spyglasses and your infrared scopes. The

attorney general's office has just announced a bounty for any information pertaining to the Governor's whereabouts that leads to his arrest."

With a grimace, he pushed the button for the jingle music. The reggae thump bounced off the cistern walls.

"I smell a rat."

Coki Beach

~ 45 ~

Bounty Hunters

GIVEN THE SIZEABLE reward posted by the attorney general's office, it didn't take long for all of St. Thomas to get in on the hunt for the Governor. News of the bounty quickly spread across the island. The information-disseminating power of the KRAT broadcast had been undiminished by the attempts to shut down its transmission.

Citizens peeked out their windows, cagily eying their neighbors. Over the course of the next five minutes, the intensity of person-to-person scrutiny ratcheted up to a heretofore unimagined level.

But when this passive approach failed to yield results, the island's residents swung into action.

Chickens were rousted in backyard coops; cluttered garages were foraged. Pruning shears were used to attack patches of overgrown greenery in side yards and culverts. Anywhere the big man might be hiding was the subject of a diligent search.

The overwhelming public consensus seemed to be that the Governor must still be in Charlotte Amalie, not far from Government House. Streams of people flowed into town from the interior, hoping to get in on the reward. The narrow alleyways between the shoreline shops soon saw more foot traffic than on days when the largest cruise ship was in port.

Regardless of their personal feelings about the Governor's guilt or innocence, money was a powerful motivator.

No one was more inspired by the potential prize than a charismatic Crucian coconut vendor–turned–Coki Beach braid entrepreneur.

"THAT'S THE LAST one," Mic said as he tied off the final braid for what had been a very thick head of hair. The long locks of wild curls were now neatly arrayed in several dozen braided rows.

The hair belonged to one of his regular customers, a woman who worked at the aquatic center.

"You're the best, Mic," she said, handing him a five-dollar bill as she stood up from the sand. "I'll be back on Tuesday."

"You know where to find me, mon," he called out, causing the customer to giggle.

As the woman walked off, Mic handed the money to Currie. He preferred to let his partner handle all of their financial affairs.

"*Ca-ching*," Mic said with an eyebrow pump as Currie tucked the cash in a shorts pocket he kept closed with a safety pin.

"Not bad for a slow day." With a sigh, Mic looked out across the empty beach. "Where is everybody?"

Currie shook his head. "They kept the day-trippers on the boat because of the mess with the Governor."

Mic scooped up a cracked shell and tossed it into the water. "Well, then those pasty boys need to come down here and get some braids done."

THE RADIO AT the rum shack squawked as the bartender switched over from his collection of downloaded beach tunes to the latest KRAT update. After hearing about the reward offer, Mic flopped backward onto the sand.

"That's a lot of dough, Currie-mon." He whistled up at the sky. "Think of what we could do with that kind of money. We could get our own place."

Currie twiddled a stray hair tie in his fingers. "You wouldn't know what to do inside a real house, Mic. You'd probably feel trapped. We haven't slept under a proper roof in years."

Mic bent his knees, digging his heels into the sand. "A tent, mon. I promise you, I wouldn't complain about being inside a tent."

The pair fell silent for several minutes. The broadcasters took another break, and the bartender turned off the radio, leaving the dull lapping of the waves to fill the void.

Finally, Mic smacked his lips.

"Currie, mon, we know a thing or two about hiding. We should head into town and see if we can't track down this Governor dude."

Currie sighed. "About all we know is how to hang out with a bunch of Jamaicans on a beach."

"You think he's here?" Mic sat up and immediately began looking up and down the shoreline.

Currie chuckled at his friend's gullibility. "No, he'd stick out like a sore thumb. He's probably still in Charlotte Amalie. That's my bet."

After another lull in the conversation, Currie hopped up from the sand.

"Come on," he said, offering Mic a hand. "Thanks to your braiding, we have a little extra cash. Let's catch a ride into town. We might as well go see what all of the fuss is about."

MINUTES LATER, THE pair climbed into the back of a safari truck. It was a spontaneous—and fateful—decision.

Currie couldn't have known that he was steering them on a direct path toward the man bent on their destruction.

The reward for information about the Governor was a minor amount compared to the far greater value that had been placed on their heads.

The West End of St. Thomas

~ 46 ~

A Deal with the Devil

THE WEST END of St. Thomas was a lightly populated terrain, scattered with private estates. Little of the commercial tourist infrastructure that dominated the island's eastern half had spread to this sector.

The area featured several stretches of inaccessible coastline along with a few tucked-away beaches that were popular with the locals but were too remote to be reached by day-tripper traffic.

It was the ideal spot to stage an unsupervised entry.

The Crucian motorboat powered swiftly toward shore, targeting one such length of sand. A dense forest flanked the rocky cove, blocking the view from the main road.

The captain slowed only slightly to navigate around a jut of boulders. No sooner had the bow pushed up onto the bank than a half-dozen thugs hopped out of the vessel.

The men carried sizeable loads of guns and ammo. Their dark skin had been heavily tattooed, the inked emblems memorials to romantic quests, family members, and various gang associations.

In addition to their weaponry, the men sported an assortment of gold chains and diamond-studded ear and nose rings.

But none was adorned as decoratively as their leader, Casanova.

He had blinged up during the ride around the island's southern rim. Who knew what St. Thomian ladies he might encounter that evening?

After all, he thought with a smile, that night, he planned to take the streets of Charlotte Amalie.

WITH THE LAST pack of supplies and ammo tossed onto the sand, the motorboat reversed out of the cove and returned to open sea. Nova motioned for his gang to gather up their gear and move inland.

The key to these surreptitious landings was to get it over and done with as quickly as possible. The longer they loitered, the greater the chance a busybody sailboat or a passing coast guard vessel might radio in a report.

The Crucian crew hiked up a goat trail to a clearing where they were met by a small fleet of jeeps and all-terrain vehicles. The transport would take them to the outskirts of Charlotte Amalie. They would wait there until nightfall to make their final incursion.

Nova smiled, spinning a gold ring he'd slipped onto his left index finger. Everything was going according to plan—that is, until an unexpected figure stepped out of the front vehicle.

The crew watched their leader, waiting for his signal.

Nova eyed the slim man in the golf shirt and chinos, pondering his presence. He knew the man by reputation—and his descriptive name.

The Fixer.

NOVA STRODE A circle around the clearing, prowling like a panther as he sized up his potential adversary.

The Fixer allowed a sixty-second inspection before stiffly introducing himself. His alias they both recognized as meaningless, merely another obligatory step in the dance. Then he cut to the point.

"I'm here on behalf of the Governor. Whatever she's paying you, he's willing to double it." The Fixer paused and then added, "Surely that's worth your consideration."

Nova was unimpressed. "That's not enough to switch sides. She's a powerful woman. Your involvement . . . complicates things."

He leaned toward the Fixer, a menacing cue to his crew, who brandished their weapons as they closed in around the interloper.

The Fixer appeared unconcerned. He had done his homework. He'd come to the bargaining table prepared.

"I can get you the Coconut Boys."

The words had their intended affect. Nova stepped back, and his men immediately relaxed.

Without further hesitation, he offered his hand for a confirming shake.

"Then we have a deal."

The Lutheran Church

~ 47 ~

Bunkered

THE BISHOP RETURNED to the cistern in time to hear the KRAT duo wrap up their broadcast.

Dread Fred rubbed a towel over his head, soaking up the sweat. There was relief in his voice. "We're signing off for now, folks. Thanks for sticking with us this morning. You can look for us the same time tomorrow. We'll do our best to get back on the air."

Whaler added a parting comment. "Stay safe, my friends."

As the DJs packed up their equipment, Sanchez grabbed her satchel and moved toward the ladder. Bobo remained in his chair. He looked expectantly at the Bishop.

The Bishop held up a cautioning hand. He stood in front of the ladder, blocking her path.

"Senator Sanchez, I advise you to stay here in the cistern for a while longer."

She bristled at the suggestion. "It's too hot in here. I don't think I can take another . . ."

The Bishop cut in, his voice calm but commanding. "The federal agents are still looking for you. There's a team sweeping the area as we speak. If you leave now, you're likely to end up with the rest of the senators, trapped in the Legislative Chambers." He smiled sympathetically. "I assure you, this is a better alternative."

"He's right, Jules," Bobo said with a stretch. He began pulling off his tunic. "We might as well get comfortable."

Sanchez watched forlornly as Dread Fred and Whaler climbed the ladder and disappeared into the world above.

The Bishop quickly followed, pausing at the top.

"I'll try to bring you some water, but it's best to close this for now."

The bottom hem of the cassock disappeared from view.

A claustrophobic fear gripped the senator's chest as the hatch swung shut and the Bishop cinched down the lid.

Across the Island of St. Thomas

~ 48 ~

Everywhere at Once

BY MIDAFTERNOON, THE local cell phone towers had resumed service, either because the ordered blockage period had ended or the person in control of the switch had tired of the inconvenience. So many St. Thomas residents had moved their phones over to the Tortola tower, the backup had begun to overload from the extra usage.

Word of the attorney general's reward offer now spread to those few residents who hadn't been able to access the intermittent KRAT broadcasts.

The volunteer-assisted manhunt for the Governor transitioned into yet a higher gear. As the islanders searched high and low for their erstwhile elected leader and, more important, the lucrative reward money, a few promising leads began to surface—and then the number exploded exponentially.

The designated hotline was besieged with callers.

Throughout the rest of the afternoon, reports continued to pile in. The Governor was sighted in every possible location in Charlotte Amalie and across St. Thomas. Other eyewitnesses placed him on St. John and St. Croix—both at the same time.

For Agent Friday, overseeing the impromptu call center from the FBI's St. Thomas field office, it was a maddening experience.

Coconut was one fruit, beverage additive, and flavoring that he would never again voluntarily consume.

THE LOCAL FBI agents had been somewhat less than hospitable when Friday requested a landline and desk space in their office.

He could understand their bitterness. It had been a poor operational decision not to brief them on the day's planned arrests. The offended feelings, he reasoned, probably explained the condition of the room he'd been offered.

The walls were dirty and scuffed, in need of a fresh coat of paint. The carpeting was so severely stained, it was impossible to tell what the original color had been. The desk was a prefab government-issue construct that looked as if one of its legs might fall off at any moment.

As for the phone, he'd been given a plastic contraption with a push-button keypad whose center number six routinely stuck in the depressed position. The receiver relayed incoming audio accompanied by a dull echo, likely a result of corroded wiring.

He had turned the phone's volume all the way up to its maximum setting, but it was still difficult to make out the voices coming through the line.

It certainly wasn't enough to drown out the occasional mocking comments from the agents on the other side of the wall. They were reveling in the mission's current state of failure.

Despite the squalid surroundings, the poor equipment, and the hostile atmosphere, the field office was a far preferable command center to the Legislature Building.

Friday shuddered at the thought.

Given the difficulties in locating the Governor, the appellate judge had ordered that the arrested senators be taken into custody aboard the navy ship. It was a decision that should have been made by the district court judge, but no one had been able to track her down since she left the melee of the early morning proceedings.

The growing armada of attorneys advising the senators had pounced on this legal technicality, challenging the appellate judge's order. The politicians had decided to stage a sit-in, obstinately refusing to move.

The situation had reached a stalemate, with no resolution in sight.

FRIDAY LOOKED DOWN at the map he'd spread across the wobbly desk. He'd used his color-coded grid scheme to allocate agents into different sectors, so that they could efficiently chase down as many leads as possible on the missing Governor, to no avail.

While they were typically unable to identify the look-alike who had triggered each report, it became clear that they were dealing with more than just the occasional case of mistaken identity. An army of doppelgängers had been let loose upon the territory, preprogrammed to pop up in choreographed locations that were timed to generate maximum confusion and distraction.

As the afternoon wore on, a concentration of Governor sightings were reported at eating establishments. A doppelgänger made an appearance at Gladys' Café, a popular West Indian place in the alleys along the waterfront. Almost simultaneously, another look-alike was seen at a diner in Frenchtown on the southwest edge of the harbor. Before those two instances could be investigated, a third Governor was spotted by the poolside kiosk at one of the island's high-end resorts.

For the increasingly frustrated—and hungry—federal agents sent to investigate these sightings, the temptation to stop for a quick bite had been too great.

Friday listened to the latest garbled-mouthful report from the field.

"Another false alarm, sir," the agent mumbled through an inartfully suppressed munch.

"Anything else?"

A loud swat echoed through the transmission.

"The mosquitoes down here are vicious."

AGENT FRIDAY STARED at the scuffed wall inside the tiny office and pondered the strategic implications.

The Governor's pre-indictment efforts had extended far beyond the series of last-ditch pleas he had submitted to the executive branch in the days leading up to this morning's invasion. He had made extensive preparations to elude capture and arrest—activities that apparently went undetected by his top aide.

Either the FBI's Government House source had been wrong about the Governor's mind-set in those last days or the whistle-blower's betrayal had been discovered and he'd been intentionally cut out of the loop.

This much was clear. The Governor had no intention of making an easy surrender.

Government House

~ 49 ~

His Whistle Blown

UP THE HILL from Friday's impromptu call center, Operation Coconut's second headquarters was seeing far less productivity.

Little had changed inside Government House since the discovery of the second governor impostor at the construction site and the sacrificial chair being tossed over the office balcony—other than Agent Hightower had slipped into a rum-induced nap.

The office remained in a state of disarray, with Hightower at its center, sleeping on the leather recliner behind the Governor's desk. His head was tilted back in an openmouthed drool. Every so often, a slobbering snore broke the silence, but otherwise, the Gorilla was quiet.

The Government House employees—minus the burly maid in the high-necked dress—were still being held in the first-floor lobby, but the group had grown restless. Their patience had run out, and tempers were rising to match those inside the Legislature Building.

So far, nothing had been thrown at the luckless agents standing guard, but it was only a matter of time.

CEDRIC FOUND HIMSELF once more pacing inside the Governor's office. He shook his head at the deplorable sight of the room and the special agent in charge passed out behind the desk.

It was yet another aspect of the day's scheme that had failed to meet expectations. The Gorilla's alcoholic rage had petered out much faster than anticipated. He had hoped Hightower would make a far bigger spectacle of himself.

Right now, Cedric considered that the least of his problems. He was deeply troubled by the latest KRAT transmission.

The Governor kept a portable radio in the office so he could listen to the KRAT broadcasts. Despite the frequent grilling he received from Dread Fred and Whaler, he was a big fan of the show and rarely missed an airing.

The interview with Senator Bobo had left Cedric perplexed. The Reverend was supposed to be tied up in the Legislature Building, protesting the indignities of the lawmakers' unlawful detention. Instead, he was running loose around town, spouting off all kinds of nonsense. He should never have been allowed to ad-lib on air.

Cedric cringed, recalling the rambling speech. Locusts, frogs, a sea of blood—Bobo wasn't a credible spokesperson for the separatist movement.

He tugged indignantly at his tie.

That was his role.

CEDRIC COMPLETED ANOTHER lap around the room, but the typically calming action did little to quell his anxiety. He was stuck in limbo, a no-man's-land of his own creation.

With his cover blown, there was little chance the Governor might contact him or seek him out. By now, the Fixer would have conveyed the information he'd learned during the construction site debacle—if indeed the Governor wasn't already aware of Cedric's betrayal.

He had been deliberately duped during the caper to elude the feds that morning. The Governor must have been told about the aide's cooperation with the attorney general's office—but when?

And how, he wondered again, had the Governor communicated with his accomplice?

Cedric crossed to the balcony, stepping into the spot where the Governor had so often stood, particularly in recent days. Taking a similar stance, he placed his hands on the railing and imagined that he had assumed the territory's top leadership position.

It was an outcome that appeared increasingly less likely to occur.

DRUMMING HIS FINGERS in frustration, Cedric stared out at the city.

Afternoon shadows had begun to creep across the rolling streets. A sticky humidity still bathed the harbor, but the sun's intensity had noticeably waned.

The crowds that had flocked to Emancipation Park and the surrounding waterfront streets were enjoying a temporary lull. Even the sporadic gunfire had petered out. After a day of frenetic confusion, exhaustion filled the air—along with a morbid curiosity of what might happen next.

These were emotions Cedric shared with the masses.

He paused.

There was something different in the scene, other than the weary pedestrians loitering in the streets. It took him a moment to identify the anomaly.

The flapping flags attached to the pole above his head had been diminished by one. Someone had removed the Stars and Stripes.

A cheeky response to the day's events, Cedric mused. Unlike Bobo's radio ramble, this rebellious action made him smile.

Gripping the railing, Cedric returned his gaze to the leafy rooftops below.

Just north of the post office, he spied the woman from the local attorney general's office hiking up the public stairs. Wendy was accompanied by a pair of federal agents, flanking her on either side. It was an unnecessary security precaution, in his opinion, but then she was an important figure both in her official legal capacity and with the clandestine separatist movement. She had taken numerous risks in both roles and, consequently, had made her fair share of enemies.

No doubt, she was on her way up to Government House to assess Hightower's condition.

He glanced over his shoulder as the Gorilla snorted in his

sleep, shifting his position on the recliner. A rum-scented burp wafted through the doorway and onto the balcony.

Cedric grimaced at the stench. If the agent awoke, the armed accomplices were far more likely to be needed inside the building than out.

He looked once more at the trio climbing the steps and then lifted his gaze toward Emancipation Park. An opening in the crowds revealed an empty picnic table, seemingly innocuous—and yet . . .

He blinked as the realization hit him.

On a normal business day, that same table was routinely occupied by elderly men, gossiping and playing backgammon.

Spinning around, he stared into the office at the upended table and the scattered backgammon checkers strewn across the floor.

This is how the Governor and the Fixer had exchanged messages.

He had been a fool to let it slip past him.

This whole time, they'd been sending signals to each other right under his nose.

~ 50 ~

Obsolete

WENDY WALKED UP the public staircase from the post office, easily keeping time with her FBI security team. Despite her formal skirt and blouse, she wasn't the least bit flushed. She'd lived her entire life in the tropics and was accustomed to both the heat and Charlotte Amalie's endless supply of steps.

It was a route she had taken countless times during the five years she'd been assigned to the local attorney general's office. There was a constant need to liaison with the numerous USVI officials located either inside Government House or nearby offices.

From the sloping field to the left of the staircase, she heard the familiar rustle of feral chickens scratching through fallen leaves. The hens were guarded by an overprotective rooster, who eyed everyone who passed with leery suspicion. The cagy bird looked up at the lawyer and gave her an extra head-bobbing nod of concern, as if he sensed the duplicity in her step.

Wendy continued up the staircase, unfazed by the animal's accusing stare. She was a pro at concealing her true beliefs and loyalties.

Most humans she dealt with were not as discerning as the rooster.

As she topped the steps, she glanced briefly at Hotel 1829's flowering veranda and the adjacent parsonage, but neither piqued her interest. Her focus was trained on the brilliant white facing of the building at the end of the row, the symbol of the territory's seat of power.

Brimming with ambition, she prepared for the next performance.

CEDRIC WAITED IN the second-floor hallway as Wendy marched into the Government House lobby. The attorney's arrival sparked an eruption of pleading and frustrated voices among the building's employees.

With practiced professionalism, she quieted the riot. Assuring the captives that she was headed upstairs to address their plight, she started swiftly up the central staircase.

The accompanying agents peeled off to join their counterparts. Wendy was alone when Cedric met her at the top banister and motioned her aside.

"What's the latest?" he whispered tensely. "I've been out of the loop since early this morning."

"When you lost the Governor," she replied, trying to mask her annoyance. The attempt was only halfway successful.

"He gave me the slip. He must have found out about my testimony." Cedric hesitated, trying to decide whether to divulge how the Governor had been communicating with the Fixer.

At her dismissive expression, he bit his tongue. Best to hold on to any leverage he had left. He switched topics.

"Did you hear the KRAT broadcast? Bobo put himself forward as governor."

"I've been rather busy, Cedric. I haven't had time to sit around listening to the radio."

Cedric's lips pressed together. He sensed he was pushing Wendy too far, but he had to know.

"It's just that—Bobo as governor. That's not what we agreed . . ."

With an exasperated sigh, Wendy brushed past the aide. She took a few steps down the hallway, distancing herself, before she turned to look back.

She wanted to prevent Cedric from causing any unnecessary disruptions, but the governorship wasn't a promise she was committed to keep—if, in fact, it was ever in play at all.

"Relax." Her voice was quiet but far from comforting. "No one takes Bobo seriously. Think about it. This plays to your advantage. You versus Bobo? Who do you think will gain the people's support?"

For Cedric, uncertainty was quickly morphing into desperation. "Wendy, I may be in trouble. My cover's blown. I don't know where to go."

"Just sit tight and wait for everything to play out. We're in a fluid situation right now."

With that, she strode purposefully to the end of the hallway and into the Governor's office.

CEDRIC WATCHED IN panic as Wendy disappeared around the corner.

Without the Governor, he had become obsolete.

He started down the stairs, his pace increasing with each step. He had no choice but to try to find the big man.

They'd always had a good rapport, and Cedric knew how to be persuasive. He might still be able to convince his boss that he had been looking out for his best interests all along.

Plus, he held one last piece of critical information—the identity of the woman leading the separatist movement, the woman who had so deviously plotted the Governor's downfall.

Cedric reached the foot of the stairs and headed for the front doors, trying to ignore the lobby full of condemning stares. As far as the Government House employees were concerned, the aide's guilt was permanent and inexcusable.

Moments later, Cedric scurried down the hill toward Emancipation Park.

With the Governor still in hiding, the aide's best bet was to check for backgammon players congregating at the park's tables—on the off chance he was still using that method to communicate with the Fixer.

Emancipation Park

~ *51* ~

An Epic Showdown

CEDRIC PUSHED HIS way through the crowds lingering inside Emancipation Park, trying to reach the area where the old men set up their backgammon tables.

The park's numbers had lessened from earlier in the day, but enough people remained to make it difficult to maneuver. In addition to the pedestrians clogging the paths and grassy areas by the grandstand, several vendors had moved in, lured by the concentration of thirsty, hungry customers. There were ice chests with cool drinks and other cold-serve items; a portable barbecue had been set up to grill a variety of meats.

While the vendors were doing a roaring business, the carnival atmosphere had grown ragged around the edges. On the grandstand, a persistent speaker or two soldiered on, hoarsely hollering into the microphones, but the speeches were rapidly losing steam.

The pickpockets who had retreated at the sight of the federal agents that morning were now circulating in full force, undeterred by the few hapless Guard members ringing the park's perimeter. With the potential pockets mostly belonging to locals, the pickers had to be careful when making their selection. These pocket-owners were much more wary of their tricks than the day-trippers, and there was a far greater risk of retribution.

Cedric looked up at the dark clouds swelling above the harbor. At any moment, the approaching storm would dump its load, causing the crowd to disperse.

If the Governor and the Fixer were still using their signaling system, he wouldn't have long to find it.

He slid around the throng surrounding the barbecue, urgently searching for a West Indian man with a backgammon board.

⌒⌒

"CURRIE-MON, GET A load of those chicken wings that guy is cooking on his stove." Mic closed his eyes and sucked in the smell. "We got to get us some of that meat."

Currie checked his pocket and shook his head. "Sorry, Mic. We have just enough to make it back to Coki." Muttering under his breath, he corrected, "Well, maybe halfway back."

Mic leaned over Currie's shoulder and whispered, "See if your cousin can hook us up."

Currie shook his head, adamantly rejecting the idea. His cousin—in truth, a far more distant relation than the shorthand term implied—was circling the park with his fellow gang of pickpockets.

Mic and Currie had briefly stayed with Cousin Spike in Charlotte Amalie when they first arrived on St. Thomas. After a disastrous attempt to practice the trade, Spike had encouraged the Coconut Boys to leave the city before they were arrested—or worse, set upon by the other pickpockets.

Currie glanced once more at his near-empty pocket. He couldn't blame his cousin for the paltry sum it contained.

CURRIE SHIFTED UNCOMFORTABLY as he watched Mic make another pass by the barbecue stand. He had been ready to leave several hours ago, but Mic had resisted his suggestions that they head back to the beach.

This was Mic's kind of event: full of jocular camaraderie and open to anyone who wanted to join in. The unifying concern for the territory's siege had forged alliances among strangers. The Governor had been maligned repeatedly throughout the day, the aspersions another commonality among the park's rallying participants.

Mic had readily thrown his own verbal punches, more as a way of fitting in than out of any deep-seated conviction.

"Hey, mon, I always knew he was a thieving son of a gun," Mic had pronounced with gusto, clasping the shoulder of a taxi driver who had nodded his head in agreement.

Throughout all this banter, Currie had remained silent. As the afternoon wore on, he became increasingly worried about the risk of being so publicly visible, particularly when Mic mugged for one of the television news cameras that had ventured into the area.

Mic remained unfazed. Even now, he was happily enjoying the festivities.

Having completed his latest tour of the barbecue, Mic returned with Cousin Spike.

Spike had Currie's short stature and Mic's slender build. It was a perfect combination for slipping through crowds—and lifting wallets. Currie didn't ask how the afternoon's haul had gone. The pickpocket's creed forbade any such discussion until the picker was a much safer distance away from the pocket.

Mic had thankfully moved on from the topic of chicken wings; the discussion of the Governor's guilt had also grown stale.

He and Spike had launched into a debate on an altogether different subject.

"The Goat Foot Woman, mon, I'm telling you, that is the most fearsome creature in these here islands. We see her all the time down on Santa Cruz."

The St. Thomian pickpocket looked at Mic as if he'd lost his mind.

"Goat Foot Woman," Spike sputtered derisively. "I never heard of such a thing. Let me tell you what we've got up here on the Rock. This'll really creep you out—the Cow Foot Woman. Now that's something to be afraid of . . ."

Currie stared up at the approaching storm, frowning as the bickering continued.

"I'm telling you a cow's foot is far more dangerous than a goat's."

"Just because it's bigger? A goat, mon, she can climb straight up walls, sneak up on you when you aren't looking. I never heard of a sneaky cow."

"Say, Mic, what do you think would happen if the Goat Foot Woman battled the Cow Foot Woman?"

Mic considered the question, his face one of serious reflection. Finally, he weighed in.

"Epic showdown, mon."

STILL SEARCHING THE park for the elderly backgammon player, Cedric overheard Mic and Spike's conversation and shook his head. He knew from his many years in VI politics that it took very little to generate a heated discussion between the residents of St. Croix and St. Thomas.

Just then, Cedric spied a figure on the opposite end of the crowd—not the backgammon player or the Governor, but perhaps someone just as valuable.

The Fixer.

~ 52 ~

The Next Best Thing

CEDRIC SHOVED HIS way through the crowd as the Fixer ducked out of sight, disappearing behind the Freedom Statue on the west end of Emancipation Park.

A new speaker stepped up to the grandstand mike. Unlike the previous petered-out voice, this one was filled with vigor. The words bellowed in Cedric's ears as he struggled to see past the machete-wielding statue.

"Once again, we have been excluded from the decision making process . . . our slavery masked by terminology . . ."

Cedric glanced up at the speaker. The face was unfamiliar, but not the words. It was a line he had written for the separatist cause.

He felt somewhat unnerved by the successful deployment of his propaganda. His monstrous creation was now flourishing on its own, uncontrolled by its creator.

There was no time to ponder the implications.

Weaving through bystanders, Cedric reached the edge of the park. He broke free from the pedestrian area and slowly pivoted in place, scanning the scene for the Fixer.

A low-hanging tree blocked his line of sight near the statue. He took a few steps to the side, trying to peek around the drooping branches.

Where had the thin man gone?

A kaleidoscope of moving bodies and jarring sound swirled around him, overwhelming his senses.

Then, suddenly, Cedric spied a figure in a golf shirt and chinos turning the corner in front of the post office across the street.

"There you are."

He set off at a sprint, fumbling for his cell phone as he ran. He punched the button for Wendy's number and clamped the device to his ear. The droning buzz cycled three times before going to voice mail.

"You've reached the US district attorney for the Virgin Islands, Wendy . . ."

Cedric clicked off the connection. There was no point in leaving a winded message.

He had no idea where the Fixer was headed—or, for that matter, how he would apprehend the man once he caught up to him.

He slid the phone into his shirt pocket. He would figure something out.

Desperate times called for desperate measures.

CEDRIC RACED ACROSS to the post office, rounded the corner, and skidded to a stop by the front entrance. The building had been locked up tight, its green shutters clamped down against the yellow ochre walls.

Panting, the aide scanned the sidewalk. Not seeing the Fixer near the post office, he turned to look up the hill.

A row of iron busts lined the bottom of the slope. Solemn faces of luminaries from the territory's past stared down at him—educators, journalists, and civil rights leaders who had been honored for their sacrifices and achievements.

Cedric had grown up learning the stories of these and other local leaders. What had he contributed to the cause?

He squirmed beneath the iron eyes, but the surge of guilt quickly dissipated. His actions were justified, he told himself, even if his motivations were rooted in self-interest.

He had long ago stopped believing in martyrs and heroes.

At this point, he was down to self-preservation.

AT THE SIGHT of the Fixer scrambling up the hill, Cedric dismissed all introspection. The thin man sprinted across the side slope, dashing through the trees—disrupting the flock of chickens and drawing a stern squawk from the resident rooster.

He landed midway up the public staircase and paused to look back at the post office, as if taunting the aide to follow.

Cedric needed no encouragement. He darted to the foot of the stairs and began the long chug toward the top.

By the time the Fixer disappeared over the crest, Cedric had narrowed the distance between them. He was only about thirty feet behind.

Out of breath, Cedric staggered onto the one-way street that ran in front of Hotel 1829. He glanced up and down the road with despair.

The Fixer had once more slipped from his reach.

A woman sat on the hotel veranda, watching him over the railing. With a shrug, she motioned east with her camera.

Cedric gulped for air and turned as she had indicated, frantically searching the street. He didn't see the Fixer until he reached the signpost for the 99 Steps.

He let out a groan. The thin man had scampered up the stairs.

"The guy's half-goat."

SUMMONING A SECOND wind, Cedric pounded up the walkway. His lungs burned; his calf muscles ached.

A strengthening breeze pushed against his back, fluttering the blooms in the adjacent bougainvillea bushes. Cedric glanced over his shoulder at the harbor. Purple and blue shrouded the horizon, the front edge of the evening storm.

The first drops began to spatter against the bricks, giving Cedric a much-needed boost of adrenaline. He surged up the rest of the steps, clearing the top with a sense of triumph.

Fowler had once more escaped from view, but Cedric heard the smack of the man's feet against the asphalt drive that led up to Blackbeard's Castle.

Charging past a curving wall of landscaping, the aide rounded the corner. The hilltop and Blackbeard's Tower came into view.

Cedric no longer questioned where the Fixer was headed. The landmark property at the summit was his obvious destination.

It never occurred to him that instead of giving chase, he was being led into a trap.

CEDRIC TRAVERSED ANOTHER line of terracing, taking him past the rolling lawn and the fountain of the three young women. A ring of floodlights flickered on, illuminating the iron figures through the rain.

The steps slickened as the initial coating of moisture mixed with the previous layer of dust, but Cedric refused to slow his pace. He reached the open gate to the main guest area and dove through.

He was so close. He could sense it.

He would have it out with the Fixer. He would demand to see the Governor. Everything was salvageable. He just needed a chance to plead his case.

SOAKED WITH SWEAT and, increasingly, rain, Cedric hurdled the last step up onto the pavilion and entertainment area. Rasping for air, he scanned the perimeter.

The pool shimmered with pattering raindrops. The surrounding statues glistened, the liquid sheen increasing their lifelike appearance.

Unaffected by the climb, the Fixer stepped out from behind a pair of dueling pirates.

"You should have stayed at Government House, my friend."

Blackbeard's Castle

~ *53* ~

Blackbeard's Bum

BLACKBEARD'S CASTLE HAD been relatively quiet since the departure of Agent Friday and team yellow.

The sole hotel guest slumped in a cushioned rattan chair on the far side of the bar's pavilion, his arms draped over the sides, his spindly legs propped on a matching footrest. The limp log of wasting flesh was dwarfed by the surrounding pillows, the body barely visible from the lawn.

The serving station was vacant. The bartender was on a break, having sated his demanding customer with another potent rum concoction.

For his part, the guest had come to terms with the mojito substitution. He would never admit it to the bartender, but he was starting to enjoy the rum punch variation. There had been a nice kick to the most recent glass; he felt a pleasant numbness in his toes.

He gazed blearily across the pavilion at the expansive view overlooking the harbor, the storm-streaked sky, and the undulating cityscape. A pleasant breeze swept in, soothing his aching bones.

This is what he had envisioned for his final days, he thought with another slurp from his straw. Blackbeard's was quite an upgrade from the scene at his last hospital room.

The flat walls, uninspiring décor, and antiseptic smell of

the place had been more than he could stand. He'd spent far too many desolate hours sealed off in a world of plastic tubing and beeping equipment—before checking himself out and heading for the Caribbean.

There was no comparison, really, he thought with a peaceful sigh.

He just wished he'd been more specific about mojito supplies when he made the reservations for his intended deathbed location.

He set the glass on a table beside his chair, a shaky motion that nearly spilled the remaining liquid. His head tilted back into the cushions, and his mouth dropped open. He felt the cloud of another stupor coming on.

His fingers fumbled for a packet of pills tucked into his shirt pocket. Two of the blister foil compartments had already been ripped open, the contents dumped inside his glass. Rousing himself, he dissolved a third pill in the last third of his cocktail and then drained the mixture in one long gulp.

As his condition had deteriorated over the past year, he had gradually modified the delivery mechanism for his pain-numbing narcotics.

Alcoholic beverages, specifically mojito cocktails, were his chosen method of administration—a prescription modification that had been frowned upon by the staff at the hospital where he'd been admitted.

The man's dry lips slurred out a mumble.

"Bollocks to you, Dr. Killjoy."

SPITTING RAIN DRILLED through to the Mojito Man's subconscious, drawing him back to the foggy edge of reality. He hovered in a hazy atmosphere of hallucination and pain, before a disturbance across the lawn caught his attention.

"Where's the Governor?"

He shifted his weight, silently bringing his feet to the ground. He leaned forward in his chair. Blinking, he tried to focus his vision.

Two figures glared at one another from opposite sides of a statue of dueling pirates. One stood closer to the pool, with his back turned to the hotel guest. He wore an oversized mint green golf shirt and baggy chinos; both garments flapped in the wet wind.

The Fixer's voice rose above the gale, taunting Cedric through the fencing statues.

"The Governor has no use for you. He makes no concessions for traitors."

Bent at the waist, the hotel guest crept across the bar toward the pool. Crouching behind the corner of the rock wall that separated the two areas, he was now close enough to hear the Fixer's sneering chuckle—and to see the shocked expression on the aide's face.

"What happened, Cedric? Have they thrown you overboard already?" The Fixer began to edge around the pirates. "Did you really think she was going to appoint you king?"

"She." Cedric repeated the pronoun, stunned by the revelation. "So . . ." He gulped. "He knows."

And with that, the last hope of a desperate man was gone. Cedric had nothing left to bargain with, no more chips to play. He was alone, vulnerable, and abandoned by both sides of the civil war. His words lashed out across the pavilion.

"You tell the Governor that he needs me. I have too much information for him to shut me out. I know all his secrets."

The Fixer rounded the far end of the dueling pirates.

"You seem awfully sure of yourself—especially for someone who's just been kicked to the curb."

Cedric pushed his bluff a step further.

"I know your real identity. And I know how you've been communicating with the Governor."

"Yes, Cedric. You're the only one who knows. Don't you see what that makes you?"

The wind howled through the verbal silence.

"A loose end."

The Fixer lunged toward the aide, and the pair scuffled to the ground.

But what happened next was lost to the Mojito Man.

A second wave of pain medication kicked in, and his vision faded to black. He crumpled to a heap behind the wall.

Government House

~ 54 ~

The Conspirator

WENDY SURVEYED THE scene inside the Governor's office, appraising the upended chairs, ripped upholstery, and the books, papers, and backgammon pieces strewn across the floor. Hightower's drunken rampage had destroyed the place.

The Gorilla had played his role well. Her nose crinkled at the stench of spilled rum on the desk where he was sleeping.

Perhaps a little too well.

Unlike Cedric, Wendy had never expected the federal agents to find the real governor. In fact, she and her fellow separatist conspirators had never intended for there to be a public arrest, but they hadn't trusted Cedric with that information.

They had a far more permanent outcome in mind for the former head of state.

PICKING HER WAY around the debris, Wendy crossed the room to close the balcony's sliding door, shutting out the rain, which had dampened the nearest throw rugs.

On her way back through the office, she bent to pick up one of the backgammon pieces and slipped it into her pocket, a souvenir of the monumental events that were still unfolding.

Sensing her presence, Hightower began to stir, causing the recliner to creak as he shifted his weight.

Wendy moved in behind him, placed a careful hand on his shoulder, and lightly pressed down. "It's time to let those people downstairs go home."

The Gorilla's eyelids fluttered. "Yes, I suppose you're right." His thick lips struggled to form words. "I can't believe the Governor got away. The guy slipped right through our fingers." His hands clenched together. "I'll be blamed for this, you know."

Wendy reached for the open bottle on the desk and dumped the remaining liquid into Hightower's glass.

"Thank ya, Wendy."

"My pleasure, Agent Hightower."

AGENT FRIDAY ARRIVED at Government House as the last employees departed the lobby. The rain had soaked his cap and shoulders. He'd trekked up from the FBI field office in the hopes of getting a word with the attorney general's local representative—who had been difficult to reach by phone.

Wendy managed a pleasant greeting, while internally suppressing a grimace. No one had expected Hightower's second in command to be so diligent at addressing his leader's shortcomings.

I'd give anything for a docile yes-man, she thought wearily. Outwardly, she opted for an assertive stance.

"What do you have to report, Agent Friday?"

"No word yet on the Governor, ma'am." His cleared his throat. "I thought I might have a word. You're headed back to the Legislature Building?"

"Yes," she replied, tapping a large umbrella she'd borrowed from the lobby—even though she had no intention of returning to the Legislature's hotbed. The senators had indicated they were prepared to extend their sit-in through the night.

"I'll escort you, then." Friday held the door as Wendy walked through. He waited patiently under the front porch while she opened the umbrella.

Friday wasted no time getting to the point. "We've got to track down this radio station. The two missing senators found the KRAT broadcast location. There has to be a connection there."

Wendy glanced up at Hotel 1829 as they passed. She smiled

at the woman sitting on the veranda, an action meant only to stall while she considered her response.

"Yes, I agree. Can you spare some men to search for them?"

Friday nodded a grunt. "I'll manage."

She paused at the top of the stairs leading down to the post office.

"Is that all, Friday?"

"Yes, ma'am." He tapped the brim of his cap. "I'll get to it, then."

FRIDAY BROKE AWAY from the umbrella and waved the lawyer good-bye. He watched her continue down the staircase, her heels planting firmly on the slick brick steps.

He'd spoken to the attorney general in Washington, DC an hour earlier. The AG had been unable to reach the woman since early that morning.

Friday was beginning to think Hightower had been right about one aspect of Operation Coconut.

Don't trust the locals.

⌒

FRIDAY'S BULGING EYES followed Wendy all the way to the bottom of the stairs. She crossed the street in front of the post office without looking back.

She knew exactly where the radio station had been broadcasting that day—and where the missing senators were hiding. Despite her best efforts to conceal her thoughts, she sensed Friday had suspected the truth.

It was important to keep Senator Sanchez securely muzzled for the next twenty-four hours.

Surely, she could put the agents off for that long.

The Lutheran Church

⌇

~ 55 ~

Unwelcome Confinement

SENATOR SANCHEZ STARED up at the cistern's sealed hatch, sweat pouring off her face. She'd drained the water bottle the Bishop had brought earlier. Her clothes stuck to her body, and she felt woozy from the stench of Bobo's hair oil.

She refused to look at her co-senator, for fear of what she might see. Similarly sweaty, he had stripped down to his loose-fitting harem pants. He sat on the floor, leaning against one of the cistern sidewalls, courteously giving her the sole fold-out chair the DJs had left behind.

Dark and stuffy, the cistern was far more humid than before. Water had begun to trickle out of the trough near the roof. It must have started raining outside, Sanchez concluded with worry.

How much longer are we going to be trapped in here? she wondered, vowing she would never again venture inside a cistern holding tank.

Just then, a grinding cinch of metal sounded from the roof, and the hatch swung open. Water ran over the rim as the Bishop poked his head through the hole.

"It's dark enough now. I think it's safe to move you. The FBI agents are still in the area, though, so please be quick."

Bobo jumped up from the floor, threw on his tunic, and scrambled around Sanchez to get to the ladder.

While waiting for Bobo to exit, Sanchez secured the strap

for her leather satchel around her shoulder and slipped off her heels. Gripping the shoes in one hand, she scaled the ladder and stepped out, barefoot, onto the cistern roof.

The Bishop crossed the roof and hurried down a ramp to a side yard that curved around the chapel. Bobo followed, leaving Sanchez standing alone while she wobbled back and forth, slipping on her shoes.

With a glance at her surroundings, she realized why the two men had moved away from the hatch. She had a clear view down the front walk and out the closed iron gates to the corner of Emancipation Park and, beyond, Fort Christian.

The pedestrians still mingling in the area south of the church had a similar view of her.

Sanchez scrambled across the concrete roof, down the ramp, and over to a newer L-shaped annex attached to the church's main chapel. The Bishop ushered the senator through the doorway and then shut it securely behind her. They were once more hidden from any observers on the street.

And, Sanchez couldn't help thinking as the Bishop secured the lock, they were trapped inside yet another bunker.

"MAKE YOURSELVES AT home," the Bishop said smoothly.

Sanchez blinked, letting her eyes adjust to the shaded interior. None of the annex's artificial lights had been turned on. The windows on the building's courtyard-facing walls let in beams from the lampposts that surrounded the church grounds, but that provided only minimal illumination.

The Bishop walked his guests down a hallway that cut through the building's two wings. He pointed out a series of multipurpose rooms, a nursery, and a bathroom equipped with shower stalls.

The space was typically used for vacation Bible school, visiting clergy, and church-related child care, but the senators would be the only occupants that evening. The resident minister, he explained, was on vacation.

Circling back to the entrance, the Bishop led the senators into one of the larger dormitory rooms.

"I hope you'll find these accommodations acceptable. It was the best I could put together on short notice."

Sanchez surveyed the offering, trying not to cringe.

Set against the steep slope, the rear wall contained a row of narrow windows that ran just below the ceiling. The panes had been propped open to their fullest position, but the portals provided little venting. The Bishop bent over a dusty fan, plugged its tattered cord into an outlet, and turned the knob. The subsequent whirring filled the room with more sound than breeze.

He dusted his hands together, careful to avoid staining the cassock. "You are welcome to stay here until the situation with the FBI has been resolved. The present difficulty will not last too much longer."

Bobo appeared at ease with their confinement. He pulled off his wet tunic, shook out the garment, and draped it over a chair near one of the cots to dry. With a tired sigh, he dropped onto the bed, kicked off his sandals, and stretched out for a nap.

This was all fine and good for Bobo, Sanchez thought. There was no chance of him making it back to St. Croix that night. But her apartment was less than a mile up the hill. That was a far better option than sleeping here with a hair-oil-reeking, half-naked Bobo.

The Bishop read the expression on her face.

"They'll be looking for you. It's not safe for you to go home right now."

Reluctantly conceding, Sanchez walked to the cot farthest away from Bobo and took a weary seat. She reached into her briefcase for a tissue and instinctively pulled out her phone.

The Bishop watched her, his dark eyes flashing with concern.

"They'll track you the instant you turn that on."

Bobo spoke up from the cot, "I don't trust those things. I tossed mine into the mop bucket in the closet back at the Legislature Building."

Sanchez wrapped her hand around the device.

"My family must be worried sick."

The Bishop didn't budge. There was something immensely intimidating about the way he looked down at her.

"Write out a message. I'll make sure it gets to them."

Sanchez returned the phone to her bag, more certain now than ever that this was no ordinary clergyman—if indeed he was a religious official at all.

Seemingly satisfied, the Bishop turned toward the hallway.
"You must be hungry. I'll see what I can find in the
pantry."

THE BISHOP RETURNED with a plate of crackers, cheese, and
fruit. Bobo rose, instantly awake, and began munching.

Meanwhile, Sanchez finished writing her message. She'd
left the text intentionally vague—as to both her whereabouts
and her estimation of when she might be able to again make
contact. No doubt, her relatives had already been informed of
the arrest warrant and FBI's takeover of the local government.

"Please see that my family gets this." Sanchez folded the
paper and handed it over.

The Bishop slid the note into a fold in his cassock—tucking
it into one of the many pockets that were always accessible but
never visible.

"Of course," he replied.

The senator stared up at him, doubting that assurance.

SANCHEZ MANAGED TO snatch a few bites before the food
was devoured. His stomach full, Bobo returned to his cot.
Within minutes, a wheezing snore wafted up from his side of
the room—along with the potent scent of his musky hair oil.

Ick, Sanchez thought, silently easing herself off of her cot.

Carrying her shoes and satchel, she crept to the door, which
had been left slightly ajar.

Two steps into the hallway, she heard a polite cough, accompanied by the swish of heavy fabric.

Blushing, she turned to see the Bishop standing a few feet
behind her.

"I've just received word that your message has been deliv-
ered," he said, slipping his cell phone into the cassock. "Your
family was greatly relieved."

"Thank you."

The Bishop took up a seat near the hallway's courtyard exit.

"I'll stay here so I can deflect any questions, should the
federal agents stop by looking for you."

Sanchez nodded, but she sensed his watchful eyes were

more intent on preventing any attempt she or Bobo might make to escape.

She pointed to the bathroom at the end of the corridor, miffed that she had to provide an explanation for her movements.

"Just going to the ladies' room."

The Parsonage

~ 56 ~

His City

WITH DUSK SETTLING across Charlotte Amalie, the Governor risked his first foray onto the parsonage balcony. Still cloaked in the brown cassock, he pulled its hood over his head, hiding his features.

The wet breeze stiffened with the brunt of the approaching storm. Before midnight, a squall would sweep through, bending palm trees, shredding bougainvillea blooms, and rinsing the grit and rancor of the day down the hillside, through the streets and gutters, and out into the bay.

Wary of any curious passersby that might be traveling on the street below, the Governor edged to the railing and looked out across the darkening harbor. The cruise ship had finally departed for its next port of call; the deepwater dock would remain vacant until the island's political turmoil could be sorted out.

He scowled at the empty slot, disturbed by the economic loss it represented. The temporary halt in cruise ship traffic was an unfortunate side effect of this whole wretched business, but he hoped the damage could be quickly repaired.

He shifted his gaze inland to the rolling spread of red-painted iron roofs that with nightfall had faded to charcoal brown. The curving outline of the surrounding streets began to glow, the streetlamps creating a lighted map against the blackness.

Through the rain, he listened to his city.

The damp air carried the thumping audio of a passing car, its chassis loaded down with an overamped stereo. With a chuckle, the Governor thought of his nephew, who had spent every last dime of his earnings outfitting a similar rig. After the triumphant debut night on the town, the young man had to take the vehicle in for servicing. The mechanic had advised that the acoustics were causing the car's nuts and bolts to vibrate loose.

"Your bumper's going to fall off if you don't turn down the volume, son."

THE STEREO WOUND around the shoreline, and quieter sounds emerged.

In the public gardens that descended across the road, the Governor heard the soothing tones of an elderly West Indian man who lay on the ground beneath a tree as he did almost every night—rain or not—feeding chunks of mango to an iguana of similarly advanced age.

Not far from the balcony, a tiny coqui frog began its love-sick call, a high-pitched whistle finished with an audible question mark.

Cook-ee?

The rough English translation: *How about me?*

The call was a romantic invitation to any female amphibian in the vicinity. The first frog was soon challenged by a second male, who sang out a similar solicitation.

Or how about me?

The Governor took comfort in the frogs' familiar vocal competition. Oblivious to the silly troubles of the island's humans, the coquis had no greater concern that night than finding an agreeable mate.

Reflecting on the day's adventures—and his own good luck—he reached into his pocket and pulled out a backgammon checker. Then he turned his gaze to the white mansion lit up on a nearby ridge overlooking the city, where his wife waited for news.

The Governor's Mansion

~ *57* ~

Coqui

THE FIRST LADY sat on a covered bench in the gardens outside the Governor's Mansion, listening to the coqui frogs' whimsical flirtations as she stared at the darkening city.

The damp blackness was soon pierced by round circles of light. Each glowing streetlamp illuminated a familiar patch of earth, a tiny plot of well-defined normalcy surrounded by a much larger, increasingly dangerous unknown.

The light posted outside the parsonage on Government Hill appeared dimmer than the rest, a subtle indicator of the fugitive hiding within—and perhaps, a reflection of the tenuous nature of his position.

A coqui frog moved closer to her bench. His perky song interrupted her thoughts.

Typical, the First Lady mused, reflecting on the early days when she and the Governor first met. The persistent frogs had been a favorite romantic ploy.

She would often complain that the frogs camped outside her window and kept her awake at night.

The Governor always replied in a serious deadpan tone.

"My dear. It was me."

The First Lady smiled, a moment of humor despite the dire circumstances.

No matter how much she and her husband disagreed over

public policy issues, Native Rights, and the future path their territory should take, the lovesick frog line still had its intended effect of tugging at her heartstrings.

For the first time since setting her plot in motion, she felt a twinge of sorrow—not regret or any diminution in the strength of her resolve, merely a moment of sadness.

She wondered what the Governor would say if he discovered the truth: that she had turned his favorite aide against him, engineered the federal indictments, and opened the door to an invading force that could be repelled only by the Virgin Islands declaring their independence.

What would he think if he knew that she had turned his favorite game of backgammon into a twisted war of chess?

"Yes, love," she murmured into the rain. "It was me."

A GUST OF wind sent water splashing across the bench. Unbothered by the storm, the First Lady shifted farther under the cover. She'd sent the dogs into the mansion, but she preferred to stay outside, where she could monitor the movements on the ground below. There was nothing to do inside the residence but stare back at the federal agents stationed to watch over her.

Useless beings, she thought crassly. She couldn't wait to evict them from her home.

As for her husband, he'd become a necessary casualty, far too closely aligned with the nation to the north. The people had lost faith in him—even she didn't trust him anymore.

He would be remembered much more fondly as a martyr. She would see to that, as his sympathetic widow and heir apparent.

After the coup was complete, his coqui serenade would be silenced—forever.

The Lutheran Church

~ 58 ~

Not My Type

THE ANNEX ATTACHED to the Lutheran church fell quiet as the hours drifted into late evening.

Senator Sanchez lay on her cot, listening to Bobo snore. Through the open doorway, she had an angled view of the Bishop—and, she was well aware, he of her.

She closed her eyes and forced herself to take slow measured breaths, but she did not sleep.

The stench from Bobo's hair oil was enough to keep anyone awake.

AFTER FORTY-FIVE MINUTES of willing her eyelids to remain shut, Sanchez finally heard the sound she had been waiting for. There was a slight creak to the floorboards, accompanied by the swish of the Bishop's cassock.

She held her breath, waiting to be sure.

The hinges on the door leading out to the church courtyard creaked, signifying its opening. The light tap of wood followed by a lock's twisting grind confirmed the exit had closed.

Sanchez propped herself up into a seated position and peered into the darkness. The narrow wedge of hallway that she could see from the bed revealed the Bishop's seat to be empty.

The cot's canvas fabric squeaked against the metal framing as she swung her legs to the floor.

Scooping up her briefcase, she tucked her shoes against her chest, tiptoed across the room, and out into the empty hallway.

She tugged on the handle to the courtyard door, but it wouldn't budge.

Sanchez fumed in frustration.

"I can't believe he locked us in here."

Bobo's snores rumbled up from his cot as Sanchez scampered down the hallway. There had to be another way out. If her choice was between being held hostage by a crazy Bishop and arrested by the FBI, she preferred the latter.

She reached the end of the corridor at the crook of the building's L-turn and stepped into the bathroom. During her previous visit, she'd noticed an open window that might be big enough for her to fit through.

It was dark inside the tile-floored room, and she dared not risk turning on the light. The slow drip from a faucet plinked as she crept toward the window. Cautiously, she leaned through the opening.

A retaining wall had been built into the sloping ground outside. The top of the wall was several feet away. It would be a stretch for her short height, but she just might be able to reach it from the window.

Or I'll face-plant into the ditch, she thought ruefully.

Either way, she wasn't going to spend another second trapped inside the church annex.

Stuffing her shoes into the satchel, Sanchez slid her head and shoulders through the window. It was a much tighter fit than she had anticipated. Her skirt bound up around her thighs, restricting her movement. With a grunt, she shifted her weight back toward the bathroom to make a wardrobe adjustment.

There was a light *thud* on the floor behind her.

Slowly pivoting, she looked over her shoulder, certain that either the Bishop had returned to haul her back inside the building or Bobo had awoken and tracked her down the hallway.

It was neither.

There, in a dimly lit spot on the bathroom floor, a tiny brown frog sat blinking up at her.

Cook-eee?

"Sorry, sweetie. You're not my type." Suppressing a giggle, she returned her attention to the window.

This time, she hiked her skirt up several inches before easing over the ledge.

Her arms flailed out, reaching for the retaining wall. The fingertips of her left hand brushed against the corner edge—and then slipped off. She moved forward another inch. Her torso tilted downward, causing the satchel to slip from her shoulder and droop around her neck.

All or nothing, she thought.

With a heave, she lunged for the barrier. This time, her hand managed to gain a firm grip on the top bricks. Her back end slid through the window, and she hung, awkwardly, for a long moment, trying not to think of the frog ogling her from the bathroom floor.

One more push. She grunted, leveraging her knees against the window's bottom railing.

Like a teeter-totter that had tilted past its fulcrum, she suddenly slid forward. Her legs flailed outward, trying to slow her momentum—to no avail. The sound of ripping cloth accompanied her undignified dump out the window and onto the ground below.

She tossed her satchel onto the upslope and clambered over the retaining wall.

Crouching on the grass, she surveyed the damage. There were a few abrasions on her hands, and her knees were scraped from the ungraceful dismount through the window, but, all in all, she reasoned, it could have been worse.

Her skirt had split about two inches along the side seam. Nothing indecent, just ragged.

Tucking a loose lock of hair behind her ear, she straightened and reached for her shoes.

"Let's hope no one saw that," she said as she limped across the hill toward the street above.

～

MAINTAINING HIS VIGIL on the parsonage balcony, the Governor peered through the trees as Senator Sanchez made her ungraceful exit out the annex window.

He rubbed his chin, pondering this development, before a second movement caught his attention. A streetlamp outside Hotel 1829 illuminated the man in the brown cassock who had visited the parsonage earlier in the day.

The Governor watched as the Bishop strode up the one-way street, a man of distinct purpose, undeterred by the rain.

~ 59 ~

No Turning Back

SENATOR SANCHEZ SCRAMBLED up the hill in her bare feet, struggling to maintain her balance on the slick leaves and other vegetation that covered the ground.

She reached the road above the Lutheran church and stepped onto the pavement across the street from Government House. Standing in the shadows beneath a tree, she wiped as much mud as possible from her feet and slid on her shoes.

The wind whipped at her hair and clothing as she gazed down the road toward Hotel 1829. She could think of nothing better than a hot shower and a warm bed. Depending on who was on duty at the bar, she might be able to check in under a false or even no name. In any event, the hotel seemed like her best bet to both get in out of the rain and elude the feds. Plus, it was much closer than her apartment.

She was about to set off for the hotel's front entrance when she saw the Bishop walking on the street just past the coral pink building's veranda.

Sanchez nearly fell down the hill in her effort to jump off the road and hide behind the nearest tree.

Her first instinct was to turn and run the opposite direction, but curiosity soon overwhelmed fear—that and having just climbed up the slick hill, she was loath to slide back down it toward the church.

"Where's he going?" she whispered, cautiously returning to the road.

The Bishop appeared not to have seen her. He continued on his route without hesitation.

Sanchez hung back, watching him approach the next block, trying to decide whether she should follow.

It was dangerous, she knew, for a woman to be out alone at this time of night. But if she was going to get any explanation for the events of the last twelve hours, the mysterious fake clergyman was a good place to start.

With a longing glance up at the hotel, she gripped her satchel tightly to her chest and pressed on.

RAIN RAN DOWN the street, pooling in potholes and gutters, as Sanchez scurried along the asphalt road, trying to keep sight of the Bishop, but wary of being seen herself. She was soon soaked to the skin, her soggy shoes squishing out water with each step.

Sanchez followed the Bishop to the far edge of the lawn that sloped up from the post office. She waited behind a clump of trees, watching as he turned down a side street that skirted the downtown's upper edge.

Trotting across the sloping lawn, she reached the sidewalk for the narrow roadway. The going was much easier on the flat surface, but her shoes were now making far more noise than she would have liked. She had little time to worry about the sound. The cloaked man flashed around a darkened corner as if taking a well-known route.

Sanchez kept pace until the Bishop paused at the entrance to a public staircase. He turned to look over his shoulder, and she dove behind a parked car.

Peeking over the hood, she caught a glimpse of the swishing cassock disappearing beneath the leafy canopy that covered the stairwell.

She waited several seconds before crossing the street, hoping she wouldn't be seen from above. She eyed an abandoned house next to the stairway's entrance, fearful of vagrants that might be sleeping inside, before nervously moving to the bottom of the stairs.

Looking up, she saw the Bishop's shadowed figure had already climbed several terraced sections up the hillside.

Staying within the shadows next to the railing, Sanchez began her ascent.

It was a long hike up the public walkway. The concrete steps were a slightly newer vintage than the brick ones on Government Hill, but they hadn't held up nearly as well. Dim lighting made navigation over the crumbling concrete even more difficult.

The rain plastered down, funneling rivulets into the steps. Her heel slipped, and she nearly turned an ankle trying to stay upright.

Through the watery blur, the Bishop cleared the top step and turned sharply to the left.

Sanchez stopped, panting and confused. There was only one residence at the end of that path.

It was surrounded by high-level security fencing and guarded by USVI police. Given recent events, she suspected a number of FBI agents would also be at the facility.

She completed the stairs and followed the Bishop's left turn—in time to see him admitted through the front gates of the Governor's Mansion.

SANCHEZ WATCHED THE iron gate slide shut behind the Bishop. The rain continued to pour down, but she hardly noticed the drenching as she contemplated the ramifications of the Bishop's destination.

She wouldn't be returning to Hotel 1829. Nor could she risk going back to her apartment—but not for the reason the Bishop had given.

This episode had a far more local cause than she had realized.

She needed to consult her uncle. With his years of political experience, he would know how best to proceed.

She began her descent down the stairs. She wasn't far from a friend's house. Hopefully, she could borrow some clothes and sleep on the spare couch.

She would set out to look for Uncle Abe first thing in the morning.

Most likely, he would be playing backgammon at Emancipation Park.

The Governor's Mansion

~ *60* ~

Religious Guidance

THE RAIN INTENSIFIED, moving up the hillside and soaking the garden outside the Governor's Mansion, but the First Lady refused to leave her covered bench.

Her gaze remained fixed on the city lights until a member of her regular security team approached, closely accompanied by two FBI agents.

The security guard spoke first.

"A clergyman is here to see you, ma'am."

She appeared unsurprised by this announcement.

"Yes, please show him in. I could use some religious guidance."

The senior FBI agent cleared his throat. "I advise against it, ma'am. We'd prefer that you remain in complete isolation until we're able to apprehend your husband."

The First Lady's eyes flickered, even as her face remained calm. She prompted the security guard.

"Which clergyman has come to see me?"

"The Bishop of St. Thomas," the man supplied quickly, speaking the title with as much authenticity as he could muster.

"Well then, how can there be any harm in that?" she asked demurely.

The agent shifted his weight, uncertain of how to handle the situation.

"This is a deeply troubling time." She pressed her hand against his forearm. "Please."

Reluctantly, the agent reached for a two-way radio attached to his hip. Speaking into the device, he ordered the guards by the gate to let the arrival inside.

THE BISHOP STRODE up the front walk and through the mansion's porticoed entrance as if he were a regular guest. In fact, it was his first visit to the place. His previous business on St. Thomas had been with far less prestigious clients.

He paused for a moment to study the decorated interior. His expert eyes scanned the walls and display cabinets, taking note of the various pieces of artwork and mentally assessing their value, an instinctive habit of his profession. It was a routine assessment—until he reached the Governor's marble backgammon set.

He stared at the checkered pieces, pondering their position, before continuing through to the side garden.

DESPITE HIS WALK up the hill in the rain, the Bishop still evoked a commanding presence. The cassock's tight weave had wicked away much of the falling moisture. His grizzled goatee gripped his chin with the same neat trim it had possessed in the Miami airport that morning.

The First Lady greeted him like a trusted confidant.

"Hello, Bishop."

He walked her toward the garden area, resting a comforting arm across the back of her shoulders. When they were safely out of earshot, he leaned toward her ear and whispered discreetly, "Your men have arrived."

Her smile confirmed the message had been received.

Downtown Charlotte Amalie

~ *61* ~

Managed Mayhem

THE STORM DUMPED its allotment on St. Thomas and moved west toward San Juan. The night sky cleared, and the city's human residents fell into a quiet slumber, even as a myriad of insect, avian, and lizard species swung into high gear. Coiquis sang out their coital requests, mosquitoes frolicked in puddles, and iguanas rummaged through the arboreal canopy for food.

The respite was short-lived. Not long after the rains subsided, a force of a different nature arrived on the soggy streets of Charlotte Amalie. Nova and his Crucian cronies, bolstered by the locals who had met them at the beach, began their assault on downtown.

Their faces covered with black cotton ski masks, the gangsters prowled the main shopping district. Armed with baseball bats and spray paint canisters, they ransacked the alleyways, smashing windows through their protective iron-bar cages.

Spray paint ran down the wet bricks, the anti-American messages blurred but easily readable.

Following the instructions of Nova's original employers, the destruction was designed to look random, a spontaneous response to the federal invasion, a reflection of outraged public sentiment—and a warning that the islanders' resistance was primed to escalate.

In actuality, the attack had been carefully planned. Nova and his men had a specific list of stores to vandalize.

The addresses and the type of destruction had been detailed by the Fixer—the spared stores corresponding to the shopkeepers who were the Governor's known allies and financial backers, the hits falling on his political enemies and anyone who had shown apathy in the last campaign.

It was a fast operation, over and done in a matter of minutes.

The police were intentionally slow to respond. Wary of being caught in gang-related crossfire, they were well practiced in delay tactics.

By the time the National Guard troops were rousted from their bunks on the navy ship and began the sleepy one-mile jog to the downtown shops, Nova and his goons had disappeared into the blackness of the night.

~ *62* ~

A Cassocked Bundle

A TANGLE OF Guard troops, FBI agents, and police converged on the site of the alleyway vandalism. Meanwhile, a pickup containing the perpetrators rumbled up the one-way street leading into Government Hill.

Nova and his crew had one more task to complete before the night was over.

After speeding past Hotel 1829, the truck screeched to a halt outside the parsonage. Nova climbed out the front passenger seat. Two more thugs hopped from the bed.

"Drive around the block. Be back here in five minutes." Nova thumped the side panel with the palm of his hand, and the truck zoomed off, its rear end bouncing over a speed bump as it barreled past Government House.

Nova proceeded much more quietly up the parsonage's uneven steps.

The security gate had been left unlocked. It fell open at his touch.

Joined by his two lackeys, he moved stealthily across the front courtyard and into the main building. The trio reached the second floor and crept down the hallway to a room with access to the balcony overlooking the street.

A man dressed in a brown cassock lay on a cot in the

sparsely furnished space. The hood had been pulled down over his face, obscuring any distinguishing features.

Nova bent over the bed and confirmed, somewhat disappointedly, that his predecessor had already done the job of taking the life.

With a dissatisfied grunt, he motioned for help lifting the body. His Crucian cronies hefted the head and feet. Between the three of them, they were able to carry the dead weight back down the stairs and out the front door.

At the security gate, Nova held up a cautioning hand. He peeked out onto the road, looking for their getaway vehicle.

Seconds later, the pickup rounded the far corner.

Nova's hard whisper called back to the courtyard.

"Bring him out. Go, go."

Additional muscle power jumped out of the truck to help dump the stiff figure into the bed.

The dim streetlight briefly illuminated the body transfer, providing a confirming glimpse to the interested observers strolling through the garden outside the mansion on the opposite hill.

Nova returned to the front passenger seat as the rest of the gang piled into the rear.

The truck drove off, one passenger heavier than when it had first arrived.

～

AS THE PICKUP once more bottomed out on the speed bump, a large man in a T-shirt, shorts, and sneakers emerged from a wardrobe inside the second-floor room from which the body had been removed.

Taking care to avoid the streetlamps, the Governor sneaked outside and into the night.

Blackbeard's Castle

~ 63 ~

So Many Ways to Say Good-bye

THE MOJITO MAN awoke to a sunrise view overlooking Charlotte Amalie from his Blackbeard's lawn chair.

The bartender had found the hotel guest passed out by the concrete wall the night before. He had scooped him up and carefully positioned him on the makeshift bed, far enough beneath the pavilion to be protected from the rain. A maid had brought out sheets and a soft pillow, tucking him in like a small child.

The staff had also set up a mosquito coil on the ground nearby. It had burned itself out a few hours earlier. A tiny metal stand and a circular trail of ashes were all that was left.

The last courtesy had been an unnecessary precaution.

After years of tests and transfusions, the cancer patient's veins were almost impossible to harvest. His pasty skin emitted the scent of coming death; his blood was tainted with enough narcotic to dissuade even the hungriest of insect foragers.

Gumming his dry mouth, he staggered to his feet and wandered toward the lawn. He mumbled his familiar and always first request of the day.

"Mojito. Can someone get me a mojito, please . . ."

Then he stopped, midappeal, startled by the image of the dueling pirates near the top of the stairs that led down the hill.

"You," he said, pointing to the pirate on the left. "You were talking to this guy." He shifted his finger to the right. "And then you talked back."

Staggering unsteadily, he swung his arm back to the first pirate.

"What happened next?"

His hollowed face contorted as he tried to recall the sequence of events. He could have sworn there'd been a struggle, but the details eluded him.

"Must have been a good time if I can't remember it," he concluded with a shrug. He glanced across the pavilion, searching for the bartender.

"Mojito?" he called out fraily.

He listened, hopefully shifting his head sideways. All he heard was the drone of an insect hovering near his shoulder, its pinpricking proboscis wavering with indecision.

He nearly fell over in his attempt to swat at the bug.

"I said mojito—not mosquito!"

BLACKBEARD'S MORNING STAFF brought out a breakfast menu, but their guest had little appetite for food. At the maid's motherly urging, he finally agreed to an omelet and a side of roast potatoes.

While the order was relayed to the kitchen, he slurped on a mimosa—again, not a mojito, he reflected, but an acceptable substitution. He swirled his straw, stirring the tablet he'd dropped into the orange juice and champagne mixture.

He leaned back in his chair as the cold slurry seeped into his system, anticipating the medication's numbing effect. But the dose was either too little or too late to offset the sudden surge of body-raking spasms that swept over him.

His bony hands gripped the armrests, the knuckles bulging white through his translucent skin.

How much longer? he thought as he willed himself through the pain. The cancer was slowly eating at him, gnawing him away from the inside out. His bones ached, his joints throbbed, and his chest constricted.

He began to ponder ways to bring about a quicker end.

If he could muster the strength, a running jump and tumble

off the steep edge of Blackbeard's cliff would probably do the trick.

He dismissed this option as requiring too much effort. Plus, the fall might bring about more physical discomfort without accomplishing the main goal. In his view, he had already endured enough.

The idea of jumping led him to a second suicidal plan. He could climb Blackbeard's Tower and leap off the top into the shallow end of the swimming pool. If the impact of the fall didn't kill him, it would be easy enough to drown in the water.

He frowned, contemplating the energy that would be required to reach the top of the tower and clamber over the rampart.

Hmm. The drugs were kicking in. The tension in his body began to loosen, but the train of thought continued—as a morbid fascination if no longer a subject of actual intent.

The mosquito buzzed his ear, still trying to work up the nerve to taste the man's narcotic-laced blood.

Death by exsanguination, he mused, imagining the bloodletting of a thousand tiny bite-mark incisions.

"Sorry, insects," he muttered thickly. "The doctors beat you to it."

He squinted at one of the iron swords forged into the hands of the dueling pirates.

Death by impalement.

He tilted his head, trying to envision the angle that would be needed to achieve this feat. Again, he concluded, too much work—and too great a risk of failure leading to extended suffering.

The sun inched a few degrees higher, spreading its rays across his chair. After just one day in the tropics, his pale skin had started to freckle. He had never been one to tan, only redden.

Death by sunburn.

This brought about another shuddering thought of pain.

Bravery wasn't high on his list of his strengths.

He took another sip from the mimosa. The orange juice was sweet and pulpy, but the champagne wasn't quite strong enough to mask the pill's aftertaste. He puckered his lips, swallowing the sour residue.

Death by alcoholic overdose.

Now we're talking, he thought glibly.

This was the preferred method, the one he had in fact already chosen, by default or deliberate action. This is the way he anticipated his life would end. The world would become a blissful blur and then gently fade away.

When the time came, arrangements had been made for his burial in an island cemetery. He had already picked out his plot number and tombstone.

The marker had been engraved with his name.

Beneath the identifying details, he'd instructed the stonemason to carve an image of a mojito cocktail glass with a slice of lime wedged onto the rim and a sprig of mint sticking out the top.

The 99 Steps

~ *64* ~

Counting in Danish

DREAD FRED AND Whaler met by the line of statues outside the main post office, incognito except for the radio equipment they carried in their backpacks and shoulder bags.

To the casual observer, it was simply a chunky Puerto Rican in loose-fitting shorts and flip-flops calling out a greeting to a tall West Indian with an impressive Afro in skinny jeans and a T-shirt. No one suspected them of being the famous KRAT DJs.

They were headed to the morning's broadcast location, a site that promised far better ventilation and signal reception than the cistern from the day before. However, neither man relished the prospect of the hike up the hill to the new spot.

The pair traversed the first flight of terraced steps, receiving an icy stare from the overprotective rooster in the sloping field. They soon reached the one-way street outside Hotel 1829.

A short walk past the hotel, the two men paused at the signpost for the 99 Steps.

Whaler reached into one of his bundles for a bottle of water.

"There's a reason we don't use this location very often."

Dread toweled off the sweat from his bald head.

"Because most days it's crawling with tourists."

"No." Whaler screwed the lid back on his bottle. He gave Dread a withering look.

"It's because of the climb."

THE DJS STARTED up the next line stairs, walking for several minutes in silence. Despite their on-air camaraderie, their real-life personalities didn't have much in common.

More than fifteen years in age separated the pair, with Whaler bringing up the younger end.

Dread had a large family; his wife and six kids took up most of his free time. They lived out on the island's west end and socialized primarily within St. Thomas's extended Puerto Rican community. Despite the rogue nature of the KRAT broadcasts, Dread was a traditionalist. They hadn't talked much about it, but he sensed Whaler was far more radical in his beliefs.

For his part, Whaler ran with an edgier crowd, young singles from Charlotte Amalie. He was generally unattached romantically—or, at least, he never mentioned any girlfriends to his broadcasting partner.

If not for their radio connection, it was unlikely the two would have ever crossed paths.

They'd been introduced by a mutual acquaintance, an elderly gentleman with a long history in island politics who wanted to spur local debate. He had spearheaded the KRAT concept to which the two DJs readily signed on.

A reflection of their well-practiced secrecy, Dread and Whaler rarely saw each other outside of their radio broadcasts. Once they finished the day's show, each man disappeared into his respective private life, about which the other knew very little.

While the exaggerated characters that existed on the air-waves enjoyed a close friendship, the flesh-and-blood counter-parts were practically strangers.

The topic of physical exertion, however, was one that they'd discussed at length.

"How many more 'til we get to the top?" Whaler asked, sweat pouring down his face. Strands of wet hair stuck to his forehead.

Dread stopped on the steps ahead and looked back at his partner. "We go through this every time."

"Yeah, yeah, I know." Whaler turned and glanced back at

the steps they'd already covered, estimating the distance. "Ninety-nine minus . . ."

"The actual total is one hundred and three," Dread corrected with a grin.

Whaler blew out a frustrated puff of air. "I tell you, that's what was wrong with Colonialism. The Danes couldn't count."

Resuming his climb, Dread replied diplomatically, "Perhaps something was lost in the translation."

AS THE RADIO hosts labored up the hill, they were met on the steps by an energetic pedestrian rapidly making his way down.

The frail man lurched as if his legs were only loosely attached to his torso. His body wobbled like a rubber band whose brittle elastic might break at any moment.

He nodded a greeting to the two sweating DJs on the stairs, but he didn't slow his frantic pace. The morning's drugs had finally kicked in, providing a temporary easing of his ever-present pain.

About ten minutes earlier, he had leapt from his lawn chair, rejuvenated and with a spring in his step.

He had found a new sense of purpose—not for life, but for his principal enjoyment.

The bartender at Hotel 1829 had called up to Blackbeard's to report that he'd acquired some fresh mint sprigs. He had to man his counter for the hotel's breakfast service, but if their guest could make it down the steps, he would prepare him an authentic mojito.

Hotel 1829

Overheard

UNAWARE OF THE mojito missile heading her way, the author clomped down the myriad steps to the first floor of Hotel 1829 and wandered sleepily into the bar. A continental breakfast had been laid out on the counter.

"What's the word?" she asked, perusing the offerings. The bar was well stocked for the siege. She reached hungrily for a muffin.

"The Governor's still on the lam," the bartender replied with a nod to the television set mounted in the room's upper corner. "They won't restart the ferries until they catch him. Nothing's moving yet."

"Oh well," she said optimistically. "There are worse places in the world to be stuck."

After spending the previous evening writing on the veranda, she found the hotel was starting to grow on her. It had a unique history that was easy to get lost in. The building had survived several human life spans and, by all appearances, was prepared to stand through many more.

She'd gazed for hours at the black-and-white photos spread across the bar's brick walls, studying the images of islanders from the late Colonial period as well as the years following the transfer. At first, she'd found herself wondering how the people in the photographs had managed to survive without the help of modern insect repellants. Several mosquito sneak attacks later, she realized that, despite developments in technology, not much had changed in that particular aspect of island living.

When she wasn't swatting at mosquitoes or spraying on another layer of repellant, the author had watched the amusing interaction between the bartender and the hotel's resident feline.

A skinny calico with long legs and tail, the cat had distinctive black lipstick coloring around her mouth and a commanding voice that she used to boss around the bartender—who complained bitterly about his four-legged supervisor.

It was during one of these episodes that the author noticed a narrow door at the far end of the bar. A sign over the threshold indicated that it led to a public restroom.

"Check it out," the bartender suggested. "The coldest restroom in the Caribbean."

Curious, the author crossed to the door and stepped inside. She was surrounded by a stiff bank of frigid air, cold enough to cause goose bumps.

Due to the floor plan's logistical constraints, the bathroom was connected directly to the building's air-conditioning unit. The bartender hadn't been exaggerating in his boast. The writer came out shivering.

"See?" He chuckled. "I wouldn't lie to you. Even the Governor sometimes stops in to use it."

"Maybe that's where he's hiding," the author said wryly.

The bartender pumped his mustache. "I'll never tell."

AFTER ASSEMBLING A full plate of pastries and fruit, the author carried her breakfast out onto the veranda and took a seat at the table she'd used the night before.

Another guest sat quietly at the veranda's opposite end, a slim man in a golf shirt and chinos. He looked vaguely familiar, but she'd found that happened often in the Caribbean. The author traveled to the region a couple of times a year. It wasn't unusual to run into someone she'd met on one island while visiting another.

She puzzled for a moment, trying to place him. Perhaps they'd met on St. John.

St. John, she sighed. She wondered if she would ever make it to her intended destination.

Setting those thoughts aside, she dug in to her plate. After a few munches, she peeked over the steep concrete wall overlooking the street.

Rising over fifteen feet from the road below, the wall wasn't an impossible barrier to breach, but it posed an effective deterrent. A spiked security gate blocked the steps that led up to the veranda. Despite all the volatility in the city, the veranda felt secure from potential human incursion—if not insect.

She reached under the table and swatted at a mosquito perched on her leg, its round belly swelling with blood.

"Argh," she moaned at the rash on her skin.

She'd started the morning with a shower, but that cleanliness had lasted less than twenty minutes. On the landing outside her room, she had sprayed herself from head to toe with repellant. The bartender had set up a pair of citronella coils on the veranda at her feet, to no avail. She was a stinky, smoky mess of a person—and they were still biting her.

She was tucked beneath the table examining the latest welt when a familiar voice called out from the bar area. The sound nearly caused her to bang her head.

"Mojito, please!"

Instinctively, she remained crouched in her chair. If she had any doubts as to the identity of the mojito drinker, the next comment erased it.

"I'm staying up at Blackbeard's. They said you had the fixins for a proper mojito."

"Yes, sir. Coming right up."

How had he made it down the hill in his condition? the author wondered, gradually easing herself into a seated position.

Cautiously, she peeked through an open window to the bar, where she spied the Mojito Man perched on a barstool. He leaned over the counter, anxiously supervising the drink preparation.

"Now, that's a sprig of mint! You have renewed my faith in Virgin Island bartenders."

He must have come in a side gate from the 99 Steps, the writer reasoned. So far, he hadn't seen her. There was still a chance she could slip off without being drawn into a rehash of the previous day's plane ride.

"Some people frown upon early morning drinking, but I always say, 'Hey, it's five o'clock somewhere.'"

"That's the attitude."

The bartender noticed the author peering through the window, but at the panicked shake of her head and finger-to-the-lips signal, he smiled and said nothing. Plunking a straw in the mojito glass, he slid it across the counter.

"Give this a try, buddy."

The frail man wrapped his lips around the straw, closed his eyes, and sipped.

"Ahhh," he said after letting the liquid swirl in his mouth. "That's the stuff."

He took a few more pulls from the straw, his slurps getting successively louder. Then he leaned back with a contented sigh.

"I had the strangest dream last night," he began conversationally. "I fell asleep up there in one of the lounge chairs. I could have sworn I heard those pirate statues talking to each other. And then, I kid you not, they had a sword fight. It was surreal."

The bartender raised an eyebrow but didn't reply to the dream comment. He instead steered the conversation to what he thought would be a safer topic.

"You should try a Bushwacker after you finish that mojito. It's my specialty. I use fresh banana—for your health."

He couldn't have picked a worse line.

The man took another gulp of the drink, gathering his strength for an extensive rant.

"No use. My health is long gone. I came down here to die. Shoot it out with one last kabang . . ."

The bartender looked up at the window that opened onto the veranda. His expression flashed a sudden understanding of why the author was hiding outside.

Silently, she stepped away from the bar and turned toward the gated steps leading to the street below.

It would be much safer to stay inside the hotel, but there was no way she was going to risk sticking around and getting caught by the Mojito Man.

Tiptoeing to the end of the veranda, she let herself out through the security gate. Even as she descended the steps, she could hear the familiar voice echoing down from the bar.

"My mother, God bless her soul, she suffered a terrible death . . ."

AS THE AUTHOR scampered off down the street, another hotel guest remained on the veranda, listening with veiled interest to the commentary inside the bar, particularly noting the statements describing the dueling pirates at Blackbeard's Castle.

The Fixer took a sip of hot tea from his cup. The motion revealed a fresh gash on his wrist.

He set the cup on the table and walked inside the bar.

~ 66 ~

Abnormal

THE AUTHOR SLUNK up the street, distancing herself as quickly as possible from the Mojito Man inside Hotel 1829. Whatever sympathy she might have felt for his condition was outweighed by her memories from the plane ride the day before. It was with great relief that she passed the foot of the 99 Steps without being called back to the veranda. She slowed her pace, taking in the Lutheran parsonage and Government House at a leisurely stroll.

Of the two buildings, the latter was seeing the most action. Federal agents and local police spilled out of the Government House front lobby, trying to keep back an inquisitive hoard of reporters and television cameras. Local news crews still outnumbered those from the US mainland, as the statesiders were having difficulty gaining legal access to the island, but global interest in the story was growing by the minute.

Above the fray, a lone figure stood on the second-floor balcony. The overmuscled man with closely cropped hair was dressed in the same black clothing as the rest of the federal agents, but he appeared not to be on duty.

Oblivious to the commotion below, he held a glass of dark rum in one hand. In the other, he steadied a cigar, blowing a plume of smoke toward the harbor.

THE AUTHOR WALKED past the Government House hubbub and continued along the road, following the thoroughfare down a gentle slope.

Turning toward the waterfront, she found the streets relatively empty. Many of the downtown businesses remained closed. The navy vessel was now the only ship stationed in the deepwater port, leaving the cruise ship mooring disturbingly vacant.

The author shifted her backpack on her shoulders, nervously gripping the straps. A raw edge of expectancy hung over the city. Charlotte Amalie was calm but definitely not at ease.

She felt the tension lighten as she approached a tiny food stand located about a block from the shore. The modified trailer had been fortified with brightly painted plywood walls and an attached covered porch.

The sign out front read DALEENA'S. The namesake could be seen through the front counter's wide window, a plump West Indian woman monitoring a grill. The smell of sizzling meat floated into the air.

At a picnic table beneath a nearby tree, an aging uncle and his niece sat facing each other, waiting for their breakfast. Several chickens scratched in the dry dirt, pecking at the feed that had been tossed out for them earlier.

The typical Caribbean ritual was a welcome sign of normalcy. The two family members were likely gathered to discuss the local gossip, provide updates on their various shared relatives, and, yes, probably touch on the political situation.

But like everything else in Charlotte Amalie that morning, nothing was quite what it seemed.

Daleena's Café

~ 67 ~

Uncle Abe

SENATOR SANCHEZ GLANCED over her shoulder, surveying the pedestrian traffic on the adjacent road. She noticed an American woman staring at the diner from the sidewalk and quickly turned back toward the picnic table.

"Don't worry." Her uncle waved his hand dismissively. "Daleena is keeping a watch out." He grinned at the chef behind the food stall's counter. "She won't let anyone sneak up on us."

"Thanks for meeting with me, Uncle Abe."

Sanchez ran a hand over her hair, which was tied back in a short ponytail. She'd changed out of her wrinkled skirt and blouse and into a borrowed T-shirt and shorts from the friend whose couch she'd slept on the night before.

Her high heels she'd relegated to a rubbish bin. After the hills, the rain, and the escape through the church annex window, the shoes were sullied beyond repair. The friend had also provided a pair of sandals, but unfortunately, this was a more difficult fit than the clothes. Sanchez's feet were about two sizes too small for the loaners.

With concern, Abe noted his niece's stress, exhaustion, and ill-fitting clothing.

He was a widower, accountable to no one but himself, and he followed an eccentric schedule. Most nights, he carried a bucket filled with sliced mango to the grassy hill above the post office and enjoyed the night air while he fed an old iguana that lived in the tree next to the feral chickens. After a lifetime in politics, he much preferred the giant lizard's company to that of any human—except for his favorite niece.

Abe took a sip of his coffee and motioned for Sanchez to begin.

"Tell me what happened."

Leaning over the picnic table, she began a recap of the previous day, starting with her late arrival to the Legislature Building, the custodial closet encounter with Bobo, and the security guard's assistance in slipping them out the side door.

Her uncle nodded along. He was familiar with the building's layout as well as all the main characters who worked there—including the persnickety security guard. He'd kept a low profile since his retirement from elected office over a decade earlier, preferring to spend his time perfecting his backgammon game, but little of significance escaped his surveillance.

He'd kept his ear to the ground and a keen eye on the players, particularly after his niece decided to run for a senate seat. Not many knew of their family connection. That was the way Sanchez had wanted it.

Nevertheless, as the election neared, Abe had subtly exerted his influence. He was remembered by many on the island, and his opinion still carried weight in certain critical circles. Close observers knew that Abernathy Jones, Abe to friend and foe, had not lost his golden touch when it came to politics.

"They tried to detain me too." Abe gave Sanchez a wink. "But I know how to give somebody the slip."

"Funny, that wasn't one of the lessons you taught me," she said with a teasing smile.

"You weren't always listening," he replied with a playful rap against the table. "Now. What happened after you and Bobo left the Legislature?"

Sanchez relayed the path she and Bobo took through the opening in the construction fence behind Fort Christian, into the courtyard, and up onto the clock tower.

"We couldn't very well stay inside the fort, so . . ."

Abe cut in. "Why not? No one knew where you were. You were safe from the federal agents—and our separatist friends here on the island."

"Well . . ." Sanchez stuttered, feeling flustered. Why *had* she let Bobo lead her around? She stared at the wooden table-top, her brow furrowed. After a pause, she lifted her head and resumed her story.

"Bobo suggested we move to the church."

"*Bah*, Bobo." Abe snorted. "Can't trust him." This was his assessment of most politicians, but he'd never liked Bobo.

"Bobo stripped off his tunic, as a disguise . . ."

Abe winced, covering his eyes. "That detail, you could have left out."

"I lost him in the crowd, but he found me outside the church. We were met at the gate by this guy in a brown robe. Dark-skinned but not West Indian. He had a gray goatee, neatly trimmed."

She shook her head, still puzzling over the man's religious affiliation. "He said he was a bishop, but I don't think he was a member of the local clergy."

Abe leaned back on his bench, his demeanor suddenly somber. He drew in his breath and then slowly let it out, as if calming his nerves.

Finally, he spoke.

"I know the Bishop."

The Lutheran Church

~ *68* ~

Honest Work

THE BISHOP STRODE briskly through the front gates of the Lutheran church and up the walk to the annex attached to the sanctuary. The regular pastor would be returning from his vacation as soon as the island's transportation ban was lifted.

He would not have the use of the facilities for much longer.

At the annex door, he reached into the cassock and pulled out the key to the exterior lock he had secured the night before. The door swung open, revealing a bleary-eyed Bobo sitting up on his cot in the dorm room—alone.

The Bishop glanced down the hallway. "Where's Sanchez?"

Bobo shrugged. "The Lord giveth, and the Lord taketh away."

At the Bishop's scowl, he added, "She was gone when I woke up."

"How long?" the Bishop demanded as he turned toward the corridor. He trotted to the end, peeking inside each doorway but quickly dismissing the escape potential of each room—until he reached the bathroom.

Bobo caught up to the Bishop at the bathroom window. The cassocked man leaned out the opening, studying the disturbance on the muddy ground below.

"I brought her to you, just like you asked," Bobo said

defensively. "I'll be expecting my payment. I earned it fair and square. Nothing dishonest about it."

The Bishop pushed back from the window. Looking over his shoulder at the shirtless senator, he wondered, not for the first time, if the Reverend was playing both sides.

Hotel 1829

Reincarnation

THE FIXER SAT at the far end of the bar inside Hotel 1829, quietly sipping a hot cup of tea. He had positioned himself so that the gash on his left wrist was facing the wall, making the injury less noticeable to the bartender and the sickly man teetering on a stool about four feet away.

The second mojito was already halfway consumed, and the bartender feared his small supply of mint leaves would soon run out. He began muddling leaves for a third glass, which he knew without asking would be requested in short order.

The drug-laced concoction had started to kick in, and the mojito drinker had a lot to say—even if his words were somewhat slurred.

"I tell you, it's something, confronting your own mortality . . . knowing that the end is near . . . that this is it . . . this is all that life is ever going to bring. Makes you kind of wish for something more."

He slurped up the last of the second mojito. His frail hand tapped the counter. "Like more mojitos!"

The bartender shook his head in amusement. He retrieved the empty glass and replaced it with a full one.

As the man started on the new drink, a commanding feline voice issued a stern order from the veranda.

The bartender reached beneath the counter for a container of cat food.

"Excuse me." Grateful for the excuse to leave his station, he carried the container outside to the cat's empty bowl.

The Mojito Man didn't seem to notice the bartender's absence. His rambling discourse continued unabated.

"Course, my mother, she believed in reincarnation. We all have multiple lives, so you've got to watch out for karma— that's what she'd say. She always thought she'd come back as a cat." He swiveled around in his chair, trying to see out to the veranda. "Could be *that* cat. Wouldn't that be ironic?"

After almost falling off the stool, he gave up on his effort to track the cat. He shifted his attention down the bar toward the Fixer.

"What about you? What kind of animal would you come back as?"

The Fixer took a sip of tea, thoughtfully pondering the question.

"Eh, pal? What would you come back as?"

The cup returned to its saucer with a light clink.

"Myself."

THE BARTENDER COMPLETED his cat-feeding duties and reentered the bar as his demanding patron drained the last of the third mojito. The man sat alone at the counter, his mood quickly mellowing.

"What happened to your friend?" the bartender asked, removing the empty teacup from the end of the counter.

"Said he had business to attend to. Nice guy. Quiet bloke . . . I think I'll just take a breather over at your nice table."

The bartender set down the cup and jumped around the counter to help the man off his stool. The spindly legs gave way as the bartender carried his customer to the bench lining the wall on the far side of the backgammon table.

Eyes drooping, the man pointed feebly at the marble game board.

"Hey, what do you call this setup you've got laid out here? There's something familiar about it. I can't quite remember."

The bartender carefully disentangled himself from the wasted limbs.

"Backgammon. Can I get you a glass of water?"

The water was rejected, but as the man stretched out across the bench, he asked, "You ever have any pirates come down here and play?"

Washington, DC

~ 70 ~

A Face in a File

THE ATTORNEY GENERAL shivered in his cardigan as his office air-conditioning unit pushed a cold blast out the room's ceiling vent. His disheveled appearance was in as much disarray as the stacks of paper and boxes surrounding him.

He'd spent yet another night sleeping on the office couch, but the morning hadn't brought any better news from the Caribbean. If possible, the situation in St. Thomas had grown worse overnight.

The president was rapidly distancing himself from Operation Coconut, disavowing all direct knowledge or involvement in the matter. The code name had been leaked to the press—to the delight of the beltway news commentators. Calls for the attorney general's resignation were growing by the minute.

The cruise ship passengers who had been stranded in the Charlotte Amalie harbor the previous day had now reached their next destination. Many had taken that opportunity to contact lawyers and were promising to sue for the costly disruption to their vacations.

The attorney general shook his head at the television screen in the corner of the room, which was tuned to one of the national cable news channels. The sound had been switched to mute, but the tropical pictures and the scrolling news feed at the bottom of the screen were enough to convey the trouble he was in.

To make matters worse, it was impossible for him to get accurate and real time reports from St. Thomas.

The frazzled man stared down at his telephone console, glowering at the device. Telecommunications in the US Virgin Islands had been restored late the previous afternoon, but so far, few people on the ground inside the restricted territory were accepting or returning his calls.

He'd tried without success to reach the Governor's aide, the so-called impeccable source of information who had triggered the indictments and attempted arrests.

Cedric's phone rang straight through to a voice mailbox that had reached capacity and was taking no new messages. The AG's tracking technology indicated the phone was located in the vicinity of a hotel named Blackbeard's Castle. He could only hope the whistleblower had checked himself into a room and was enjoying a nice cocktail by the pool.

He suspected a far more nefarious fate had befallen their star witness.

The attorney general had received a similar lack of response from his chief legal counsel on St. Thomas. Wendy the Wunderkind was no longer looking quite so wonderful. He knew for certain that she was avoiding his phone calls. That this would lead to her termination appeared not to matter.

The AG stared woefully at the framed photo of his golden retriever.

Intelligence reports from native Virgin Islanders were quickly losing credence.

WITH WENDY AWOL, the attorney general had turned to the assistant special agent in charge for briefings on the latest developments. At least the FBI was providing prompt updates, he thought as the light flashed on his console.

The AG answered the phone, weary but anxious for news.

"Well, Friday, what's the word?"

"Cautiously optimistic, sir. The streets this morning are calm. There's no sign that the vandalism from last night has spread."

The AG sighed. "If that's all it takes to cheer you up, you're a far more optimistic man than I am. What about the Governor?"

"Still no sign of him, sir. I'm afraid he's given us the slip."

The AG rubbed his forehead. "And the arrested senators?"

"Camped out in the Legislature Building. The appellate judge stayed with them all night. He ordered in a nice breakfast for everyone. Maybe that will convince them to cooperate."

The AG shook his head. He knew there was little chance of that happening.

"And Hightower?" he asked with a despondent sigh.

There was a brief hesitation.

"He's . . . uh . . . unavailable, sir."

"You mean he's on the sauce," the AG snapped. "I saw him on the news this morning. The cameras showed him on the balcony outside the Governor's office, drunker than a skunk."

Agent Friday chose not to provide further comment. None was needed. The AG had already gathered plenty of damaging evidence on the Gorilla through other sources.

"The assistant director of the FBI is due at my office within the hour. I'll get back to you on Hightower. In the meantime, don't let him do anything foolish."

A slight edge of sarcasm crept into Friday's voice.

"That may be overoptimistic, sir."

MUTTERING TO HIMSELF, the attorney general turned his attention to the nightly reports Friday and his teams had sent in. They were digital files, requiring the AG to review them on his computer, but at this point, he wasn't complaining.

As expected, the write-ups were thorough and complete.

Slowly, the AG scanned through photos from the vandalism in downtown Charlotte Amalie, studying the graffiti that had been sprayed in the waterfront alleys and the physical damage that had been inflicted on the shop windows.

After a careful perusal, he shifted to the file compiled by the FBI agents manning the Governor's Mansion.

With a wide yawn, the AG reached for his cup of coffee—and nearly spilled it down his shirtfront at the image of the cleric who had visited the First Lady the previous evening.

The report identified the man as a religious official, but the AG had seen his face somewhere before—and not in a church-related context.

He squinted at the blurry picture on the computer screen, drumming his fingers across the desktop.

Then he leapt up and began frantically digging through the banker's boxes piled around his office.

The search appeared haphazard, with the AG skipping randomly from one stack to the next, but there was a method to his madness.

"Aha!" He yanked a tabbed manila folder from a box. Sitting on the floor, he flipped it open on his lap and thumbed through the contents.

He held up a photo, a blurry black-and-white image of a dark-skinned man with a gray goatee wearing a brown cassock. It was a match to the shot taken from the Governor's Mansion security camera.

In the background, his computer picked up the morning KRAT broadcast and automatically relayed the audio. The attorney general ignored the by now painfully familiar "I Smell a Rat" jingle.

He kept his focus trained on the file for a man known to US intelligence agencies only as "The Bishop."

Blackbeard's Castle

~ *71* ~

A Wife's Duty

HAVING FINALLY REACHED the top of the 99 Steps, Dread Fred and Whaler circled the drive leading up to Blackbeard's Castle. The pair stopped at the bottom of the stairs that cut through the sloping lawn. Dread caught his breath while Whaler drained his water bottle.

"We're almost there," Dread said patiently, starting up the last portion of the climb. He reached up to rub his shoulder. The radio equipment always seemed a lot heavier at the end of the hike than it did at the beginning.

Whaler would have made a snide comment, but he was too tired to speak. Crumpling the empty plastic bottle, he jammed it into a side pocket on his backpack and wearily followed Dread up the stairs.

THE DJS FOUND Blackbeard's pool and pavilion area empty, save for the bartender who provided the pair with fresh water bottles. Whaler pushed back his frizzy mane and pressed the chilled plastic container against his forehead while Dread went in search of the tower keys from the front office.

Today's location wasn't as clandestine as that of the church cistern, but the hotel owner was a fan of the show and had given them permission to broadcast from the premises. With the cruise ships temporarily diverted from Charlotte Amalie—and with them, the day-trippers—the area was quiet. They were unlikely to be disturbed.

And yet, no sooner had the DJs reached the platform at the top of the tower's spiral metal staircase than they were startled by an electronic buzzing.

Dread patted his pockets, checking for his cell phone. He pulled it out, but no calls registered on its display. "Is that you?"

Whaler guzzled half his water bottle before responding. "No, is it you?"

"No, numbskull, its not me."

Dread scanned the platform's circular space, searching for the source of the sound. The area was protected from the wind by four feet of additional tower height. The men typically spread out across the wood plank floor when they operated here.

A second buzz helped Dread track the hidden cell phone to a crevice beneath the stairwell. He fished the fancy, high-end device from its hole and shrugged.

"Must belong to a tourist." He studied the call log. "Whoever the owner is, there are a lot of people trying to contact him."

Whaler set down his bottle and held his hands up for a catch. "Lemme see."

Dread tossed the phone across the platform, but his aim was a little off. If not for Whaler's long-armed reach, the phone would have sailed over the top of the tower and dropped into the swimming pool below.

"Ha!" Whaler exclaimed at the difficult nab. "No offense, Dread, but short people can't . . ." His voice trailed off as he read the most recent number that had dialed the phone.

Dread looked up from the equipment he was assembling on the other side of the platform. "What's that, Whaler? You wanna demonstrate your athleticism by racing me down to the bottom of the hill and back?"

"Naw, man, you'd leave me in the dust." After scanning the call log, Whaler slipped the phone into his backpack. "Short legs have an advantage on hills."

Dread returned his attention to the equipment, humming as he plugged in the various cables to their slots.

Whaler looked down the hill toward Government House and, beyond, the Legislature Building. He'd recognized the DC area code on the display.

The number for the previous outgoing calls was even more familiar.

He wondered who had been trying so desperately to reach Wendy.

BEFORE LONG, THE KRAT team was on the air, fielding calls from their engaged listeners. The main topic was, predictably, the territory's political upheaval, with specific mentions of the senators barricaded in the Legislature Building, the vandalism that had occurred overnight in the alleyway shops, and, of course, the missing Governor.

"The US can't just swoop in here and arrest all of our politicians," one caller protested indignantly.

Dread grimaced. "I'm afraid they just did."

The dark reply was more threat than comment. "We need to kick them out and retake control of this here island."

Dread switched over to a second caller.

"What are those hooligans doing out there on the streets? Did you see what they did down on the waterfront? Who is going to clean all that up? They're going to scare off all the tourists. Then we'll see some real trouble."

"Pasty boys," Dread admonished into his mike. "It's time for you to get busy."

He was about to move on to the next caller when Whaler threw his hands up and wiggled his fingers in the air, indicating they'd been contacted by a "drop everything" guest.

Dread leaned away from the mike, listening as Whaler whispered the identity of the woman waiting to voice her thoughts on the missing Governor.

"Are you sure?" he asked, surprised. Despite numerous requests, they had never received an interview from this sought-after source.

Whaler nodded, his Afro bouncing an enthusiastic affirmation.

Dread returned to the live transmission.

"Drop whatever you're doing, folks, and listen in." His

brown eyes gleamed with anticipation. "We've got the First Lady on the line."

After a quick introduction and the obligatory niceties inquiring as to how the First Lady was coping with recent events, Dread began spouting out questions.

"What can you tell us about the Governor? What are his plans? Is he going to fight these charges?"

There was a short pause before she issued her response. Her voice was touched by emotion, but steady in tone.

"My husband is dead."

Dread stared at the radio equipment, speechless. Filling the void, Whaler scooped up the handheld mike and gently prodded. "What happened to him?"

This time her response was swift, her words confident in the message conveyed.

"The federal agents killed him. He's been assassinated."

Emancipation Park

~ 72 ~

Grounds for Divorce

AFTER PASSING THE comforting scene of the elderly uncle and his niece sitting outside the diner, the author took a short walk along the shoreline. She snapped several photos of the Legislature Building, where a line of catering trucks had pulled into the parking lot, bringing hot breakfasts to the hot-headed senators still holed up inside.

It didn't take long for her to fall into the flow of the day's foot traffic, which led her to Emancipation Park.

The crowds were once more gathering around the grandstand. The microphones hummed with speculation and vitriol, an even mix of concern about what might happen next and angst at the territory's leaders for provoking the federal invasion.

The speeches immediately stopped, however, at news that the First Lady was about to go live on KRAT.

"HE'S BEEN ASSASSINATED."

The First Lady's words hung in the air, defying gravity. The sentence dealt a stunning blow to everyone within earshot.

Mouths fell open, and all conversation stopped. Then faint murmurs of sorrow, disbelief, and outrage began to float up over the crowd.

"Bless his soul."

"It can't be."

"They'll pay for this."

Dread Fred sputtered an incoherent response, but the First Lady ignored his futile attempts to interject.

"The bribery case against my husband and the VI government was based on trumped-up lies and fabricated evidence. It was nothing but a pretext for the United States to install a puppet government over our territory—so they could impose on us a leader more compliant to their demands than my husband."

The voices of discontent grew louder. The author eased toward the edge of the park, sensing it might be prudent to return to the hotel, even if—she grimaced—the Mojito Man was still camped out at the bar.

The First Lady's next comment confirmed the author's intuition.

"In honor of my husband's memory, we must evict the federal invaders, purge their traitors from our ranks, and separate ourselves from the country of his murderers."

⌒⌒

ON HER WAY out of the park, the author noticed the man in the golf shirt and chinos that she'd seen on the hotel veranda at breakfast. Unlike the rest of the crowd, he appeared unaffected by the First Lady's announcement.

The author had the distinct impression he was searching for someone—an impression that changed when he turned her direction.

It took a moment for the woman to realize that the Fixer's attention was trained on two West Indian men who had just stepped into the space beside her.

One was tall with stubby dread locks sticking up off the top of his head. His friend was shorter, his head nearly smooth from lack of hair.

Having just arrived at the park, the men were apparently unaware of the First Lady's dramatic announcement. The taller of the pair exclaimed in a voice that drowned out the KRAT broadcast.

"I mean, really, mon. How could anyone be afraid of a Cow Foot Woman?"

~ 73 ~

Duck

CURRIE SHUT HIS eyes.

"I can't keep having this conversation with you."

Mic had been carrying on a one-sided debate of cow-versus goat-footed ghouls ever since Currie's cousin Spike left them shortly after breakfast.

Mic and Currie had spent the night on the outskirts of Charlotte Amalie, sleeping beneath some trees in a wooded area that Spike had recommended. Even with the dense canopy, they'd been soaked to the skin during the worst of the night's downpour.

Currie had agreed to one last stop at Emancipation Park before they started their trek back to Coki Beach. He was anxious to get out of town, but by all indications, it was going to be a very *long* walk.

"A cow, mon? What's scary about a cow? What's the worst it could do to you? Moo?"

Currie let out a groan.

"But a goat, I tell you what. You don't want to mess around with an angry goat."

"If you say so."

"They've got those beady eyes and tiny little teeth. And don't forget the horns." Mic shuddered. "Creepy creatures."

Tuning out Mic's commentary, Currie gazed across the crowd.

"And they eat anything, those goats, mon. Cows are vegetarian."

Suddenly, Currie spied something that terrified him far more than any cow, goat, or ruminant-human hybrid.

"Duck," he whispered harshly. He grabbed Mic's sleeve and tugged.

"Duck Foot Woman?" Mic frowned, trying to imagine such a creature. "I've never heard of one of those, mon. Why are you crawling around on the ground? Are you checking people's feet? 'Cause you can't always tell from the shoes."

Currie threw his shoulder into Mic's knees, causing them to buckle. Mic collapsed onto the grass, howling with indignation.

His protests died in his throat when he saw where Currie was pointing.

Nova and his gang were circling the park, closing in on their position.

~ 74 ~

The Hunt

MIC AND CURRIE crawled through the crowd on their hands and knees, scurrying into the nearest bushes. Branches and thorns scraped at their skin, but neither man noticed the abrasions. A much greater concern loomed at the opposite end of the park.

The pair held their breath, hoping they'd escaped detection, but the evasive maneuver had come too late. The Fixer had pointed them out; they'd been spotted.

Nova had temporarily lost sight of the Coconut Boys, but the mere glimpse of his long-sought-after targets brought a triumphant smile to his face.

He motioned for his gang to spread out across the crowd. There was no way Mic and Currie could escape his clutches.

He was going to enjoy this hunt.

As Nova scanned the park for his victims, he passed a group discussing the First Lady's KRAT announcement, and his smile broadened to a deeper level of menace. He would pay for his betrayal, but whatever the repercussions, switching allegiances to the Fixer had already been worth the price. And besides, he thought with a confident swagger, he could surely smooth things over with her.

He'd always had a way with women.

SLITHERING ON HIS stomach, Currie scooted to the edge of the bushes and peeked out at the sea of feet in the park just beyond.

"Do you see anything?" Mic hissed from deeper inside the hedge.

Currie shook his head. He lifted his chest from the ground to get a better look—and froze.

Nova's men were rapidly converging on the bushes, a wide net of muscled machines ready to tear them limb from limb. Their current hiding place wouldn't protect them. They would have to run for it.

"Come on, Mic," Currie said briskly. "We've got to get out of here."

THE COCONUT BOYS sprinted pell-mell out of Emancipation Park, dodging and diving around disgruntled pedestrians. The disturbance in the crowd was easy to spot. Nova and his crew took up the chase.

Currie scrambled onto the pavement encircling the park, trying to decide on the nearest cover. Their best chance was to try to lose their pursuers in the steep neighborhoods above the harbor. Grabbing Mic's shirttail, he veered toward the hillside, but Nova's men fanned out across the road, cutting them off.

With no other choice, the pair spun around and headed toward the waterfront.

Nova let out a whoop.

"Let's go! We've got 'em, boys."

TERRIFIED, MIC AND Currie scampered down the street. Their legs pumped at high speed; their flip-flops smacked against the pavement.

Mic, being a foot taller than his friend, took the lead as they turned in front of the Legislature Building. Despite having the advantage of speed, Mic relied on Currie for direction. He looked back at his friend, seeking guidance.

Currie scanned the road ahead of them. Past the Legislature, the asphalt curved along the harbor. They were exposed, with little place to hide. He was about to gesture toward the Legislature parking lot, which would at least provide a few vehicles to hide behind, when Mic dashed across the street to the rear of Fort Christian.

"Over here," Mic panted, slipping through the hole in the chain-link gate.

Currie felt his stomach tighten with worry. Strategically, it was a bad move; they could easily be trapped inside. But there were no better options. They would have to move fast to get through the opening before Nova's men rounded the corner.

Reluctantly, he chugged toward the fence.

~ 75 ~

Cutlass and Cassock

MIC AND CURRIE fled across the fenced parking lot surrounding the rear of Fort Christian, hopping around construction barriers and abandoned equipment as they headed toward a metal door fitted into the steep brick wall.

Currie held little hope that the passage would be unlocked, but when Mic pulled on the handle, the door swung open.

With a last glance at the street behind him, Currie followed Mic inside. Together, they closed the door and slid a rusty bolt through its interior lock.

Currie held his breath, listening for sounds on the other side of the wall.

"Did we give them the slip?" Mic asked, bending over to catch his breath.

"I don't know," Currie replied anxiously. He scanned the inner courtyard and pointed to the clock tower over the fort's front entrance. "Let's see if we can get up there and take a look outside."

THE COCONUT BOYS trotted across the courtyard toward the front entrance. Currie remained focused on the clock tower, but Mic had started to assess the fort's residential potential.

"You know, Currie-mon, we could just live here." He gestured to the sky above the courtyard. "Plenty of open air, but some areas of protection." He nodded with satisfaction. "I bet I could do a bang-up business in hair-braiding outside by the vendors' plaza."

Currie paused by the fort's museum to give Mic a sarcastic look. He glanced briefly at the displays and then turned for the clock tower.

"I might even expand my line of hair ties . . ."

"Shh!"

On the opposite side of the fort's front door, Currie heard the exterior lock rattling in its fittings—followed by Nova's voice, growling to his subordinates.

"Head around back and guard the rear. I've got a key to this door somewhere in my pocket."

SPINNING AWAY FROM the front entrance, Currie grabbed Mic and pulled him back into the courtyard.

There were few options that held any realistic prospect of concealing them from Nova's sharp gaze.

"In here," Currie whispered, pointing to the museum.

The two scurried inside. Currie surveyed the historical displays and reached for the only available weapon—an antique cutlass once used to harvest sugarcane.

It wouldn't be much of a match for Nova's pistol.

NOVA'S DARK SHADOW strode powerfully through the fort's front entrance. He paused in the foyer beneath the clock tower, listened for his prey, and then walked toward the courtyard.

Reaching into his pocket, he pulled out the pair of bullets he had been carrying especially for this occasion.

He removed his gun from its holster, released the magazine, and loaded the special bullets into the front of the round, ensuring they would be the next two shots he fired.

Two, he felt confident, would be all that he'd need.

CURRIE STOOD IN the middle of the museum, looking out through its open doorway at the man who intended to kill him.

He wasn't one for risk-taking or wild adventure. He was a careful, deliberate soul.

He would have preferred a nice quiet home in a peaceful Crucian setting, but life had thrown him some hard knocks, unfortunate—unfair—wallops that had leveled him to the ground.

Each time, he got up and tried again. He had always faced his troubles as bravely as possible, even when the odds were stacked against him.

Never had his prospects looked as dire as they did in that moment. He and Mic had only one plan, and it had a very low likelihood of success.

Swallowing his fear, Currie held the cutlass in front of his body and prepared for the worst. Summoning his deepest voice, he called out.

"Nova, over here."

HEAD COCKED TO one side, Nova turned toward the museum. There in the doorway stood the shorter of the Coconut twins.

Gun cocked and at the ready, Nova began a slow but steady approach.

"What's this, Currie? You volunteering to go first?"

Gripping the cutlass with his sweaty hands, Currie managed a hoarse reply. "Let's get it over with, Nova." He swung the blade through the air, but the action failed to intimidate. He was a rodeo clown taunting a bull.

"There's no easy way out." Nova chuckled his enjoyment as he moved closer to the museum. He stood outside the doorway, casually waving his gun. "I'm going to make you suffer."

Currie slashed out with the knife, a feinted effort meant only to draw Nova inside.

Laughing, Nova stepped over the threshold.

"You know what this is, don't you?" He held the gun up, as if giving a demonstration. "This is what's going to make you pay for running out on me in Frederiksted. You can't parry with a gun."

Currie held his breath. Just a little closer, he told himself. He flicked the cutlass once more, trying to entice Nova to take one more step.

He hadn't meant to hit the pistol, but the cutlass had a longer wingspan than he realized. The blade dinged the tip of the gun, causing it to jump out of Nova's hand.

Startled, Nova juggled the weapon, struggling to regain his grip, but it slipped through his fingers. He bent to catch the pistol before it hit the floor.

Afraid that he'd pushed Nova too far, Currie lost control of the cutlass, and it tumbled downward—the sharp blade slicing across Nova's left cheek before it clattered onto the ground.

Unaware of the injury, Nova stood, training the gun on Currie's horrified face.

It wasn't until blood began running over his lips and into his mouth that Nova realized he'd been cut.

Enraged, he moved toward Currie, intent on firing the gun into his forehead.

"Let's end this now . . ."

The subsequent *bong* wasn't the ricochet of a bullet, but the clash of Mic's skillet with the back of Nova's head.

~~

"I KNOCKED HIM out good, didn't I, mon?" Mic stared down at Nova's unconscious figure, admiring his handiwork.

"Come on, Mic," Currie said, ushering him toward the museum door. "We've got to get out of here before the goons out back realize what's happened."

"Wait," Mic replied. "Take a look at this first."

Mic motioned Currie over to the display case where he had crouched while waiting for Nova to enter the museum.

A body lay across the floor, wrapped in a brown cassock.

"Who is it?" Currie asked, aghast.

"Don't know, mon, but he's dead. Like really and truly dead."

Currie cringed as Mic pointed at the cloak. "I've got an idea."

Currie looked up at his tall friend and sighed.

"I already know I'm not going to like this."

SECONDS LATER, A tall humpbacked figure dressed in a brown cassock staggered through Fort Christian's front entrance and hobbled, with difficulty, across the lawn.

Washington, DC

76

Relieved of Duty

"FRIDAY! HOW DID that woman get on the radio?! Don't your men have her under surveillance there at the Governor's Mansion?"

The attorney general hollered his frustration into the speakerphone. The assistant director of the FBI sat in a chair in front of the AG's desk, looking miserable, as together they listened to Friday's latest report from St. Thomas.

"She's still in the mansion, sir. Locked herself inside one of the upper bedrooms and barricaded the door. The house phones were disconnected. I don't know where she got the cell phone she used to call KRAT, but I suspect the Bishop slipped it to her the previous evening."

The attorney general reached for his bottle of pink tablets while his counterpart from the FBI took over the conversation.

"What's all this about the Governor being murdered?" the assistant director demanded plaintively. "We have to immediately deny any involvement in this."

"We've been unable to locate him, sir. I can't say if he's alive or dead. Just that we didn't kill him."

"That's not terribly helpful, Friday."

"We're doing the best we can, sir."

The attorney general swallowed his antacid tablet without chewing it. "We're working the Bishop angle here in DC. I think that's the only chance we have of finding a way out of this mess. Stay close to your phone, Friday. We'll be in touch."

The assistant director leaned toward the speaker console. "And, Friday . . ."

"Yes, sir."

"Please relieve Agent Hightower of his duties."

There was no hesitation in his response.

"With pleasure, sir."

Hotel 1829

77

The Brokered Deal

SENATOR SANCHEZ WALKED beside her uncle as they traversed the steep steps on the hillside above the post office. She held her hand near his elbow, ready to brace him if he stumbled, but the old man's footing was as sure as ever. Sanchez, still wearing the borrowed T-shirt, shorts, and oversized sandals, was more at risk of slipping than her uncle.

Midway up the stairs, the pair passed the feral rooster, who gave Abe a conspiring nod, as if commending the wily politician's plan. The bird was far more confident in the outcome than Sanchez. She had at first balked at his idea and had only agreed to accompany him because she didn't want him to make the attempt alone.

Minutes later, they reached the one-way street at the top of the steps. On the opposite curb stood the coral pink fronting of Hotel 1829.

The bartender buzzed them through the front gate. They were the first to arrive for the morning's impromptu gathering—which is what Abe had intended.

Given the guests he had invited, he wanted to make sure he and Sanchez had seats against the front wall with easy access to the exit.

IN ITS LONG history, Hotel 1829 had witnessed important meetings among politicians, Danish landowners, and other island power brokers. The establishment had hosted tête-à-têtes between governors, premiers, ambassadors, and presidents.

But never had it seen a caucus quite like this one.

Abe chose his spot on the large wooden table inside the bar. Then he rotated the marble game board so that the two participants would be seated in the appropriate player positions.

Backgammon was a two-person game. He was just there to referee.

Knowing the players' preferences, he preordered their drinks.

An iced tea for the Bishop.

A hot tea for the Fixer.

And a lemonade for himself.

Senator Sanchez opted for a glass of water.

The bartender prepared the requested drinks and set them on the table before excusing himself. He tugged on his graying ponytail as he departed through the veranda gate.

Where Abe was concerned, some proceedings were best left unobserved.

THE FIXER ANNOUNCED his presence by ringing the buzzer at the front gate. Abe nodded for Sanchez to trigger the door's release inside the small office attached to the bar.

The thin man walked quietly across the length of the veranda and stepped inside the hotel. He nodded at Abe and took his seat next to the cup and saucer.

Sanchez shifted her feet, anticipating the arrival of the next participant.

A swishing brown cassock appeared from the bar's courtyard entrance. The Bishop swept into the room, quickly assessed the settings around the table, and took his seat next to the iced tea. He acknowledged Sanchez but focused his attention on the Fixer.

The Bishop picked up the iced tea, his ruby ring clinking against the glass. He took a casual sip, but his eyes never left his opponent.

Abe cleared his throat. "Thank you both for coming. Shall we begin?" He placed a pair of dice in front of each man. "Each of you roll one die, and we'll see who goes first."

The Bishop tapped a finger against his numbered cube. "Is this really how we're going to settle this?"

Abe continued with his preamble as if he hadn't heard the comment.

"I believe you're both familiar with the principles of the game. You're each assigned fifteen checkers. They have already been arranged in their starting positions. You can move them around the board according to the numbers rolled on your dice. The objective is to be the first man to remove all of your own checkers from the board."

Warily, the Bishop rolled his die. Silently, the Fixer did the same. Abe leaned over the table, comparing the two numbers.

"Right, then. The gentleman in the green shirt will go first."

The Fixer slid two checkers across the marble board as Abe wrapped up his instructions.

"Move your checkers according to the numbers shown on the dice, but you cannot both occupy the same point on the board—just as, it seems, your clients cannot both occupy the Governor's Mansion." He looked at the man in the brown cassock. "Your turn, sir."

The Bishop dropped his dice into the marble cup and gave them a gentle shake.

"The Governor has already been removed from the mansion." He looked across the backgammon board as he released the dice. "Permanently."

The Fixer lifted his teacup with his left hand, revealing the red gash on his wrist. "I assure you the Governor is very much alive—and about to make his own public announcement on recent events."

Sanchez glanced at her uncle. Abe had yet to touch his lemonade.

"I see." The Bishop rolled his dice and then stroked his neatly trimmed goatee. "That leaves us at a bit of an impasse." He moved his requisite two checkers and set the dice cup in the middle of the board.

Abe strummed his fingers on the table's edge. "Of course, either one alone is weaker than the two acting together, however fractious their union."

The Fixer grabbed the cup and shook it, letting the dice

clatter against the sides for several seconds before letting them tumble onto the board.

"The Governor doesn't feel the differences are irreconcilable."

He looked across at the Bishop, who, in turn, shifted his gaze to Abe.

"And the attorney general?"

Abe finally took a slurp of lemonade. "I believe I can resolve that aspect." He set down the glass and smacked his lips. "If we're all in agreement, there's just one more matter to discuss."

He tilted his head toward his niece.

"My commission for brokering the deal."

ABE COLLECTED THE dice and checkers as the Bishop and the Fixer stood to leave.

"I'll let you know as soon as I have conferred with the First Lady," the Bishop said solemnly.

As he turned for the doorway leading out onto the veranda, there was a disturbance in the refrigerated bathroom attached to the opposite end of the bar.

The flushing whoosh of water was followed by a feeble voice that echoed off the inner tile floor.

"Mojito? Bartender, can you bring me another mojito? I can't bear to leave this nice cold place."

~ *78* ~

Funeral Plans

IT TOOK THE author far longer than she'd anticipated to make the return trip back up to Government Hill from Emancipation Park.

She'd been detained for almost forty-five minutes by a surly FBI agent with a bulky gorilla build who reeked of stale rum. The agent had ordered several apologetic National Guard troops to corral her while he demanded to see her camera's digital storage card.

It wasn't until a second agent arrived on the scene—a harried man with a horsey face—that she was finally released with her camera and digital photos intact.

She returned to Hotel 1829 to find a curious assortment of individuals walking out its front gate. It appeared a meeting of some sort had just broken up, and the participants were departing.

There was the elderly uncle and niece who she'd seen eating breakfast outside the diner earlier that morning. They were followed by the man in the brown cassock who had taken the author's flight from Miami. In her head, she reluctantly called him the Bishop, although she was more convinced than ever that that was not his religious affiliation.

Lastly, the author passed the flat-faced man in the golf shirt and chinos. He held the gate open for her and smiled, ever so slightly, as she stepped through.

The author hurried across the veranda, reaching into her backpack for her notebook and pen. She was so eager to take notes on this odd assortment of characters that she forgot to watch out for her thirsty travel companion.

The bartender looked up from his counter as she stepped inside. A moment too late, she caught his warning expression—and the glass of muddled mint leaves at his station.

"HELLO, LOVE."

The author closed her eyes, wincing at the voice that called out from the bench along the wall next to the door. She turned as the Mojito Man pulled his frail figure up into a seated position.

He gripped the edge of the backgammon table, trying to stand. Instinctively, she lunged forward to keep him from falling.

She felt his weak arms wrap around her shoulders for an indulgent hug.

"Nothing like the healing powers of a woman."

The bartender finished preparing the mojito and set it on the counter.

"Here you go, sir."

The man's attention shifted from the author to the drink.

"Help me, over, can you?" he asked, nearly breathless from the effort it had taken to stand.

She eased him onto a bar stool, and his mouth found the straw. After a long slurp, he seemed to recover a bit of his energy.

"Have you been inside that bathroom?" He pointed to the door at the end of the bar. "You could chill a corpse in there. I told 'em that's where they should stick me when I'm gone. You know, before the hearse comes to pick me up."

With a sigh, the woman slid onto the adjacent stool. The bartender smiled and began making a frozen daiquiri.

"Mango?" he suggested with a pump of his mustache.

"That'll be fine."

Her neighbor swiveled in his chair to look at her.

"Will you go to my funeral?" His bloodshot eyes pleaded pathetically. "No one else will be there."

The bar fell silent. The author pressed her lips together, knowing she would regret answering the question, whichever way she responded.

Finally, she nodded the affirmative, making a promise she knew she didn't intend to keep.

Emancipation Park

~ 79 ~

Judas

IN THE HOUR since the First Lady's startling announcement on the KRAT broadcast, the crowds at Emancipation Park had quadrupled in number. Spurred on by news of the Governor's assassination, residents from across Charlotte Amalie converged on the area to express their sorrow, outrage, and anger.

While the grandstand microphones were in full use, the noise in the crowd exceeded the amplified voices on stage. The agitated atmosphere was growing more unstable by the minute.

All of this activity ground to a halt, however, when a line of shiny black SUVs circled the park's perimeter and stopped along the street next to the post office.

The crowd shifted its focus, several hundred people turning in unison to stare at the official-looking arrivals. Speculations soon began to float through the masses.

"It's the First Lady."

"It's the feds, come to arrest us."

A cheeky pickpocket piped up. "It's the Cow Foot Woman, ready for a brawl!"

The first SUV disgorged the Governor's regular security team. Several members of the cabinet—including those who had been indicted—stepped out of the second.

The third and fourth vehicles carried the USVI senators who had just been released from the Legislature Building. The politicians quickly spread through the crowd, mingling with their constituents, rumpled but triumphant.

The crowd waited, eagerly anticipating the last reveal, as the security team surrounded the fifth and final vehicle. The door to the rear passenger compartment swung open. A suited leg and formal leather shoe kicked out and planted firmly on the curb. Then a large man with a sturdy build, rotund middle, and a beaming smile exited the vehicle.

His identity was spoken in a single stunned whisper.

"It's the Governor."

THE GOVERNOR STRODE to the grandstand, nimbly climbing the steps to the platform. Few people noticed that he was accompanied by the fifth SUV's second occupant, Senator Sanchez, who had hastily changed into a suit and heels.

The Governor wasted no time in addressing the crowd. He approached the nearest microphone and spread his arms wide, embracing his listeners.

"We've been through a dark and troubling time, my friends, but I'm pleased to tell you that reports of my death have been greatly exaggerated."

A cheer exploded across the park. Even those who had, hours earlier, derided the Governor as a thief and a coward, now clapped enthusiastically.

"My fellow islanders, I know that you have been distressed by recent events. Believe me, I share your concerns about the foreign troops who have spread across our territory."

A number of hisses and boos rose up from the audience.

"But I must tell you the truth. It was a traitor in our own family, a trusted source close to me, who betrayed us."

The crowd's anger quelled, replaced by morbid curiosity. Who could it be? The question circulated through the park, quickly followed by a myriad of wild guesses. Someone even dared to suggest the First Lady.

"This sordid individual spun a twisted web of lies and deceit—a hoax that fooled the justice department officials, law enforcement, the FBI, and most of all, me."

The Governor detached the microphone from its stand so he could pace back and forth across the stage.

"Who was this Judas?" he asked, leaning toward the crowd. "This betrayer of our beloved islands?"

The question hung in the air. The murmurs fell silent, waiting for the Governor's next words.

"It was my closest aide. A young man who was born and raised here. He served in my administration for many years, and he was a trusted member of my staff. But now he is a fugitive from the law. A wanted man."

The Governor shook his head. His expression conveyed sorrowful disbelief.

"Cedric, I encourage you to turn yourself in."

THE GOVERNOR PAUSED, waiting for the impact of his message to sink in. A member of his security team offered him a water bottle. He reattached the microphone to its stand and took several long gulps. Handing back the near-empty container, he resumed his speech.

"My fellow islanders, there are long and difficult days ahead of us. This callous act of sabotage has caused severe damage to St. Thomas. We must now rebuild our reputation with our friends in the tourism industry. We must redouble our efforts to welcome the cruise ships and their guests to our port."

The crowd nodded in agreement. The Governor's silver tongue had always served him well. Scooping the mike once more from its stand, he bent over the platform to deliver one more blow to his opponents.

"But know this. We will not rest until all those involved in this treacherous crime against our territory have been apprehended and brought to justice."

While another round of raucous applause swept through the park, the Governor motioned for Senator Sanchez to join him at the front of the stage.

"I want you to know that Senator Sanchez has worked diligently, throughout this ordeal, to rectify the harm that has been done to our territory—even while being wrongfully accused herself. She has shown true leadership and skill."

Sanchez blushed at the Governor's words and tried to stifle the surge of guilt she felt for the honor she was about to receive.

"I am pleased to announce that she has accepted my

invitation to join my cabinet as a senior advisor. She will play a key role in liaising with the tourism industry, our most vital and important economic partner, and rebuilding that relationship. She is a bright and rising star, and I expect great things to come from this young woman. I know she will succeed."

Sanchez nodded and smiled through the subsequent polite applause, drawing heavily on her weatherperson's media skills. After the earlier dramatics, this was merely a perfunctory administrative matter. Few, if any, realized that Sanchez's position had been negotiated by her uncle Abe at the Hotel 1829 backgammon table.

"And now, if you'll excuse me," the Governor said with a wink. "I have to get home to my wife."

◦～

FRIDAY STOOD AT the outskirts of Emancipation Park with several of his fellow agents. His was a skeptical stance. He had observed the spectacle with a wry expression on his face, his arms folded across his chest.

With the Governor's political rebirth complete, Friday shook his head and turned toward the sidewalk leading to the deepwater port. The US Navy ship would soon be departing for Virginia with its load of National Guard and FBI agents.

He had hastily conferred with his assistant director and the attorney general prior to the Governor's arrival at the park. While Friday didn't yet know all of the underlying details, he recognized a politically contrived solution when he saw one.

His team had been diverted onto a new mission, a global search for the Bishop.

He glanced back at Charlotte Amalie's curving hills, taking a last look up at Blackbeard's Tower with a sigh.

"So ends Operation Coconut."

◦～

THE GOVERNOR STEPPED down from the grandstand and was once more surrounded by security personnel.

A slim man in an oversized golf shirt and chinos, however, managed to slip through the heavily armed barrier to pat the Governor on the back.

"Congratulations, Guv."

The big man stopped to clasp his arm around the Fixer's shoulders. "I can't thank you enough." He lowered his voice. "We'll be in touch—through the regular channels."

"I'm glad we were able to work things out, sir."

But as the Governor turned toward his waiting SUV, the Fixer leaned over and whispered in his ear.

"We've got one more loose end to tie up."

The Loose Ends

~ *80* ~

The Last Mojito

THE AUTHOR WATCHED the Governor's grandstand appearance from the television set in the bar at Hotel 1829. The remarkable performance was immediately followed by news that the island's transportation ban had been lifted. The ferry schedule would recommence shortly.

The bartender leaned over his counter and pumped his thick eyebrows.

"If you get on over to Red Hook, you might make it out tonight."

"I'll grab my bag," she said, hopping off her stool.

The shuffling sound was enough to wake the Mojito Man, who had been snoozing fitfully on the bench against the far wall.

"What happened?" he asked, suddenly alert. "Where's everybody going?"

"I'm headed to St. John," the author replied and then added a muttered aside: "Hopefully."

Her pale friend jumped up from the bench. The most recent dose of pain meds was still in full effect. "Time for me to get back to Blackbeard's."

The bartender reached for his phone. "Let me call you a cab."

"Don't bother," the man waved him off. "I'm going to walk. I feel spry as a spring chicken."

He staggered toward the marked door on the other side of the bar.

"Just going to make a quick pit stop first."

The bartender motioned toward the courtyard. "Now's your chance. Better make a run for it."

The author gazed at the exit for several seconds before throwing up her hands. She couldn't stop thinking about the earlier funeral conversation.

"I'll take him," she said reluctantly. "Blackbeard's is just at the top of the 99 Steps, isn't it?"

The bartender grinned. "It's going to feel like a lot more than ninety-nine."

FORTY-FIVE MINUTES LATER, the author staggered up the last set of stairs leading to Blackbeard's pool and pavilion area.

The Mojito Man leaned heavily against her, gasping for breath. He had at first enjoyed the excuse to drape his arm over her shoulders, but the last set of switchbacks had nearly done him in.

"Stay for a cocktail, dinner . . ." he panted as she escorted him to a lawn chair by the pool. "There's plenty of room. I've got the whole place to myself."

"I have to catch a ferry," she said firmly. "Are you sure you'll be okay up here?"

"I'm a special guest," he replied with a goofy grin. "They've got a full staff to take care of me."

"Okay." She backed slowly away from him. "Well, good-bye, then."

And with that, she turned for the stairs.

"Alone again," he said pathetically as he watched the brown-haired woman disappear down the steps at the edge of the pool.

A voice spoke up from inside the pavilion.

"Don't look so sad."

Still dressed in a green golf shirt and chinos, the Fixer walked over with a tall glass filled with muddled mint leaves.

"This will dull the pain."

THE MOJITO MAN leaned back in the lawn chair, happily sucking down a drug-laced mojito—this one loaded with triple its regular dose.

The Fixer watched the drink disappear in the glass, waiting for confirmation of the kill—and the elimination of the witness to his duel with the Governor's aide.

It didn't take long. The glass slipped from the man's grip and tumbled onto the grass. His gray eyes, drained of color, had seen life's last look. His troubled spirit drifted peacefully into whatever the next life had to offer.

Are you ready? the dying man had often asked himself.

At some point, fate moots the question and makes the decision for you.

⌁

IT WAS A better death than the one that had been suffered by the Governor's former favorite aide.

Emancipation Park had almost emptied—along with the surrounding downtown streets—when Senator Bobo scurried furtively up the front walk to Fort Christian. In their hurry to depart, Nova and his crew had left the front door unlocked. Bobo slipped through the entrance and made his way to the museum.

He stepped gingerly across the dusty floor, carefully avoiding Nova's spattered blood and the cutlass that had generated the messy facial injury. He would clean that up later. He had another matter to attend to first.

Bobo bent behind the display counter to Cedric's sprawled body. The corpse was far more gruesome without the brown cassock that had covered the young man's wounds.

The Reverend touched the points of a cross on his chest and murmured a silent blessing. Then he hefted the dead weight into a shipping crate and nailed down the lid.

With a groan, he lifted the crate onto a rusted dolly. The wheels creaked as he shoved the load out of the museum and into the courtyard.

"Just another day's honest earning."

~ 81 ~

Fresh Coconuts

"CURRIE-MON, THIS ISN'T the turnoff to Coki Beach."

Mic and Currie had hobbled almost a mile outside of Charlotte Amalie before abandoning their brown cassock disguise. After a short walk, they'd caught a ride on a passing safari truck. The other passengers had shared the news of the Governor's return and the lifting of the island's transportation ban.

Currie had watched the road, carefully gauging the length of ride they could afford. At the appropriate moment, he'd signaled for a stop.

The pair had been heading due east for about fifteen minutes when Currie steered Mic toward the Red Hook ferry building.

"Aren't we going back to Coki?" Mic asked again as Currie hurried to the ticket window. He reached into his pocket and took out their last few dollars.

There was just enough left to buy one ticket on the next departing ferry to St. John.

"One ticket, please," he said, pushing the crumpled money through the slot to the attendant. Gulping, he turned and handed Mic the ticket.

"Nova won't stop looking for us. Our only choice is . . ."

The words were too difficult to speak. Currie cleared his

throat and finally completed the sentence. "Our only choice is to split up."

"No," Mic replied, shaking his head. "No, we can't do that."

"We have to," he insisted solemnly, pressing the ticket into Mic's hand. "Besides, I'm the one who cut Nova's face—he'll remember that. I'm too dangerous for you to be around."

Mic shook his head. "No, mon, I can't make it without you."

"You can set up a hair-braiding business in Cruz Bay. I'll send Spike over with your kit. You'll do great there. I'm sure of it."

Mic swallowed hard. "What will you do?"

Currie shrugged wearily. He hadn't thought that far ahead. "When it's safe again, I'll come find you."

A voice came over the terminal intercom, announcing the ferry's imminent departure.

"It's time to go," Currie said, gently turning Mic toward the gate. Mic took a step forward and then turned back.

"Curie-mon, I refuse to say it."

He gave his short friend a tight squeezing hug.

"To fresh coconuts."

Currie could hardly push out the words.

"To fresh coconuts." Then he added a choked, "Mon."

THROUGH TEARS, CURRIE watched the ferry turn away from the dock, carrying the only thing in the world that he cared anything about.

The boat powered up its engine and rumbled toward the open water, shrinking in size until it disappeared into the horizon of the Pillsbury Sound.

THE AUTHOR SETTLED into her ferry seat, relieved to at last be on her way to her intended destination. She glanced out the side window as the boat picked up speed for the short ride east to St. John. Then she began her regular routine of cataloguing her fellow travelers.

A few rows up, a tall West Indian man with a head full of stubby dreadlocks stared morosely at the floor. She wondered for a moment what calamity had struck the poor fellow—before a second passenger grabbed her full attention.

It was the Bishop, or at least, it was a gentleman with the same distinctive goatee.

She blinked, trying to be sure. He sat on the far side of the ferry's passenger compartment. He had abandoned the tailored brown cassock for far more ragged clothing.

I must be mistaken, she thought—until he ran his hand over his smooth brown scalp and the light reflected off the ruby ring on his index finger.

THERE WERE TWO more passengers of note on the day's first departing ferry.

Seated five rows behind the writer, well out of sight of the other passengers, the couple appeared to be enjoying their unexpected getaway. They had packed their bags in a rush that afternoon. Neither was sure how long they would be gone or when they might return.

The KRAT DJ turned his head toward the nearest open window, letting the sea breeze ruffle his frizzy mane of hair. He wrapped an arm around his girlfriend, who was ready to take a much-needed vacation after quitting her job at the local attorney general's office.

~ 82 ~

Aground on St. Thomas

THE GOVERNOR'S BLACK SUV left Emancipation Park and circled through downtown Charlotte Amalie, a victory lap, of sorts, celebrating the most unlikely of political resurrections. The Governor looked out at the passing city—still, remarkably, *his* city.

Eventually, the driver steered the vehicle onto the curving road that wound up the hill to the Governor's Mansion.

The SUV pulled to a stop in the driveway, but the passenger remained seated for several minutes. Finally, he opened the side door and climbed out. The reckoning could be delayed no longer.

The house was quiet as he approached. He crossed through the front entrance and walked inside.

The place felt oddly different to him. It was uncomfortable, like an ill-fitting shoe. He tried to attribute the sensation to the fact that federal agents had been camped out there for the past twenty-four hours. Perhaps they had moved a piece of furniture or disrupted some other established pattern—but he knew it was the residents who had changed, not the building or its décor.

The Governor paused in the living room by the backgammon table. The position of the checkers still meant nothing to him. Even after all this time, he had no idea how to play the game. Uncle Abe had given up trying to teach him.

Their frequent backgammon lessons had been nothing more than a subterfuge for information exchange. When it came to summoning the Fixer, the old politician was the only reliable means of initiating contact.

A movement on the second floor caught the Governor's attention.

He turned away from the game board and met the gaze of the woman standing at the top of the staircase. The First Lady stared down at him, her expression unreadable.

He called out with gusto, "Honey, I'm home!"